THE NICK STONE SERIES

Ex-SAS trooper, now gun-for-hire working for the British government, Nick Stone is the perfect man for the dirtiest of jobs, doing whatever it takes by whatever means necessary . . .

REMOTE CONTROL

◢ Washington DC, USA

Stone is on the run with precious cargo, the only person who can identify a vicious killer – a seven-year-old girl.

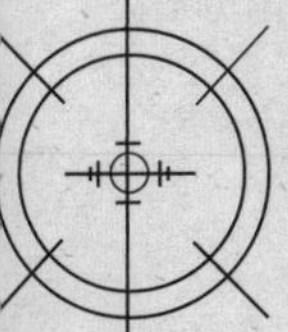

CRISIS FOUR

◢ North Carolina, USA

A beautiful young woman holds the key to a chilling conspiracy that will threaten the world as we know it.

FIREWALL

◢ Finland

At the heart of a global espionage network, Stone is faced with some of the most dangerous killers around.

LAST LIGHT

◢ Panama

Caught in the crossfire between Colombian mercenaries and Chinese businessmen, Stone isn't comfortable.

LIBERATION DAY

◢ Cannes, France

Behind the glamorous exterior, the city's seething underworld is the battleground for a very dirty drugs war.

DARK WINTER

◢ Malaysia

The War on Terror has Stone cornered: the life of someone he loves or the lives of millions he doesn't know?

DEEP BLACK

◢ Bosnia

All too late, Stone sees he is being used as bait to lure into the open a man whom the West are desperate to destroy.

AGGRESSOR

◢ Georgia, former Soviet Union

An old SAS comrade calls in a debt that will challenge Stone to risk everything in order to repay his friend.

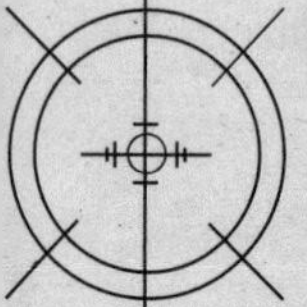

RECOIL

◢ The Congo, Africa

A straightforward missing persons case quickly becomes a headlong rush from the past.

CROSSFIRE

◢ Kabul, Afghanistan

The search for a kidnapped reporter takes Stone to Afghanistan – the modern-day Wild West.

ANDY McNAB

REVIEWS

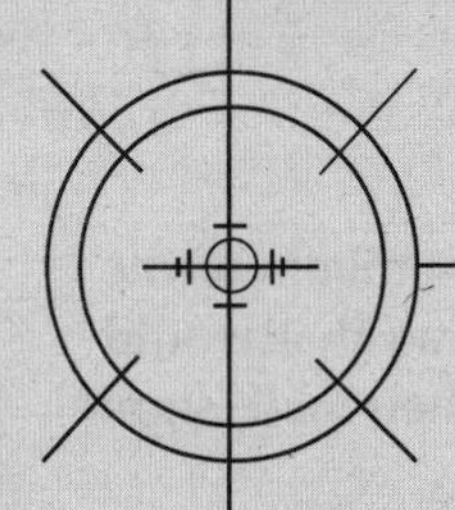

'One of the UK's top thriller writers'

Daily Express

'Like his creator, the ex-SAS soldier turned uber-agent is unstoppable'

Daily Mirror

'Could hardly be more topical'

Mail on Sunday

'Other thriller writers do their research, but McNab has actually been there'

Sunday Times

'Sometimes only the rollercoaster ride of an action-packed thriller hits the spot. No one delivers them as professionally or as plentifully as SAS soldier turned author McNab'

Guardian

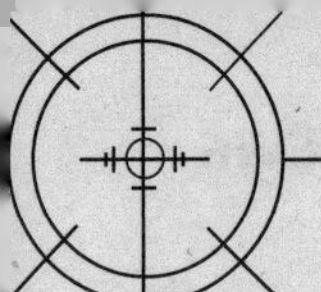

BRAVO TWO ZERO

In 1991, Sergeant Andy McNab led eight members of the SAS regiment on a top-secret mission in Iraq that would send them deep behind enemy lines. Their call sign: Bravo Two Zero.

IMMEDIATE ACTION

The no-holds-barred account of an extraordinary life, from the day McNab was found on the steps of Guy's Hospital as a baby to the day he went to fight in the Gulf War.

SEVEN TROOP

The gripping true story of serving in the company of a remarkable band of brothers. But he who dares doesn't always win. Every man is pushed to breaking point, some beyond it.

THE GOOD PSYCHOPATH'S GUIDE TO SUCCESS

As diagnosed by Professor Kevin Dutton, McNab is what they call a 'Good Psychopath' – he's a psychopath but he's also a high-functioning member of society. Learn how to be successful the McNab way.

SORTED! THE GOOD PSYCHOPATH'S GUIDE TO BOSSING YOUR LIFE

Together, Andy McNab and Professor Kevin Dutton are here to show you how to dial up your inner 'Good Psychopath' to get more out of life.

BRUTE FORCE

◢ TRIPOLI, LIBYA

An undercover operation is about to have deadly long-term consequences.

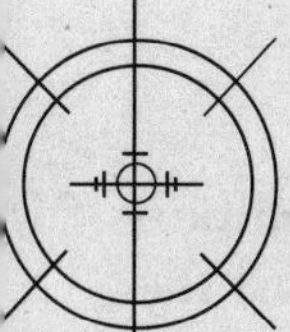

EXIT WOUND

◢ DUBAI, UAE

This one's personal: Stone is out to track down the killer of two ex-SAS comrades.

ZERO HOUR

◢ AMSTERDAM, NETHERLANDS

A terrorist organization is within reach of immeasurable power – but not for long.

DEAD CENTRE

◢ SOMALIA

When his son is kidnapped by pirates, a Russian oligarch calls the only man he can think of, Nick Stone.

SILENCER

◢ HONG KONG

Stone must return to a world he thought he had left behind in order to protect his family.

FOR VALOUR

◢ HEREFORD, UK

Called to investigate a death at the SAS base, Stone finds himself in the killer's telescopic sights.

NICK STONE

DETONATOR

◢ The Alps, Switzerland

When someone Stone loves is murdered, he can no longer take the pain. He wants vengeance at any cost.

COLD BLOOD

◢ The North Pole

Accompanying a group of veteran soldiers on an expedition to the North Pole, Stone learns quickly that it isn't just the cold that might kill him.

LINE OF FIRE

◢ London, UK

The Nick Stone series comes closer to home in more ways than one.

STANDALONE

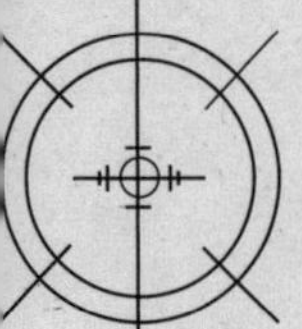

WHATEVER IT TAKES

◢ New Zealand

James Mercer will do anything to right the wrongs against his family. Even if it means breaking the law . . .

THE SERGEANT TOM BUCKINGHAM SERIES

RED NOTICE

Deep beneath the English Channel, Russian terrorists have seized control of the Eurostar to Paris and are holding four hundred hostages at gunpoint. But one man stands in their way. An off-duty SAS soldier is on the train; his name is Tom Buckingham.

FORTRESS

Ex-SAS and working for a billionaire with political ambition, Buckingham will have to decide where his loyalties lie as he is drawn into a spiral of terrorism, insurgency and, ultimately, assassination.

STATE OF EMERGENCY

Undercover inside a frighteningly real right-wing organization, Buckingham uncovers a plan to kill the party leader. But beneath that lies a far more devastating plot to change the political landscape of Europe for ever.

Andy McNab and Kym Jordan's novels trace the interwoven stories of one platoon's experience of warfare in the twenty-first century. Packed with the searing danger and high-octane excitement of modern combat, they also explore the impact of its aftershocks upon the soldiers themselves, and upon those who love them.

WAR TORN

Two tours of Iraq have shown Sergeant Dave Henley how modern battles are fought. But nothing could have prepared him for his posting to Afghanistan. This is a war zone like he's never seen before.

BATTLE LINES

Sergeant Dave Henley returns from Afghanistan to find that home can be an equally searing battlefield. The promise of another posting to Helmand is almost a relief for the soldiers but, for their families, it is another opportunity for their lives to be ripped apart.

DOWN TO THE WIRE

Andy McNab

PENGUIN BOOKS

TRANSWORLD PUBLISHERS
Penguin Random House, One Embassy Gardens,
8 Viaduct Gardens, London SW11 7BW
www.penguin.co.uk

Transworld is part of the Penguin Random House group of companies
whose addresses can be found at global.penguinrandomhouse.com

First published in Great Britain in 2022 by Bantam
an imprint of Transworld Publishers
Penguin paperback edition published 2023

A CIP catalogue record for this book
is available from the British Library.

ISBN
9780552174299

Typeset in Palatino by Jouve (UK), Milton Keynes.
Printed and bound in Great Britain by Clays Ltd, Elcograf S.p.A.

The authorized representative in the EEA is Penguin Random House Ireland,
Morrison Chambers, 32 Nassau Street, Dublin D02 YH68.

Penguin Random House is committed to a sustainable
future for our business, our readers and our planet. This book
is made from Forest Stewardship Council® certified paper.

PART ONE

1

Villefranche-sur-Mer
Saturday, 10 July 2021

A big twist of the throttle took the electric outboard to max, but it didn't seem to make much difference to our relative speeds. The *Alamat* looked just as far away, and Gabe was going ballistic. 'He said it would be staying put all night. Your fucking bossman got it fucking wrong!'

The inflatable bounced up and down in bigger swell as we reached halfway into the bay, and Gabe had to grip his seat with both hands. Jack was still at the bow, using his lard to keep it down.

I glanced across to Rio, perched on the other side of the outboard. 'Keep hold of that bag!'

The yacht wasn't exactly going flat out, but its position was changing in relation to the bay's ribbon of lights left and right. Our own motion was just about fast enough to blow everyone's hair back, apart, of course, from Gabe's. The moody Jock hadn't had that much to start with, but in the last few months what was left of it had all fallen out.

Four bodies on board and only four horsepower to move them would have been fine for closing in on a static target, but not one that was on the move. But we were where we were, and that was it. If we caught up with the yacht, then all well and good. If not, we'd just have to revert to Plan B, as soon as I'd thought of one. At least the *Alamat* wasn't completely out to sea yet: there were still lights running both sides of the bay ahead of it. In this harbour, vessels were under a speed restriction until they reached open water.

'We're gaining!'

Either Jack had a better perspective from ahead there on the bow or he was bluffing himself.

Straining my eyes into the gloom, I triangulated *Alamat*'s stern lights with points on the shore. Jack was right. We were gaining on it, not fast, but fast enough, and the closer we got the easier it was to use its lights as a marker to check our relative speeds.

There were many newer models than the sleek white three-master out there in the bay, available as charters for the super-rich to swan about in, but this was the only one named after a nineteenth-century Ottoman Empire battleship. It had left Marmaris in Turkey and made its way to the French Riviera via Tunis, but the journey was about a whole lot more than having fun. Serious work had been done *en route* and during the two stopovers, first in Tunis and then here. The problem was that the work being carried out on board was a danger to the West, and The Owl had ordered that it had to be stopped.

Soon, salty water splattered our faces as we bounced on the remains of *Alamat*'s wake.

Just a minute or two later, I could make out the faint rumble of engines, more like the gentle throbbing hum of an electricity generator.

Jack was up on his knees, gripping the loose end of the thin white nylon bow-rope in both hands.

Two more minutes and we were no more than four or five metres from the rear platform, which was just above sea level. At anchor, a ladder would go down from it into the water for swimmers, and a jet-ski was lashed on either side for those who wanted to be noisier.

The inflatable bucked and I had to hold on. Rio knelt behind Gabe and used his body to steady him as the spray drenched us. What he said to him carried to me on the wind: 'Last chance, mate. It's not too late.'

Gabe shook his head. 'Don't worry. I know what I'm doing – and why.'

He wasn't going to change his mind. We all knew that. Back on the quay, just before we jumped aboard the inflatable, his eyes had locked onto ours, one by one. He didn't say anything at first. We waited for him. It was his moment.

'Thanks, lads,' he finally muttered. 'It's been a fucker these last seven months, and especially this last one. But it's yous cunts have made it bearable.' Finally, Gabe had taken a deep breath and had one more good look into our eyes. 'Right then, shitheads. Enough, before it turns into a fucking prayer meeting. Let's go save the fucking world, yeah?'

2

The yacht's engine was so loud now it drowned out any other sound, and moments later the inflatable jolted as the bow connected with the swimming platform. We rebounded, and I had to keep the throttle on full so we recovered enough distance for Jack to make his move. He leapt, belly-flopping onto the deck, the line still in his hands, keeping himself flat as he rolled and crawled to tie it off against one of the jet-ski's strapdowns.

The moment it was tethered, the inflatable thrashed from side to side. I used the outboard as best I could to counter the motion while Gabe, with Rio's help, made his way to the bow. Jack was on his knees on the swimming platform, arm out, ready to pull him aboard.

Rio passed me the bag to sit on, then thrust his shoulder into Gabe to steady him. Jack soon had a hand on Gabe and pulled him as Rio pushed from behind. Gabe slithered onto the deck, like a walrus flopping onto an ice floe.

He rolled out of the way so Rio could follow, and then it was the bag's turn. I closed down the outboard and hauled the heavy holdall in my left hand, clambering to the bow. The inflatable swung violently left and right in the yacht's wake as I stretched out my arm. Jack grabbed the bag and I half jumped, half threw myself to join the others. All four of us were soaked and already fucked, but so what? We were on board.

Gabe had the leg of his cargoes pulled up and was busy getting a grip of his prosthetic. He'd been on industrial amounts of painkillers since the transtibial replacement was fitted three weeks ago, courtesy of The Owl. 'Transtibial' meant he'd lost his leg below the knee, which was what tended to happen when you stepped on an IED in Helmand. He, Jack and Rio were all physically disabled outcomes of the two post-9/11 wars, but here we still were, after five years of fucking around together.

I unzipped the bag and distributed our only weapons, the four steel belaying pins, each twenty-three centimetres by two and a bit, which Gabe had also bought at Decathlon. Each was still in its packaging, and if we'd been caught with them we'd have said we worked on a big boat with old-fashioned rigging. Not that any of us had the remotest idea about anything to do with masts.

The sea motion had stopped. The massive yacht was solid on the water. From here, even the wake that had flung us about was a smooth, constant wave. The inflatable trapped in it, however, was bucking like a bronco, and I hoped the nylon line held.

Three of us gripped our belaying pins, but not Gabe: he tucked his into his waistband. If all went to plan, he wasn't going to need one. He was the star, we were the supporting cast. We were all here for him.

I tossed the empty holdall off the back of the yacht. 'Gabe, you ready?' He was still sorting his prosthetic, turning a small blue dial just above his Nikes where his ankle once was.

We waited for his answer.

His cargoes went back down over the titanium shaft. 'Yep.'

Rio poked him gently in the shoulder with his belaying pin. 'Mate, you sure? You really sure?'

He nodded without hesitation, and I stood up. 'Okay, let's get on with it.'

The plan was short and sharp: get to the target, and kill him. Taking out anyone else doing business with him would be a bonus. Plans didn't come simpler than that, and that was good. When the pressure goes up, the IQ goes down.

I took up position at the bottom of the curling gangway on the right that led up onto the rear lower deck, ears pricked for any sounds above the low, powerful hum of the engines. Everything down here was sparkling clean, and no doubt the interior was even cleaner. Any other day, somebody would have been very unhappy that we hadn't taken our trainers off on deck.

I studied each of the three in turn, waiting for their nods. I got them. We all wanted this over and done with, each for his own reason.

As I put my foot on the bottom step, I hoped that being under way meant security would be concentrating on what happened inside, that as far as they were concerned, everything out here was good. According to The Owl, he travelled with just two bodyguards. But The Owl had got the *Alamat*'s movements wrong, so now we had to consider the possibility that the other information we'd been given might also be wrong, including how much security was on the boat. Whoever, whatever came our way, we would have to deal with it the best we could. That was why we still worked for The Owl: we had gone past caring about dramas. We'd all had enough of those over the years to know how to deal with whatever was thrown at us. For The Owl, that was good; for us, not so much. But that's what happens when you begin not really giving a fuck.

When you start out in this business, you don't care because it's about the thrill, action, mission, challenge, whatever you want to call it. Then, after a while, you get into maximum damage with minimum risk. You want to enjoy the benefits of the work and spend the money. Then you get to where we were: back to not giving a fuck, but not for the reasons the younger versions of ourselves once had. Maybe it was because at this stage none of us was under any illusion as to what he was involved with. No tears, no fears. Just get on with what you've chosen to do.

As my head came level with the top step, I spotted an outdoor dining table and chairs, and beyond them a wall of glass. Then, beyond that, the brighter, almost yellow, lights inside.

And there was movement.

Bodies sat on a sofa with their backs to me and I saw three male heads. None of them matched photographs of Isar. The hair was either too thin, or too grey. They were laughing, but I couldn't hear what about through the wall of glass. The three heads were acknowledging somebody to their right: there was at least one other body out of sight to me.

Above them, two decks higher, was the bridge, and everybody on it was going to be far too busy looking ahead to look down. I couldn't see bodies out on deck.

I climbed down to the other three. 'I have three confirmed bodies, inside, the other side of the glass doors. No Isar yet.

There's another unsighted possible. I'm going to move closer.' I laid my good hand on Jack's shoulder. 'You back me. Rio, stay with Gabe. If there's a drama, you two come in and get among it. You know what to do.'

Gabe was impatient. 'Get on with it, for fuck's sake.' His eyes drilled into mine.

I gave him a quick nod and started up the stairs, secure in the knowledge that Jack would be right behind.

3

Crouched in the shadows, behind the table and chairs on deck, I'd been enjoying having an extra obstruction between me and the wall of glass, but it was time to move. I needed a better view into the cabin.

I edged my way towards the centre of the deck, and as my perspective changed, Isar finally came into view to my right. He looked exactly like he had in The Owl's photos. Dressed in a short-sleeved blue shirt and green sleeveless pullover, he looked like he was propping up a golf-club bar as he pontificated to his guests. His moustache was as jet-black as his short, immaculately groomed hair, which seemed unlikely. We knew he was in his mid-fifties, and even if we hadn't, the dad-bod bulge under the green said it all.

I tried to stand stock-still but there was a bit of motion under my feet. I swayed with it. Isar held his cigarette between his forefinger and thumb, and took a drag. He was happy, confident. He was enjoying holding court to the three guys on the sofa, who all looked about the same age as him. He had a tumbler of amber liquid in his free hand, gave them a toast and took a sip.

The yacht did another gentle up and down and I glanced behind me. The mass of lights to the right were Nice, the ones to the left Monaco: we were coming out of the bay.

It was shit or bust time – but between me and the four in the cabin was a wall of massive glass panes. They would be marine quality, maybe laminated. The two attached to the body of the *Alamat* on the left and right were solid panels, and the two in the middle pulled apart like patio doors. We had an entry point, but was it locked?

I couldn't see any other entry points into this part of the yacht, though there were certainly more, via other doors on the way towards the bow. We had all watched the charter company's video promoting *Alamat* and its crew, yours for only $136,000 a week. But these entry points weren't in the running as options: that would entail moving around the yacht and heightening the possibility of a compromise. The important thing was that the target was close – once we started, we wouldn't have any time to waste. By whatever means we got him, it would have to be from here. Apart from anything else, two of the Special Needs Service hadn't that many legs to run about with.

The minute or two I stared into the haze of nicotine felt like twenty, but Isar finally turned his back on the guests to face a highly varnished, dark-wood drinks cabinet. Stubbing out his cigarette in an already overflowing ashtray, he put down his glass tumbler, reached inside the cabinet, and pulled out a fresh pack. His jaw never stopped working as he turned to the rest of them, all smiles through perfect, expensive-looking teeth. Shoulders on the sofa heaved with laughter. He lit a new cigarette to add to the haze, then picked up his glass and turned again to his guests. That was when I made my move.

4

Jack's head was where it needed to be, just peering over the top of the steps, covering me, checking for movement forward and above. He leant out to one side to let me go lower to join the other two, then he descended a few steps behind me, staying about halfway down, partly to provide early warning of movement above, but also so he could hear what I had to say. I told them what I had seen. None of them looked directly at me: they were in their own worlds, picturing in their minds what I was describing.

'So, order of march: me, Jack, Rio, Gabe. I go straight for the doors. If they're open, Jack, Rio, make entry and dominate the room, I'll back. Gabe, wait for me to shout you in. If they're locked, I'll go for it – top right-hand corner of the far-right pane.' I didn't wait for any form of reply. 'No matter what, we get through, same order of march. It might be a bit scrappy, but we clear the route for Gabe. Short and sharp, yeah?'

I took two nods and didn't wait for words, instead turned and made my way up the steps once more, Jack leaning out to let me pass. To focus on the job and accept the outcome, one way or another, was always best. I went into auto-mode, as we all would.

I strode straight up to the doors, with the four bodies still in the positions I had left them. I gripped the two handles, and pulled.

Nothing.

There was a bit of reaction from inside, but nothing of concern. Not yet, anyway. For all they knew, I was crew, but that would change in the next couple of seconds.

I didn't try again. I jumped back, moved to the right, and took a run at the right-hand glass panel, belaying pin raised in my left, like a dagger. Arm straight, I twisted my body for extra momentum and slammed it hard into the top right corner of the pane.

All four bodies inside jerked round as the pin bounced back. Fuck: not enough power from my left hand. Another swing at the corner and the bodies now moved, brains scrabbling to process what the fuck was going on. If you're in a secure area, it takes several seconds to understand that there's a problem. With luck, they'd had enough drink to slow them down even further, but it wouldn't last for long. They'd switch on soon enough.

As I gave the pin a third swing Jack came in from behind. 'Move!'

Passing me as fast as his different legs would take him, he jumped as best he could, pin raised, and made contact. The impact made a dull thud and the hole was only small, but the 1960s safety glass frosted and turned into a giant spider's web.

I put my shoulder against the frosting and Jack immediately threw his weight into me, pushing me through and down onto the room's carpet amid a shower of thousands of little glass shards. Jack and Rio scrambled over my back before I could get up and follow. There was no screaming from either of them: there was no need yet.

After the freshness of the sea air outside, the haze and stench of cigarette smoke hit my eyes and nostrils, like I was being tear-gassed.

As I pushed deeper into the room I could make out two of the sofa crew on the floor, hands raised, pleading. Jack and Rio had their pins up, ready to smash them down on anyone who moved. The third guest tried to scramble to the far wall, but Rio brought down his steel onto his back and flattened him. He fell with his arms spread wide and sobbed into the plush carpet. I wasn't concerned about them. It was Isar: he was more alert and had started towards the corridor in the top left corner of the room. He turned and hurled his tumbler in our general direction, and it ricocheted off a brown leather chesterfield chair and onto the shower of glass splinters. Brandy sprayed my face and filled my nostrils.

'Stand still! Stand still!'

I pointed my steel at him and saw that my hand was covered with blood. I wanted him to obey but he pivoted. He wasn't going to take direction from anyone.

'Gabe! Gabe!'

I threw my pin left-handed at his back, hoping at least to slow him as I ran for him. It missed.

Gabe was in the room now and level with me, totally in his own world, not looking at me or anybody, totally focused on where his pin needed to go. It made contact and Isar went stumbling with a yelp before dropping to his knees, but still moving into the corridor, screaming for back-up.

Gabe was so fixated on his task he wouldn't have felt the

pain from his leg. He closed on Isar just as the Lebanese reached the corridor and threw himself onto his target's back. It was a messy sort of rugby tackle, but it brought them both to the floor.

Gabe was now where he needed to be as bodies came running down the corridor from the decks above.

Gabe had seen them too. His scream was muffled as he fought to keep control of Isar. 'Going early, gotta go now!'

We all knew what was coming.

The three of us dropped behind the sofa a split second before the explosion.

5

The pressure wave rammed us into the floor, blasting the contents of the corridor into millions of pieces as it tried to find a way out of the confined space.

My ears rang and everything became muffled, as if I had dived into a swimming-pool. I finally stood up in the cloud of smoke and dust. The sofa crew and the new bodies deeper into the corridor weren't moving, their clothes ripped from them, their bodies torn apart in a mass of tissue and bone. The brisance of all the debris shattering and being carried away by the pressure wave at high velocity had done its job on them. Thousands of wooden and glass shards had joined the fragments of titanium shrapnel from the one-kilogram device built into Gabe's prosthetic. There was nothing left of Gabe and Isar. The floor and side panels of the corridor about the detonation site were just gaping holes.

It took a couple of seconds for it to sink in. Seconds we didn't have to lose.

'Move! Move!' I had to push Rio to make him follow Jack onto the deck. He'd taken some glass from the wall as he first came into the room and blood poured down his face, but he was breathing, and head leaks always look worse than they are. But it wasn't the loss of blood that had taken its toll.

We fell down the stairs to the inflatable. The wake wasn't as big as before – the yacht was slowing. There were shouts from up in the bridge area, shouts from the bow. A fire alarm had kicked off with a strident two-tone wail.

Jack unleashed the inflatable, held the rope and jumped in with it. I wanted us out into the darkness, out of sight, not fucking about and wasting time trying to get aboard methodically. Grabbing Rio, I had a sudden thought. 'Can you swim?'

'Fuck off!'

He jumped, and I followed. Nothing mattered apart from making distance from the yacht.

I didn't look back, just kept swimming. The bay lights were about a kilometre away. The inflatable was silhouetted against them, and there were two bodies on board. Rio was at the outboard and it was Jack who was going to have to drag me over the inflatable's side. Getting aboard from the sea was a two-handed job. I grabbed the side line with my left hand and pulled myself up some of the way. Then he grabbed my belt and helped me slither over and in.

Rio twisted the throttle to get us back into the bay.

Looking back, I could see the yacht was now fully lit, its emergency beacons strobing the sky. Someone fired a red flare from the bridge that illuminated the darkness, but it wasn't needed – to our right, as we looked back, clusters of lights were heading fast from Nice.

Rio turned away to face the bay as he worked the outboard, and all he could say was 'Fuck, he did it. He did it.'

I had to get everything back online. 'We stick to the plan.'

As soon as we were on land, we would split up and head

for our hides, where our passports, personal items and cash were stashed. Then it was every man for himself to get back to the UK.

My hide was in the wheelie-bin area behind the Best Western near Nice railway station. Cheap and impersonal hotels are always found near city stations, but my plan wasn't to catch a train. The station would be a key point for the police to check. In my hide I also had a change of clothes. One by one, we would walk out of the city and eventually head to Italy, a couple of hours away. All the security at the border was outward-facing in an attempt to stop migrants crossing into France from Italy at Ventimiglia. Movement the other way, there was far less vigilance about.

From there, none of us knew each other's plan for getting back to the UK. It was good Operation Security. My own plan ended with a flight to Scotland, as the last part of this job had to be done alone.

PART TWO

6

Glasgow International
Monday, 19 July 2021

The sky, what little of it I could see through the blanket of condensation on the rear windows, was as cold and grey as Aberdeen granite. Almost like the weather gods were setting the scene for my afternoon's work.

The cab driver had his wipers on intermittent and they slapped against the sound of the radio, tuned to a local call-in. The world was still turning in its normal fucked-up way, with the added joy of us all having to wear masks. Covid was still with us, and politicians were still bickering at each other over trivia, while Russia was still busy fuelling polarization in the US and ensuring no real leadership in the West – and super-busy using Ukraine as a testing ground for its cyber-war capability.

As for our attack on Isar and his business partners, it had been seen just as The Owl had said it would, as an inside operation, a power struggle. It's a universal law that if you have something of value someone will want to take it from you for themselves. It had been attributed to a suicide bomber, armed with a device made from Russian plastic explosive sourced in Syria and an Iranian detonator that had landed up in Iraq. The bomber had infiltrated with all the illegal migrants coming in from North Africa, just like all the right-wing groups in Europe had warned – and he had then attacked and killed the middleman, the guy who made his money by providing safe routes around the world for the three illegal activities that underpinned most Western banking systems.

If it wasn't for the international businesses of drugs, people trafficking and terrorism the world economy would show deep cracks in its foundations. It wasn't just the money made illegally, then filtered into the mainstream economy that kept us going: it was also the taxpayers' funds spent on vast resources trying to counter these big three money-spinners. Both sides knew that this war would never be won, but so what? Both sides were enjoying the sort of revenue that made Jeff Bezos look like the owner of a corner shop.

It was people like Isar, a middleman, who made all this pain and money happen. People like him guaranteed that goods and cash got to where they needed to be. The big three use exactly the same routes around the world, for the simple reason that they are secure. That's why money from drug cartels in Mexico or Albanian brothels in Germany will fund terror groups in the Middle East: it's simply business. Of course, there are always bumps in the road, like a middleman being killed. But no matter what, the world keeps revolving. That was just the froth, the surface scum, of what Isar getting blown to bits was really all about.

The killings had made half a page in the French broadsheets

with a big picture of the bomb-damaged *Alamat* being towed away by tugs. The rest of the pages were shots of glamorous people on red carpets as the Cannes film festival was happening just thirty kilometres along the coast, at the same time as the hit. Post-Brexit, the UK press didn't give a shit. As for the US, where was France anyway? All just as The Owl wanted. There was too much out there in the public domain about targeted assassinations masterminded by the US, and any one of them could escalate to war.

7

Isar had expanded his portfolio of work into a technical area that was making him even more rich and powerful, yet at the same time more vulnerable to getting fucked over. It was a fickle world: no one was indispensable.

For years, US intelligence had had opportunities to kill one of America's High Value Targets, Iran's Qasem Soleimani, but decided against it because of the possibility of a large-scale retaliation by Iran, which would lead to a war in the Middle East we'd all get dragged into. But Trump ordered the hit anyway and a US drone strike killed Soleimani in Baghdad in January 2020.

The nightmare scenario of Iran's heavy retaliation didn't play out, and Trump denounced the intelligence community as wimps and wanted more Iranian High Value Targets eliminated. But what the intelligence community knew and Trump didn't, because he couldn't be arsed with proper security briefings, was that Iran now had an easier and more destructive way to retaliate. It had taken years to construct, but the Iranians had already prepared the battleground for an easier conflict and at the time of their choosing.

Iran conducted a front-of-house attack by firing ballistic missiles at two joint US-Iraqi air bases, but that was only to show an instant response and keep the home team happy. The real battleground was America's critical IT systems, which Iran had infiltrated, inserting various malware and denial-of-service attacks. The biggest attacks, the ones that most shocked the West, were the Iranians hitting the US with 'Zero Days' – security vulnerabilities that hackers could use to attack systems. Zero Days referred to the fact that if the creator learnt of a flaw in their software because it had been hacked, they'd have 'zero days' to respond with patches or workarounds. Once the flaw had been corrected the attack was no longer called a Zero-Day exploit. It was just called history. Usually, a very expensive history. It was like shutting the door to the chicken coop after the fox had already been in and ripped all the heads off. You can prevent future attacks, but there's still a lot of dead chickens.

Sometimes the developer did know about the vulnerability but wouldn't secure their software as they thought no one would ever be able to discover their mistake. By not acknowledging the problem, they kept their credibility. Or it was out there without anyone discovering it, apart from hackers searching for their money shot.

Iran had bought their Zero-Day exploits from Isar, the middleman, who represented hackers selling their discoveries everywhere from the backstreets of Buenos Aires to the hi-tech office blocks of Hong Kong. This was a worldwide underground market, with effective Zero-Day exploits changing hands for millions of dollars. Even the West's intelligence agencies were customers and, of course, the middlemen got their cut.

The Iranians had spent their cash wisely with Isar and were deep inside the IT systems of major US commercial businesses, from casinos to supermarket chains, the banking system and big oil. But, more importantly, they were also inside America's critical infrastructure: energy, water, defence and emergency services. After the Soleimani drone attack, the Iranians demonstrated their cyber capability to the US. They had attacked more than four hundred hospitals in the middle of the pandemic, the largest cyber-attack in history. Patients had been turned away and staff reduced to using pen and paper. At the same time, they opened a dam's floodgates in Pennsylvania while all the critical staff could do was watch the horror on their screens. Multiple states had to declare an emergency when US oil-supply pipelines were closed down. Then, just to tighten the screw, the Iranians attacked the computer systems of several southern states with ransomware. Their court and justice systems screens went black, along with their social-welfare departments, so the courts were closed and benefits cheques went unpaid. Acts like that made sure the US knew that Iran had a loaded gun aimed at it and made it very clear to the White House that they would fully retaliate at the time of their choosing. Trump would only have understood the severity of the situation when the lights went off in the Oval Office and the country's air-defence system went with it.

That made targeted assassinations by the US even more problematic because there were other countries with their own cyber-gun pointed at the US. Iran was now also a member of the cyber Mutually Assured Destruction club, but without a blue-water navy capable of cutting the underwater cables that supply almost all of the world's data traffic. That capability belonged to the other two players in the cyber MAD club: China and the really big one, Russia.

Why else had Russia been able to saunter into Crimea and take it from Ukraine in 2014 with just a few stern words from the White House in reply?

The White House knew, loud and clear, that if Russia retaliated with their cyber-weaponry, there was no Pentagon planning model or even a fairground clairvoyant that could predict what might happen.

8

I rubbed the condensation to look out at the less than welcoming tenement blocks, and tried to make the most of the downtime. The afternoon was going to turn very uncomfortable for me – and for Gillian and the two boys, if they were there, Anthony and Michael.

Gabe had served in 14 Sigs. The regiment's role was to provide an electronic warfare capability to enable operations in the electronic battlespace. Which basically meant: once a geek, always a geek, even if he was the unlikeliest-looking geek you would ever see and had bits missing.

His life, and his family's, had been unbearable since his last tour of Afghanistan had fucked him up, physically and mentally. He'd basically become a domestic health hazard, to the point where he had a court order banning him from seeing his kids after he slapped their mother, and she feared the violence would spread to them. As Rio shouted at him after he confessed it to us one day: 'You want to hit something? Get a fucking tambourine!'

Rio had wanted to ride shotgun today, but I needed to

keep him in reserve as Rio-the-good-guy card. Someone else, a stranger, should be the bearer of bad news. Rio fitted the bill. He used to go with Gabe to Glasgow and wait outside the house in his car while Gabe stood on the doorstep with his tail between his legs and begged for forgiveness after his latest outburst. That wouldn't work, of course, as they would kick off on each other. Before Gillian could call the police to serve the restraining order, Rio would step in and smooth the situation before it got completely out of hand. It was an indication of what a nightmare that particular marriage was if it was Rio Gillian got to like and trust.

Jack didn't even contemplate coming with me. It was a smart move, as he found it hard to deal with any woman, let alone a strong-minded one. I would have vetoed it anyway: Jack had an accent that would have got him a job as an announcer for the BBC in the 1950s, and for all I knew Gillian was a Nationalist with a four-hundred-year-old grudge against the Westminster oppressor.

Gabe had tried so many, many times to patch things up with Gillian and the kids, but the patches never stuck. It left him feeling a complete failure, on top of feeling guilty for surviving the IED in Afghanistan when the others in his vehicle had had their body parts thrown about in all directions across the desert. He felt he had failed as a husband. He felt he wasn't a good enough father for his sons, and sometimes not a good enough friend even to us. The emotions would churn around and take him over. His temper was a defence mechanism, when all along the only thing the once ginger-haired midget probably needed was a cuddle. Rio and I weren't offering, but occasionally others did, and Gabe's response was to push them away. All of us were concerned about him. Gillian, I knew from Rio, was more concerned than any of us, but she had to draw a line. He had to sort himself out before he could even dream about coming back. He might have made it, but the diagnosis was the final straw. It was aggressive and it was final, and for Gabe, all bets were off.

Mesenchymal chondrosarcoma was a primary bone cancer that was rare and very aggressive. It wasn't anywhere else in his body apart from the proximal femur of his complete leg, and the irony didn't escape him. The tumour was only picked up when Gabe went for his three-yearly MRI scan on his damaged leg. Both limbs went through the scanner together, and that was when the mass in the good one was discovered. He'd had pain and swelling over the past six months, but he'd put that down to his good leg overcompensating. Gabe didn't have much time for medics and he didn't bother getting it checked out. Further tests confirmed the disease and, worse, it was at Stage 3. The NHS oncologist suggested either a complex reconstruction of the femur and hip joint, or proton therapy, a new approach that gave a much higher dose of radiation into a more defined area. The problem was, there were only two centres in the UK, one in London and the other in Manchester. And the waiting list was years long.

But if Gabe could make his way to America . . .

9

To people in London or New York, or posing along the Croisette in Cannes, the collapse of Communism didn't stop the Cold War. It was just an updated version that had been raging since the nineties and still was. And just like with the old post-Second World War Cold War between the USSR and the West, neither side, be it the US, Russia, China or Iran, wanted a direct conflict, face to face. Of course, that would always be the option of last resort.

But why bother when Russia could influence US elections from the comfort of a room filled with desktop screens?

The West – really meaning the US's NSA (National Security Agency) and UK's GCHQ – were just as proactive against the opposition, but unfortunately not as good as them when it came to defence of their own systems. This was due to arrogance in the early days of this new conflict, thinking that no one, or no country, could possibly be as advanced at producing cyber-weapons as they were. But they forgot one fundamental world truth: that just because developing countries couldn't access the digital economy as easily as rich

Westerners were able to, it didn't mean no one else wanted to enjoy it just as much.

Teenagers from developing or sanctioned countries had to reverse-engineer and hack into software to access games, apps, Netflix, even regular satellite TV. This young generation of streetwise Russians, Chinese and Iranians now continually beat the brightest from Harvard, Princeton and Stanford at the International Collegiate Programming Contest, the oldest, largest and most prestigious programming contest in the world. An Argentinian teenager could hack into an iPhone in under sixty seconds at one of the world's so-called hacking conferences. Just like the conventional weapons trade, cyber-weapons also have their conferences. But unlike tanks and guns showing off their capabilities at a glitzy trade fair, cyber-weapons are sold in the dark corners of the world. This is where hackers rub up alongside cyber-criminals and security organizations from the US, Europe, Middle and Far East to sell their ransomware and, of course, the digital holy grail: Zero-Day exploits.

Isar had been one of the many middlemen in this business who also descended on these conferences from all over the planet to make sure these mostly teenage hackers would be getting the highest price without understanding who the buyer would be. If the price was right, Isar would even sell to the NSA and GCHQ, but once the Iranians had attacked the US with Zero Days that he had sold to them, it was the middleman who had to take the fall, so Isar became an HVT, ensuring he wouldn't do it again.

The Owl had given the rationale for why Isar had to die by quoting Joseph S. Nye, a political scientist: 'The defense of democracy in an age of cyber information warfare cannot rely on technology alone.'

It must have been quite the TED talk, but I thought it was more that the US had acted like a jilted lover: if I can't have her, no one else can. At that point The Owl took over from political theory and the system being pissed off with Isar.

That was fine by me: anyone with more than two brain cells understood that this new cyber Cold War needed to continue, because the only alternative was for any cyber-attack of magnitude to be declared an act of war, and then it would tip over into a full-scale global conflict. On the plus side of this cyber mutually assured destruction structure, the move from a conventional conflict to a nuclear exchange wasn't as clear-cut as it once was. Cyber mutually assured destruction was now a halfway house of threat between conventional and nuclear that would hopefully prevent or at least slow down the escalation, giving time for more stable minds to prevail. Hats off to street-kids everywhere.

So, killing Isar had had to be carried out in such a way that it looked like an internal dispute, non-attributable to the US, and done quickly before another high-profile drone attack was ordered. The quick and simple solution was to use a suicide bomber.

10

We'd made some cash doing what we did for The Owl a couple of years ago, and contacting him again was an obvious route forward. Or so we thought. Rio, Jack and I jumped in and said we'd work it out for Gabe to get to one of the proton-therapy centres in the US, but Gabe said thanks, but no thanks. He'd had enough. Of his disability. Of his life. Of the universe. Fuck it. For Gabe, it wasn't the fact that he was going to die: none of us get out of here alive. It was the fact that he had no control over the when and the how. He needed to be the one who arranged his travel plans, no one or nothing else. He chose to die, but he also chose the way he wanted to, and when. On his terms.

And that was where The Owl came up with a plan. If it worked, it could be rolled out. There was a market for people like Gabe in The Owl's world. People for whom there was no hope, and who wanted to be compensated for the inevitable.

It wasn't a new concept. It had been going on for decades: bombers with suicide vests, people driving car bombs, even sometimes insider attacks in Iraq or Afghanistan where local troops or police would open fire on their own side. In less developed countries where no social welfare or health system exists, and most of their populations are living on a dollar a day, it makes sense to be paid to sacrifice yourself for the wellbeing of your family.

In Afghanistan, the Taliban even had a suicide training school called the Paradise Facility.

I'd seen a number of car bombers hit by gunfire while attempting to drive into a checkpoint and killed before they could detonate, and two of them were adults with Down's syndrome. People might think it outrageous that terrorists, organized crime or even sovereign states were exploiting disadvantaged people, but another way of looking at it was: why not? Why not accept the offer to bomb or kill someone? Why not actually achieve something in their death, making sure their family got money, making sure their family were helped out of their poverty? Mostly they didn't give a fuck about becoming a martyr. Ideology was left to the low achievers, who believed the hype and just thought about themselves.

Orphanages were ideal places to radicalize children, who had the added bonus of being cheaper to detonate. The only payment was a bribe to the orphanage for access to the pool of potential bombers. Kids as young as eleven, who had no future or no understanding of what they were doing, would be guided onto a target by their mentor. Just before the attack their mentor would give the last few words of encouragement, while arming the device that could be a suicide vest, bag or even a bicycle, then leaving the kid to make the final distance to target and detonate.

Even the Provisional Irish Republican Army played with the idea of using suicide bombers. They would have recruited young guys from housing estates in Dublin. It would have been easy to rev up eighteen-year-olds to kill themselves for the cause – it always had been. But the social and political fallout would have been disastrous for the Republicans, because at the time PIRA were already killing more of their own people than the Brits were.

11

The Shawlands area, two kilometres south of the River Clyde, wasn't at all what I'd been expecting. It was a nice middle-class area with tree-lined streets, red sandstone terraced houses and a trendy coffee shop every fifty metres, not a location I would have associated with the rough, tough Glaswegian I'd known. Then I suddenly knew why Gabe was skint: he was brick rich, cash poor. His wife and kids had benefited from all his guilt.

The cab driver must have been as new to the area as I was, because he religiously followed Google Maps off the mobile stuck to the windscreen. He stopped outside a terraced house in Tantallon Road and took the thirty quid I offered him. He made no effort to give me the £2.60 change as I jumped out, tucking the A4 Jiffy envelope under my duvet jacket to protect it from the rain.

The envelope contained letters from Gabe to his wife and each of his boys, the death certificate, and details of funds that he had arranged for her to access. There was his army pension, of course, and the MoD would sort that out for her, but he'd also made sure The Owl paid upfront for the Isar job and the cash was sitting in his account. What he didn't know was that there was four times as much in the account as he had planned. Rio, Jack and I had had a chat, and it seemed the right thing to do. We could always go back to the well. He couldn't.

There was darkness at the front of the house and through the frosted-glass panel on the front door, so there was a chance I'd be drinking lattes in the local café.

Behind the wooden gate was a small, neat front garden, and I had to negotiate a row of recycling bins.

I got to the doorstep, and ran through my lines one final time in my head. She would have spent years waiting for a knock on the door when he was in Afghanistan. Every time the doorbell went, she would have thought: This is it. And now it had finally happened, and she was going to open it to me.

I put my finger on the doorbell, and as I pressed, my finger trembled. Not because I was worried about the lies I was going to tell Gabe's widow, but because that was what it had been doing for weeks now, every time I put pressure on it.

Then the rest of my hand began to shake, a little at first, then uncontrollably, and finally it locked completely in a painful spasm.

12

The other side of the frosting was suddenly bright and a fuzzy shape got larger as it approached from the rear of the house.

I'd only seen her once before and a long time ago, in an old photo-booth shot out of Gabe's wallet. Even so, the woman in front of me didn't look at all like I was expecting. Her hair was still dark brown but much shorter than in the picture, cut in a sort of take-no-prisoners bob, and her expression was severe. She looked like she had an axe to grind with any man who came to her door, raising an arm to block the entrance, waiting for me to talk.

I tried my hardest not to look like a threat or a dodgy door-to-door salesman. I was probably smiling a bit more than I should have been.

'Hello. My name is Nick. You're Gillian?'

I got a slow who-the-fuck-are you-and-what-the-fuck-do-you-want nod.

'I'm Gabe's friend. We haven't met, but—'

Her face contorted. 'He doesn't live here.' The Glasgow

accent was as aggressive as Gabe's. 'I don't know where he is.'

My hands went up in submission. 'I know. Can I come in?'

She looked at me like I was crazy. 'No way! What's he done?'

'He's dead.'

Her face dropped, in shock rather than sadness. Maybe that would come later. 'Oh.'

I let it sink in a while longer.

'Oh. Oh. How?'

'Could I come in? It'll be better if I explain it inside.'

She bounced back into the real world and beckoned. I stepped past her into a narrow hallway and pulled the Jiffy from my duvet. She saw but didn't ask.

The walls were freshly painted – I could still smell the last of the oily residue. They were covered with pictures of the boys playing football on the beach, the boys holding trophies, all that sort of stuff. There were plenty, too, of the boys with Gillian, but none with Gabe.

'Are the boys home?'

The door closed behind me and she switched off the hall light.

'No. Nick, right? I'll get the kettle on.' She headed down the passage, to where light was trying hard to push through a doorway.

I followed her into what looked like a newly knocked-through kitchen-diner. A couple of Papa Johns sat defrosting in their boxes on the draining-board. Through the patio doors I could see two pairs of very wet and muddy football boots neatly lined up outside on the patio, and all around was the normal shit that normal people have in the main room of their house. There was a bowl of fruit on the dining table, opened letters stacked up, to-do style. Attached to the wall on the other side of the room was a flat-screen TV, near it a sofa with throws, and in between a coffee-table covered with football and gamer magazines. What really drew my gaze, though, was a picture hanging next to the flat-screen. It was Gabe in Afghanistan in standard squaddie pose, rifle in hand, butt in the shoulder and grinning ear to ear into the camera.

Gillian checked inside the kettle a bit too long and decided it needed more water. She followed my gaze. 'The kids need to remember what their father looks like, don't they? I put it next to the TV since they spend all their time glued to it.'

She turned back to the sink and flicked the tap on, but she couldn't finish filling it. Her shoulder dropped. Tears rolled down her cheeks that fell into the sink. I gestured, which seemed a waste because she didn't see me. 'Shall I do it?'

'No, no.' She pointed to the table, her eyes still fixed on the sink. It was an order. I did as I was told and placed the Jiffy next to the to-do letters.

She got a grip of herself as she filled the kettle. 'How did it happen?' She kept her eyes now fixed on the spout as if that would make it fill quicker.

It was pointless beating about any bushes. 'He had bone cancer in the good leg.'

By now the lid was back on the kettle. Gillian put it on its circular receiver and gave the power a flick. 'What? Why didn't I know?'

Both her hands were on the worktop, and she supported herself with straight arms as tears fell onto her thin blue sweater, producing dark spots. 'You know, I spent years waiting for a knock on the door when he was going out there.' Her head jerked at the picture on the wall. 'Every time the doorbell went, I thought, This is it. And now it's finally happened. I've opened it to you.'

She finally broke down. She sobbed, her shoulders heaving up and down.

The kettle boiled and switched itself off. I stood up, trying to show respect, help her make the tea, whatever I needed to do, just knowing I wanted to get out of the house as soon as I could. I hated this even more than I'd thought I was going to. Not because of the loss of Gabe, but because she was about to get lied to big-time about a man she obviously still cared for. I wasn't expecting that.

'Why didn't he tell me?'

Her hands came away from her face and she wiped her nose. Little pools of mascara stained her bottom lids.

'Fucking idiot.'

I thought the sobs had finished but they hadn't. The black mascara ran down her cheeks.

'It was quick. He only knew six months ago. He didn't want you to know. He didn't want to complicate things even more. He just wanted to get sorted as if nothing had happened, and hopefully get back to the point where things were with you before the war.'

'Where was he, where did he . . .?'

'Cleveland in the States. They've got this advanced proton laser that can really define and kill the cancer – but it was too late in his case. I'm sorry.'

She came towards the table and I jumped up and held a chair out for her. She sat, her hands in her lap, shoulders heaving. I sat opposite her. 'I'm here because Gabe asked me to tell you a few things. First of all, that he loves you, he loves the kids, always has and always will. He just didn't want to put you and the boys through any more pain than he has already. But he also wanted me to tell you that he's made sure you're going to be financially secure. There's the army pension, of course – they'll sort it out for you – but he'd been working really hard and had savings put aside for you and the kids. What he's provided for you will be deposited every month, just like he normally did, but now it's going to be six thousand a month for the next ten years. He wanted to make sure you and the boys are looked after.'

She didn't move her head. Her eyes were still on her lap. She fiddled with her fingers. 'Six? How did he . . .?'

She looked up. She wanted an answer.

I slowly shook my head. 'Please, don't. Just – it's six thousand a month for ten years. Think about yourself and the boys, because that's all he thought about. This is what he wanted for you.'

She stared. 'Who are you?'

'No one.' I shrugged. 'We worked together.'

She pulled a tissue from her sleeve and wiped her nose. The heels of her palms went up to her eyes, which made the mascara spread even more over her cheeks. 'Okay, so you're telling me he died of cancer? Is that the story?'

'It's the truth. He had cancer. I'm sorry.'

'Can I bury him?'

I shook my head slowly, giving myself time to make sure I got the lie straight. 'He wanted to be cremated, in Cleveland, no fuss, and then I was to scatter the ashes in the Clyde. I did that this morning on the way in. I'm so sorry. I should have thought about it. I should have asked if you wanted to be there. But he was adamant he'd put you through enough trouble all these years and he didn't want to add to it. He made me promise to come here, scatter his ashes, and tell you that you and the boys will be looked after.'

She jumped up and for a split second I thought she was going to attack me. Instead, she headed for the kettle before turning it back on for a quick reboil. 'Did he leave a letter for me? The boys?'

I laid a hand on the Jiffy. 'It's all in here for you. To you *and* the boys, the death certificate, details of the account he arranged for you to access the cash.'

She threw a teabag into a mug and poured water from the kettle.

Her head jerked up. 'You say you worked with him? In the army?'

I shook my head.

'You know Rio?'

'Yes.'

She nodded slowly. 'Oh, aye.' It was starting to come together for her. There had been quite a lot of cash come Gillian's way for her and the kids – Gabe had always made sure of that. Gillian was no idiot. She knew never to ask. She dug out the teabag and added milk, then a couple of sugars, which I didn't want, but I let her get on with it. The tears still fell. 'Do you know, we would have got back together. All he had to do was sort himself out. I just couldn't have him the way he was, living in the house. He was a good father. He once was a good husband. He could have got back there.'

The tea came to the table along with a coaster that she placed in front of me. I left it. It would be too hot. She slumped back into the chair opposite, no tea for herself, her head in her hands once more. But it felt like she'd got over the initial shock. 'Was it quick?'

'Very.'

Her shoulders were going once more. I let her get on with

it. I didn't know her well enough to put an arm round her, and there was nothing I could say or do to change the facts.

After several long seconds she sat upright, composing herself, and looked over my shoulder at the far wall. 'You know, once he came home from hospital and out of the army I was so happy I would never have to tell the boys their dad was dead.'

She checked the clock again on the wall behind me. 'The boys'll be home soon.' There was no mistaking her worried tone.

I picked up the tea and took a testing sip. 'Do you want me to stay, to explain?'

She got to her feet, a bundle of nerves, and turned back to the worktop. On autopilot, she started to unpack the pizzas and turn on the wall oven at the same time. 'No, the boys don't know you. I don't know you. It needs to be just the three of us. I need to be with my boys.'

I was relieved but gave her an accepting nod.

The pizza boxes got crushed and thrown into a blue bin.

'I rehearsed this so many times in my head when he was away, how to tell the boys. The knock on the door, the guy in uniform telling me the worst. I had that when he was blown up, but it was different. He was still alive. But this – I'm not prepared. I thought that was all behind us.'

The red oven warm-up light hadn't gone out, but the pizzas went in anyway. She turned back to me. It was straight arms against the worktop again, her face a mess of black. 'I told them that one day Dad would be home, once he felt better . . .'

I was glad she was looking everywhere but at me. 'That was why he wanted the treatment so badly. Get the cancer over with. Not tell anyone, not have anyone to worry – and make up for lost time. When he was diagnosed, he was devastated, but he was adamant about not being a burden. I'm sorry for you and the kids that it's worked out this way but he made sure you were taken care of. Please, just keep his provision to yourself. No one needs to know. Could you do that for him?'

Now she was looking at me. Staring, pleading. 'Please, Nick. Did he really have cancer? He didn't do anything stupid like fuck up and kill someone for this kind of money for us?'

It was easy to keep my eyes on hers. After all, it was me who'd fucked up. 'He had cancer.'

She looked down and sighed. I still wasn't convinced she believed me, but there was nothing I could do about that just now. I stood up.

The oven pinged as the warm-up light cut out.

'You're busy – I'll see myself out. Thanks so much for the tea.'

The pings from the oven persisted, and as I made my way to the front door the sound of her sobs filled the corridor.

I closed the door behind me, wove round the bins and out onto the street. I didn't know where I was going, but that didn't matter. What did was that she wasn't convinced. All I could do was rely on money being the universal smoother of all problems, and hope that the security it would bring to her and the boys would soon erase any thoughts that might put her in danger.

Giving her a lump sum upfront before the payments started would have helped that erasing, but would also have brought a big possibility of compromise. Gillian had to be given enough that she felt financially secure and could save, but it could only be enough to be seen as sustainable within her lifestyle. Otherwise it would send red flags up where they shouldn't be. Back in my days running agents in Northern Ireland, it would have been like paying an unemployed informer who lived in a council flat a grand a week. It wouldn't take long for questions to be asked after he'd bought himself a BMW, the world's biggest Tag Heuer, and started placing chunky bets down at the bookie's.

As I turned the first corner on my walk to anywhere, two boys in black school blazers – they were maybe ten and eleven by now – came towards me from the opposite direction, ties reaching only halfway down their shirtfronts and the knots far too big, swinging their school daysacks at each other as they messed about. The closer they got, the easier it was to recognize them.

I stepped onto the road for them to pass, then stopped and looked back, so pleased for them that it was their mother they took after rather than the ginger midget.

It was a shame. They were having such fun, but they were going to have a really shit end to their afternoon.

PART THREE

13

Tulse Hill, South-east London
Saturday, 25 September 2021

I came out of the station in south London and straight away a discarded newspaper blew itself against my jeans and stuck. The spotlessness of Harley Street was only forty minutes behind me by tube and train, but it might as well have been a continent.

By the time I'd found a bin to chuck it in, I'd learnt that China had declared crypto-currency transactions illegal, and a much bigger piece told me all about the tribulations of Britney Spears. According to a former employee of a security firm, the singer's father and the security firm he hired to protect her ran an intense surveillance operation that monitored her communications and secretly captured audio recordings from her bedroom, including her interactions and conversations with her boyfriend and children.

Tough on Britney, but I had my own problems. The hour-long session with the consultant neurologist hadn't been the formality I'd hoped. I regretted not going via the NHS, and not getting an appointment until well into 2022. At least it would have bought me a few more months of ignorance. My fault for sticking to the principle that if you can afford not to be in the NHS queue, you owe it to society to give someone else your place. And as the consultant told me when I joked about feeling guilty, the NHS would fall apart if doctors couldn't earn their kids' school fees through private practice.

My right hand had been in a black neoprene wrist support for a couple of weeks now, the only way I could disguise the intermittent tremor, and the story I'd told the other two about spraining my wrist falling off an e-scooter was wearing thin. The shaking had got so bad I'd had to cave in.

Could be Parkinson's, the consultant said, could be MS, could be a form of dystrophy or motor neurone, could be one of a whole heap of neurological things or 'a combination thereof'. Or it could be none of these. It would take months of tests to pin it down for sure.

Did the diagnosis actually matter? I asked. Would the condition be curable? Unlikely, but not impossible, was the answer. From the look on his face, I got the feeling that whatever it turned out to be, it was going to be at the upper end of the bad-luck-mate-you're-fucked spectrum.

What could have caused whatever it was? Genes, most likely, he said. Though, there had been research to show that veterans in the States had had neurological disorders triggered by Agent Orange in Vietnam. And physical trauma. Had I ever been injured or beaten up in my time in the military? Morning, noon, and night, I said. If it counted, I'd also done a lot of high-altitude low-opening parachuting without oxygen. Hmm, interesting, apparently: Muhammad Ali's Parkinson's had been the type connected to head trauma.

And the consultant had treated any number of professional rugby players, all fucked up because they'd banged their heads together and been kicked to shit over the years.

Finally, with one eye on the clock, he had summed it all up in what he obviously thought was a helpful sentence: 'A condition like Parkinson's will change your trajectory in life,' he said, 'but it doesn't have to define who you are.'

I couldn't think of anything to say back but 'Fuck sake.'

14

Rio's house was on Coburg Crescent, just up on the left. I crossed what was left of the grass bank dividing the crescent from the South Circular, and wove through clumps of parked cars.

Ten minutes later, the three remaining members of the Special Needs Service were perched in our usual places in Rio's living room, staring at the unoccupied sofa. As a mark of respect, we'd cleared away the sleeping bag and empty pizza boxes when we got back, but that had only emphasized the vacuum, and we had daily debates about taking it all to the dump. I couldn't remember who came up with the name Special Needs Service, but after my trip to Harley Street, if there was a selection process to join, all of us were now shoo-ins.

The four of us had been living there for at least a year before the Isar job. None of us had anywhere else to go because nobody wanted us, but Rio had taken us in. He had been the only one to think ahead and buy himself an ex-council house, one of the scores of narrow 1960s terraced brown brick houses in this neck of the woods, with a garage as the ground floor and two floors above.

I'd only just got home, but it seemed it was my turn to make tea. It always was, as the rest of SNS took way too long. By the time they had hobbled up to the kettle we could all have been on our second brew. I threw the Co-op teabags into three large tannin-stained mugs and threw the belVitas towards the armchairs Rio and Jack were sitting in. It was lunchtime, after all. The brews were stronger than usual as we had hardly any milk left.

The packet fell short and landed next to a half-eaten bread roll on the glass coffee-table stained with mug rings, next to a spoon and a bowl, both encrusted with dried soup. Rio wasn't exactly what you'd call house-proud. If *Homes & Gardens* ever did a feature and asked him to describe the look he'd gone for, shabby chic wouldn't cut it. Freshly burgled would be closer. I'd tried to make the place look less derelict, but had thrown in my hand after a week.

Thrown in my hand. Fuck sake. I allowed myself a wry smile.

Rio was annoyingly taller, better-looking than Jack or me, and far too slim, considering the amount of calories he shoved down his neck. He was still on the ganja – too much sometimes – to help with the pain of having the lower half of his forearm missing. He was very particular when it came to terminology. It had to be called ganja, which in his mind meant it also had to be Jamaican. He wanted to boost his ancestors' homeland economy. Until seven months ago, he'd had a limp lower arm and two fingers that were fixed in a semi-permanent hook. He used to cover it with a thin woollen glove so he didn't scare the kids in Tesco. Well, that was how he joked about it, but in truth he didn't want his own twin girls to see the damage bad men had done to their dad. But he'd had enough of the inconvenience of having an arm just hanging there, and had elected for an amputation. It was a strange decision. It wasn't like there was anything new he could do, and the pain was still there for him to medicate, or so he claimed. But at least the empty sleeve was tidier to look at than his dreadlocks. They weren't anything to do with religious enlightenment: he just couldn't be arsed to go to a barber.

The dreads had come on really well when he started growing them six or seven years back. He had enough to bunch up into a woolly Rasta-cap, but I hadn't wanted him to do it in France. A big hat with Jamaican green, yellow and black bands would have been too much of a visual distinguishing mark, so instead he'd pulled them back and tied them into the world's biggest ponytail. It still stuck out, but it was much less of a multi-coloured VDM.

Those dreadlocks and the whiff of ganja were only two of Rio's Rasta features. His body certainly wasn't a temple: he ate meat, shoving Big Macs down his neck like they were threatened with extinction; he hated vegetables; he probably thought Haile Selassie was someone off *Love Island* and had no wish to go to Africa, let alone cross oceans to return to it. He didn't even like crossing the Thames to north London.

Failed-relationship-wise, Rio's issue was that he kept turning up at the family's old flat in the housing estate near Brixton, unannounced, sometimes drunk, mostly stoned, and it was affecting the kids. The lard-arse boyfriend, who, Rio grudgingly admitted, had lost a bit of weight, was now officially their stepdad, and the way I saw it he was doing quite a good job. The family had also got religion. The boyfriend apparently had always had it, and that had helped the girls get places at St Martin-in-the-Fields. It was the high school of choice for so many girls, and underpinned by Christian values. So it was well done, lard-arse boyfriend.

Maybe that was why Rio was so pissed off about him: he had never been able to make the cut when it came to stability. I knew the feeling well. At least he still had his family. His ex-wife hated him, and hated me, but Rio had always provided for the girls financially, and still did. He wanted to. Like Gabe had, he knew his responsibilities. That also meant he got to see his kids, albeit under his ex's supervision, the bonus being that he got to spend time with her as well, as a sort of fucked-up family. Just like Gabe, Rio did this shit for the sake of his wife and kids.

And now that he'd given up his big pay day, he was desperate for an injection of funds to keep it going.

15

The sofa had been Gabe's domain. He would eat and drink there all day, even sleep on it at night because it saved another flight of stairs to reach the three bedrooms. The problem was, he couldn't be arsed to get out of bed most mornings, and the rest of us had had to make do with two armchairs. It was also where he smoked, joint after joint. Rio had got the other two onto it to manage their pain. The downstairs smelt less of marijuana since we'd returned, but the bedrooms still stank. I was thinking of moving down here and sleeping on the floor.

A week's worth of the *Metro* and the *Sun* were scattered on the carpet, most of them folded to the TV page so we could fight over which sex-life-death talk show we would watch to waste an afternoon and many a night into the early hours, shouting at the housewives of LA, Atlanta and, our latest, Cheshire to get a fucking grip. But not today. The three of us had a fun-packed day ahead.

Rio was going to the Westfield Centre in Shepherd's Bush to use his Defence Discount card to chase a couple of pounds off a pair of jeans in the Levi's store. He used his discount card for everything. He even walked an extra five minutes to Starbucks instead of a closer Costa because he got a few pence off.

Jack was going with him to test-drive a Tesla. No discount cards accepted in that shop, for sure – not that Jack was in a position to put down even as much as a deposit. It was just that he worshipped the ground Elon Musk walked on and a Tesla showroom was the closest he was going to get to his idol until he dropped another pay cheque.

As for me, it was a two-bus trip to Notting Hill Gate for a meeting with The Owl. Rio had to pay for new kids' shoes, school trips, and all the other maintenance shit; Jack had to have funds to give away to some woman in distress he'd only met online; and me, I had to keep myself in neoprene supports and a drug called Rasagiline the specialist had prescribed, 'Just in case it is Parkinson's. We might as well get cracking.'

I shuttled over to the coffee-table holding two mugs in my left hand, and shoved the mess with my neoprene hand to make way. Then it was back to collect my mug before perching on the arm of Jack's brown corduroy and very saggy armchair. The rule was: first one into the room got an armchair to themselves.

I glanced down at Jack. He had been quiet when I set off this morning – but, then, he always was, thinking too much about life, death and everything in between. Maybe it was an ex-officer thing.

I kicked his titanium leg. 'Mate, you okay?'

The one thing Jack didn't have problems with was his prosthetic and its state-of-the-art adjustments. What was probably the last of the family money, spent on trips to the world's top prosthetics designers in the States, had seen to that.

His parents owed him. They'd christened him Jacobi in a moment of madness, but he'd changed it to Jack after his first playground fight. Like the rest of us he was ex-army, but he was smarter and got himself a commission. He had followed his forefathers into the army but really wasn't into running about up to his neck in Kevlar. He, Gabe and Rio had met each other in the military rehab hospital way before I had come and fucked their lives up even more.

Jack had put on a bit of lard, but had smartened himself up over lockdown. The once shiny blue eyes were still clouded and tired but gone was the county-lord look of curly matted hair, frayed shirt collars, and pullovers with holes in the elbows. To up his chances on Tinder, he had gone for the man-at-Gap look in an attempt to pass himself off as more the thirty-something he was. Well, sort of: his face looked like he'd been wearing it for ten years more than he had, and the only women he got swiped right by were almost old enough to be his mother. But he still plugged away at it. The new Jack was still out there looking to make his life even more complicated with a partner. It hardly ever got off the ground. His success rate at even attracting interest from potential online partners was low to start with, and after that he crashed and burnt. Women found him boring, usually because they couldn't be arsed to put in the time and find the real Jack. Either that or they found him boring and a good target to rip off.

His problem was that he wanted to be honest in his profile but had no idea how to write it. The result was honest-ish and not very interesting. But all was about to change for Jack: at great expense, he had found himself a profile writer.

Online, Candice would have a two-hour 'discovery session' with him so she could write up the true Jack for his profile page. Then she would write his first five email, text or WhatsApp exchanges with the next love of his life for him. There were only two issues. The first was that he still hadn't got it into his head that he lived a lie. His profile wouldn't be highlighting what had happened on the *Alamat* as some fun fact. The second was the money he would have used to pay her was now in someone else's bank account in Scotland.

16

It was Rio who articulated it. 'It's not the same without the midget, is it? Fucking pirate.'

We were all pirates. We had been coastguards many years ago, but they had fucked us over. The one certainty in my life was that being a pirate was a much better bet.

Jack hit the reality button. 'It is what it is. It's not the first time we've had bodies missing from the ORBAT, is it?'

For all the messy estate-agent look, he still had a military mind ticking away. ORBAT was the Order of Battle: which regiments and units were in the fight. He was right to use the term, even in this context. We were involved in a battle. But for me, no more. I'd been thinking during that forty-minute journey from Harley Street.

We finished our lunch and Rio was first to stand. 'Right, time to go bargain-hunting.' He would have rubbed his hands together if he'd had a pair.

Jack stood to join him. Then, as they started for the stairs, he had a thought. He didn't bother stopping, just called:

'Make sure you get some work out of your bossman. I want a Model 3 Performance.'

'Lads, about that . . . I've made a decision.'

Something in my tone got them both turning and heading back into the room.

'I'm done. France was my last job.'

Rio looked as shocked as Jack. 'Mate, you serious?'

I held up my neoprene hand. 'Something's up here. I get the shakes. It's not going to get better. When and how it gets worse, who knows? I've had enough fucking about. Time to kick back and enjoy a flight that's taking me on a holiday for once. I want to live a normal life.'

Rio jumped in. 'Really? Well, first you need to find someone to do real world with, and you being such a twat, that's not gonna happen. What then? Listen in. We're all fuck-ups.' He jutted a finger at Jack. 'What you call us?'

Jack had to think. He called us so many things, it took him a second to remember. 'Victims of biological injustice.'

Rio had always liked that one, but the half-smile evaporated as the finger turned to me.

'And you're the most fucked up of all of us. You'll be dead within a year out there. Your fucked-up brain won't be able to hack the real world. It's darker than in here, shit-for-brains.'

Jack agreed. 'Mate, you need to think about it. What have you got to offer the real world?'

Rio wasn't finished. 'Mate, you need to find someone, a real person, or you won't survive. Even Jack is out there trying. He might have the emotional brain of a six-year-old, but at least he's having a go, stepping up, know what I mean?'

Jack's face suggested he wasn't too sure if that was a compliment.

They waited for my reply, but they weren't going to get one.

Rio took the spare armchair. Jack just hovered about the room as the news sank in. They listened, faces blank, eyes on mine.

'Both of you need to stand steady. Look, it's not as if I'm one of you. The two of you instantly lost bits and had no time for thinking about the situation. It just was. But I've had a few weeks to accept it and adapt, still with my bits intact. I'm binning it because of the unpredictability. Feeling good today isn't a guide to how I feel tomorrow. Sometimes I feel totally fucked, sometimes fully switched on. I won't improve. I hope I will, but I now know I won't.'

Rio leant towards me. 'Yeah, but . . .'

I had to continue, because this part was very important for them to know. 'Listen – it was me that fucked up on the boat. I couldn't get the glass down. I gave them warning and nearly fucked up the whole job. My hand just wouldn't work. I could have killed you two as well. Not good, lads, not good. I'm sorry. I decided this morning. I can't have that happening again.'

I let it sink in for a couple of seconds. 'So, enough of that – the end. I'm going to tell The Owl the same.'

There was silence as I stood and turned to leave, to pre-empt any overtalk and concern.

Jack was shaking his head. 'Mate, we don't care that you won't be able to paint watercolours. Look about you, we're all damaged. The real world doesn't like people like us because we're not good for anything else, so why stop? Remember what Gabe used to say? It's scarier out there than in here.'

Rio slid back into the corduroy, his legs out straight, heels dug into the cheap green carpet. 'What you going to do,

Nick? Become one of those fuckers who say hello when you go to B&Q? Mate, we've all fucked up over the years, but so what? We got each other, know what I mean? You're lucky – at least you might get a timeline on when you get dead. Us two, we have to plod on without a fucking clue.'

He sucked his teeth as he rested his hand over his crotch as if my answer was going to be a kick.

Still standing, Jack was now punching the air between us to hammer home a point. 'If you knew what was going to happen tomorrow you'd give up today.'

Rio was more confused by that than I was. 'What the fuck?'

'What I'm trying to say to him, and now in a way you can understand, is this.' He turned back to me and our eyes locked. 'Get a fucking grip, Nick. We've got each other. We will all eventually go down doing what we do. We like the money and don't want to become one of the pencil-necks.' He turned to Rio. 'All for one and one for all, yeah? Better?'

He got a nod back, and I was ready to make a getaway. 'Thanks, yes – we'll always have each other. I will never let you down, but it's the end for me. I'm not going to fuck up on the job, and fuck you two up at the same time. But I'll see The Owl. I'll get you a gig.'

I was heading for the door, but Jack had one more thing to say.

'Okay, you do that. Tell the fucker that what's left of the SNS is still open for business and now we're half the price. Set up a meeting.'

Rio decided he wanted the last word. 'And pick up some milk!'

17

Nothing ever seemed to change along the Bayswater Road. Even the wind that drove the first drops of a downpour into my face as I got off the bus near Notting Hill Gate tube was gusting from the same direction as every other time I'd been there.

It was good skills to use buses. I could check if I was being followed as I boarded; I could go drink a coffee when I got off, and then check once more before boarding the next. What was more, it gave me time to think.

I wanted my hand to get better, but I had a bad feeling it wasn't going to. The doctor's face had said it all. What Rio and Jack said was true: I wouldn't function out here in the real world, with or without a shaky hand and anything else that followed. I wanted to carry on working, but I simply couldn't risk fucking up again – and, in turn, fucking my mates up. That said, The Owl had summoned me, so he must have a job in mind. I would get them this gig, help them plan it, do everything I could short of actually being on the ground.

The odd food place along Notting Hill Gate had disappeared since my last visit, maybe shut down by Covid, and those still open had big mask signs on their doors. The one place that had never changed in the time I'd known it was Café Diana. The People's Princess used to sneak in for a cappuccino and a croissant, and later took the boys there for a Full English. When she died, the café became a pilgrimage site for fans from all over the world, including, strangely, The Owl. But, then, The Owl wasn't exactly a run-of-the-mill member of one of the three-letter agencies, either in terms of looks or of the power he wielded.

The Owl's face was baby smooth without a hint of bristle. His eyes bulged and were so wide apart they almost didn't fit on his face. When I'd first met him six years back, I hadn't exactly had to dredge my imagination to come up with his nickname.

The Owl had that cosy home-cooked apple-pie Midwest accent that would invite you into his home but not really mean it. His default facial expression was a smile straight out of the fast-food guide to customer care, and I admired him for the way he appeared to breeze through drama as if he was just in a muddle. Smile, be friendly to people, but always consider how you're going to kill them: that's a skill.

Yet I still didn't get it, how someone in such authority, literally having the power of life and death over us mere mortals, could harbour this weird fascination about a dead princess. Not just him: it was his husband, Tom, too. Both had something weird about her going on in their heads. I'd met Tom once, maybe three years ago, in the café, of course. He had been early forties, clean-shaven, perfectly shaped eyebrows, salt-and-pepper hair that was very high and short. The Owl was punching way above his weight there. They were an unlikely couple – if Tom really was The Owl's husband, of course. But that was The Owl: a world of contradictions: you could never work out if what he said was the truth, a lie, or a mixture of both. For all I knew, his whole life was just one big cover story.

What organization he belonged to, I didn't know, and he wasn't going to tell. The four of us had kicked it around often enough in Coburg Crescent, and had eliminated the CIA, NSA, Secret Service, all the usual suspects. His powers seemed to straddle several of them. All we knew was that we had seen him in operation, and he had the authority to move whole battalions of agents around the world's chessboard, arrange for classified Pentagon records to be rewritten or go missing.

'People like me,' he once told me, 'we're needed because we're fighting a backroom kind of war. Sometimes things happen that mean desperate actions are taken.'

If there was going to be harm done, The Owl wouldn't be the one who was doing it. He wasn't the sort to get his hands dirty – he didn't have it in him. His super-powers were tucked away in his head. His body was just for getting that brain of his from one place to another to tell people to do shit. He didn't need strength: he had power.

Another time, he'd said: 'My job, Nick, is to pour oil on troubled waters. American waters, Russian waters, anywhere I see ripples. I clean things up before the world finds out, and if it does find out, I pour even more. Anything to stop our so-called leaders going to war with each other.

'Hey Nick, look at it another way. During Liechtenstein's last military engagement in 1886, none of the eighty soldiers sent to fight were killed, and all eighty-one returned. Yup, eighty-one. They picked up a new Italian "friend" along the way. That's kinda what I do, make friends of the enemy. You know, be nice, but be ready to cut throats the first chance you get. I'm one of the good guys – but sometimes I've got to do bad. It's good for us all.'

It was what it was. I'd always tried not to worry about it too much. My only concern was The Owl's obsession with loose ends. Would he allow me to become one? I wanted out, but I also wanted this gig for the other two. Maybe The Owl didn't let his worker bees off the hook so easily. As the saying goes: if three people know a secret, the only way to keep it is if two of them are dead.

18

I entered the glass door into the shrine that still had the look of a fry-up palace, which was fine by me. Press cuttings and pictures of Diana plastered the walls. A couple of tourists in face masks sat with cameras in front of them on the table, cross-checking it all with the menu to see if there was anything that said this was the sticky bun She liked. And if there wasn't, the management were missing a trick.

A group of men from the roadworks outside, in high-vis jackets and muddy boots, were filling their faces with tea and toast. The remaining occupants were the same you saw in any café offering free Wi-Fi, their laptops and phones plugged into the banks of sockets, seated at individual tables two metres apart.

I took a four-seater in the corner, and a young woman with bottle-blonde hair came over for my order, the pocket of her apron bulging with notepads and a card reader. There was still a small turnaround of young European women working there despite Brexit, even though the new home secretary reckoned all these jobs would be taken by Brits. Good luck with that one.

I scanned the menu. No mention in the hot section of what combination of sausage, bacon, egg, tomato, beans and mushrooms the People's Princess had gone for.

'Fried egg on toast and a large tea, please.'

The Owl was never the first to arrive. I was sure he was tucked away somewhere, watching me come in, making sure I wasn't being followed. He was never more than three minutes behind; it was too much of a coincidence.

I sort of liked him. His friend-next-door approach had always worked on me. Maybe it was just different from what I'd come up against over the years.

My tea arrived in a basic white mug with the teabag still in it and a little jug of milk, just the way She would have liked it.

A few minutes later the food came. I grabbed the tomato sauce bottle and was mid-squeeze when I heard a familiar voice.

'Jeez, Nick.'

I looked up to see him busy wrestling off a formal-looking belted raincoat, the sort you'd wear to protect a suit. His uniform, however, was a navy blazer, polo shirt and jeans, and it made him look like a travelling American mattress salesman. It wasn't hard to picture him with a carry-on full of pressed chinos, neatly folded button-down shirts, and suede loafers, all ready to sell some memory foam.

I smiled. He looked like a middle-aged man who'd been working hard on his dad-bod and failing, rather than what he really was: someone with the power to order pain and death.

He finally managed to work out he had to let go of his copy of the *New York Times* so he could get one hand out of a sleeve to shake mine.

The Owl was all apologies. 'I'm so sorry I'm late. London, you know how it is. People. Traffic. Rain. It's crazy out there, isn't it?'

'Yep, the whole world is full of weird.' I checked through the window. It was still dry.

He glanced around the walls, stage-struck as ever. 'I love this place.' He patted his light brown short-back-and-sides-with-side-parting, as if to tidy himself up for a royal audience. 'The Queen of Hearts.'

I glanced at the headline of his *NYT*: *The Surveillance Apparatus That Surrounded Britney Spears.*

'What – Britney?'

'Nick!' The Owl's face was still baby smooth, but he'd put on a lot of lockdown lard. He was looking big enough to burst, his neck gripped by the dark blue buttoned-up polo.

He pulled out a chair, draped his coat over the back and sat. He placed his soft, well-manicured hands in front of him on the table and finally switched his expression to one of concern. 'It's good to see you, Nick. How are you?'

'Mate, I've had better.'

The Owl nodded down at the neoprene as my fingers wrapped themselves slowly around the mug. 'You okay?'

'Little boating accident.'

He liked that one and came back with a smile. 'Good to hear, Nick. Got to take care of yourself.' I couldn't tell if the concern was mock or genuine, but in the same breath and tone he got back to work. 'Yes, of course, Nick – it must be a bad day for all of you guys.' He shifted the condiment tray out of the way so there was a clear view between us.

'Anyways, I just wanted to say: it was a job monumentally well done. And the Scottish angle? It standing up?'

My teabag was still brewing in the mug. I liked that. It gave me power to decide how strong it wanted to be. The waitress came over and The Owl ordered a cappuccino with a niceness thicker than the froth he was going to get in his cup. We waited for her to leave.

'All good.'

'All good is the way I like it. I'm still kinda nervous having something like that hanging out there, with no control. It was your idea, so you're my go-to guy. It's on you. Any problems you see coming down the road?'

'None.'

'She's happy with the official line? She won't go trawling Cleveland clinics for the truth?'

I shook my head.

'The two sons. They won't go digging one day?'

'People don't get interested in family-tree shit until they're about forty.'

His coffee arrived and he radiated a million watts of Greeter's Grin. We waited again for her to leave.

He turned the grin to me. 'And, of course, she has plenty of money. That was very generous of you guys.'

I must have raised an eyebrow involuntarily.

'Don't look so surprised, Nick. Obviously we checked her finances after your visit in July. The nineteenth, yeah?'

Bastard – but why should I be pissed off? He not only had the power to corrupt information at the Pentagon, but also to summon up nuclear submarines to carry out his bidding. Why wouldn't he have known?

His eyes strayed to the newspaper. 'Civilian surveillance capability is so first-generation, isn't it? The stuff we've got up in the air now, most people wouldn't believe.' Then his head jerked up. 'So your bank accounts are empty. It's kinda back to work early.'

He gently placed his hands on the table and leant forward as if there was a secret about to be told.

'It just so happens you're in luck.'

19

I took another mouthful of runny toast, then paused to wipe some of the yolk off my chin, which The Owl took as hesitation.

'Get you all back in the saddle, take your mind off things. What say you?'

Like he thought I had any choice. Once you're in, you're in.

But not today.

'I told the other two I'd take a back seat on this one. They're very capable – you've seen what they can do.'

He moved his hands away from the table and sat back.

'No, Nick. Big fat no. It has to be you. I've already done the big sell.'

'What if I say no?'

'Then I'll get it done another way. It would be a shame.' He gave the words a couple of seconds to hang about and establish their significance before he kicked back in. 'You could have named your price.'

Okay, that changes things.

How could I turn down the chance for Jack to have his

Tesla and Rio to send his girls to Ibiza? I should go along with this a bit longer, find out what it was all about. For all I knew, the job might be something I could do with a wonky hand.

'Just trying to give this thing a rest. Any reason neoprene's not in the dress code?'

'You'll be fine.'

'Yep, yep, okay, then. Who, what, where, when?'

I was so pissed off with myself I pushed back into my wooden chair. Why hadn't I strung him along a bit more, maybe got more details, before I committed? I overcompensated for my self-anger by taking far too long mopping up the last of the egg yolk with the remaining piece of toast at arm's length.

The Owl leant in to claw back the extra gap I'd created between us. 'Yep, let's start with the who because it's a big pot of weird.'

It wasn't too late. I could still call his bluff, insist I was out, that it was the other two who should be listening to this, not me. But I didn't. No one ever paid anyone what they were worth in this game. Worth had to be defined and justified by the person getting paid. I was prepared to do that on Rio and Jack's behalf.

'Mary Gaskell, late twenties, intelligent – no, not just intelligent, whip smart. But, unfortunately for her, she's gotten herself mixed up with a boyfriend who's gotten himself mixed up with a cult.'

'That doesn't make her sound intelligent or smart to me. Susceptible and weak maybe.'

His jaw hardened. I'd never seen The Owl's face change so quickly from genial salesman to what was maybe his real self, eyes cold and steely.

'No, Nick. You're wrong. It could happen to anyone. The

more confident you are that you'd never succumb to these fucks, the easier it is for them to suck you in. It's happened to you in the military – think about that.'

That was something I wasn't going to do, so instead a last swig of tea followed the solids and I made him wait. For just a few seconds the pause gave me the illusion of power.

It wasn't going to be a normal job. That was clear to see. This guy usually made our briefings sound as if he was ordering a tuna wrap at Subway. Then the steel softened and he was becoming emotional. That was new.

'She's so overwhelmed by this boyfriend of hers.'

He took a long breath. The Owl only ever gave the minimum amount of information before the formal brief, but it felt like he was gearing up to deliver all the ingredients of a long ramble. Fuck that: I wanted to get this over and done with. I had a pharmacy to get to before closing time.

'So where?'

'Norway–Russia border, way, way up on the north coast.'

His voice betrayed the fact his head was already there, and he couldn't control himself thinking or, more likely, worrying about Mary Gaskell.

'She doesn't sound Russian – that's the cult?'

The Owl nodded slowly, like the thought made his neck hurt.

Was this his daughter?

'When?'

He stood up, retrieved his coat and draped it over his shoulder. 'Four days. I'll meet you in LA for a full brief, then – well, just as soon as you and the guys can get yourselves on the ground.'

'What about the Covid restrictions? You guys letting people in?'

'You'll be going AMC. I'll have details for you tomorrow.'

He checked through the window and discovered the raincoat needed to go on. But it didn't. He turned on his heel and left so fast he forgot his *New York Times*.

I stayed where I was, and signalled for the bill. It was 17:00, just about enough time to pick up my prescription while I wondered how he'd got me onto a flight with Air Mobility Command.

20

'I knew you weren't leaving us.'

Jack was jubilant as we both blagged ourselves an armchair. He swivelled and looked up at Rio, who hadn't been quick enough and had to perch on an arm of Jack's. He was usually a bit stoned and slower on the uptake, so he was used to it.

I coughed. 'I'll be leaving you if you keep smoking that shit in the house. Come on, lads, please. I'm gonna get lung cancer here – we all will.'

They both laughed, thinking I was joking, but I wasn't.

Jack was the one who read. 'Actually, bronchitis is more likely than cancer.'

I shrugged as if everything was all right then, and launched into the who, what, where and when of The Owl's brief. That done, I added my own piece. 'I'm thinking she might be family. He got carried away, and that's the first time I've ever seen him like that. I never get a twinge out of him, but he really started to throw one at me.'

Rio got up and headed for the kitchen. 'Fucking melt.'

Jack knew the possible implications. 'That could mean he's paying. Does it affect the cash? I'd rather be taking American taxpayers' money – personal cash could bring problems, even be less.'

I had to agree with him. 'Maybe that's why I'm going to the US.' I shrugged again. 'Guess I'll find out when I get there. It's pointless worrying about things we know nothing about. We have no control. I'll go and make sure you get the gig – and that you're paid properly.'

I heard the tear of a ring-pull, a couple of swigs, then the fridge door being closed. He came back cradling a couple of Camdens under his arm, a pack of sliced cheese and a mega pack of crisps in his hand. They all landed on the coffee-table and he took a long drag on his can. 'I suppose you want us to stop drinking here and all, do you? You want a Coke, get it yourself, weirdo.' He took another swig looking down at me, jutting his jaw. I knew he'd be more annoyed if I didn't take the bait. I leant over, grabbed the crisps and started to open them. Jack grabbed a can and pulled back on it.

'Lads, as much as it pains me to say it, I really need to thank you for the reality check this morning. If I do it again, I want you to grip me.'

Rio was still pissed off trying to work out how to get me to bite, but then seemed to give up. 'You think you're the only one with the hump? You don't get it. We're all fucked up, one way or another. Remember this morning when you said you've had a few weeks to get to terms with having a touch of the old Elvis?'

He shook his hips in a bad Presley impersonation.

'Whereas us two and Gabe, we didn't? One minute we were okay, the next we were blown to shit. That plays with your head. So don't worry. There's a lot of it about.'

Jack had to agree. 'We've all got physical and mental problems, but on the upside, that's why we're here. That's why we're the SNS. What you have to remember, Nick, is that you need this job to get your head out of the mud – that's what we do. Just keep concentrating on something else. That's what you need to do.'

Rio finished the Camden and crushed the can one-handed before tossing it onto the table and helping himself to the last slice of cheese. 'You eating those crisps, or what?'

I dipped my hand in, took as many as I could grip, and threw the packet over to him. He clamped it between his knees and reached in.

Jack adjusted his leg, stretching it out. He'd been thinking again. 'Listen, Shaky Boy. I think you may have Alzheimer's and all.' I knew what was coming because he was pointing towards the kitchen. 'You forgot the milk.'

I pushed up, grabbed my coat and headed for the door. The one who emptied the carton was the one who replaced it.

It wasn't as if I was the only one with any responsibilities today. It was Jack's turn to sort out the food for tonight, but he had other ideas. 'While you're out, get the vindaloos in – Brixton Curry Delight. The naan is much better.'

Zipping up before descending the stairs, I turned because I had a better solution. 'Why don't you just call them? Get the Deliveroo guys.'

'It's not as funny as you having to go and pay for it.'

I headed out onto the South Circular. Soon I was walking faster than the jammed vehicles, and a couple of cars honked as the lights changed to red far too quickly. Admittedly a little win, but one all the same.

PART FOUR

21

California
Wednesday, 29 September 2021

The frenzy of lights on Santa Monica pier and the Ferris wheel to my left looked so familiar, like I'd spent half my life on this stretch of Californian coast. I hadn't, but I had passed big chunks of it in front of the TV watching pulpy American beach dramas and cop shows.

Up in front of me in the Tesla X – what else would these guys be driving here? – Tom was at the wheel and The Owl was beside him. Sam, he'd told me to call him today

Sam was probably his 'government name', his real name, as his husband kept using it. I liked the term coined by the extreme right in the US. Being anti-government, they didn't like being called by their given names. I had no idea about Sam and Tom's government surname. They were married so I presumed it was the same for both of them, but I didn't need to know, and I didn't care. These guys up front, in their matching beige chinos and brown loafers, they just weren't my kind of people. Tom, his hair still high and tight, wore a blue Ralph L button-down shirt with the cuffs rolled up, Sam a button-down red shirt and, clearly being the conservative one of the pair, his cuffs fastened. The extra tight material around his stomach really did emphasize his lockdown lard, or maybe it was only noticeable when he sat next to ever-perfect Tom.

The car interior strobed with all shades of neon, and Tom took the opportunity to check me out in his rear-view. He had perfect teeth, and a pirate smile. 'Not long now, Nick. Ever been to Malibu?'

I shook my head.

'It looks much better at night – less tired, you know. This is the good view. We prefer the east coast.'

I bet they did. Both had the look that said they had a holiday home on the coast of Maine, along with a firm belief in the benefits of prep school and the superiority of wooden sailing boats. All made up in my head, of course, and I had no idea what Tom knew or thought about me, or if he even knew what his husband did for a living, but he would certainly have known all about this job.

Mary, they'd just revealed, was Tom's niece, his sister's daughter.

The light-show continued as we drove north along the Pacific Coast highway or Highway One, or whatever the Hoff called it. The beaches and shuttered lifeguard towers to the left were straight out of *Baywatch* and the surfy drug-smuggling films I'd lapped up as a kid – and beyond. Hours and hours I'd spent late at night sitting with those other three dickheads in Tulse Hill, none of us able to sleep, hoovering up reality shows, rubbernecking the lives of the rich and famous and their kids. They were totally at the extreme of life and, if what Tom and Sam had told me was correct, totally at the other end of Mary Gaskell's existence right now.

The Air Mobility Command flight from the US Air Base at Mildenhall had taken me on a C5 Super Galaxy to Dover Air Force Base, Delaware. On board the massive tank-carrying aircraft were rows of fully laden pallets, along with forty-odd US Air Force personnel and some families using the Space-A Travel programme. US military can hop on a flight if space is available, and The Owl had made sure there was space for me. From Dover it was another AMC flight to March Air Reserve Base east of Los Angeles.

Almost the moment I disembarked, they had propelled me into the back of the Tesla and pumped me with even more information to add to the stuff about cults I'd been reading up on during the flight.

According to these two, she was being held by a cult whose compound straddled a river, the Jakobselv, which was the border between Norway and Russia.

'Check this out. It's from one of the Kennans.' The Owl turned in his seat to show me his iPad. Glowing on the screen was a black-and-white aerial shot of groups of buildings, with a river running through them.

'What's the scale?'

The Owl had already worked that out. 'The compound's just under two square K. Most of it on the Norwegian side.'

Kennan spy satellites are basically big digital cameras orbiting the earth at about three hundred kilometres. The problem is that because they're in orbit, they cannot hover over a target or provide real-time footage. Unless imagery was needed of a secured or sensitive area, wherever it might be on the planet, that wasn't covered by commercial companies, Google Earth was just as good and in colour.

'Can't you get a drone up for some real-time footage? It'll be good to confirm she's there?'

'Can't do, Nick. Since the Iranians shot one of ours down along their border in 'nineteen, it's something we don't do. Too much tech heading Moscow's way if they take it down, plus we then have to deal with the sabre-rattling from both sides.'

I held out the iPad for The Owl to take back.

'But that's why you're here, Nick. There are some things that just can't be handled by microprocessors. It's gotta be boots on the ground.'

From what I'd googled before the flight, there was a lot of confusion about cults. She could just have found herself part of a religious group, a commune into magic mushrooms, or some paranoid preppers gathering for the end of the world. Whatever it was, she had gone with Gedi, some Austrian guy.

Tom had given me the only picture Mary's parents had of him. It was a selfie close-up of them both on the beach, her head resting on his shoulder.

'She "met" him on the beach during lockdown.' Tom had added air quotes as he let the Tesla do its auto-drive thing.

'Or he just met her?' I had an attempt at making the conversation more objective, hoping to learn a little more than just their version.

'He said he was "stuck" in Los Angeles until Europe let in flights from the US again.'

'You think he was in LA specifically to recruit rich young women?'

Tom shrugged. 'Or men.'

'And Gedi?'

'Short for whatever Gideon is in German. A biblical name – hotel Bibles, right? And this one Mary got lured by is a member. God's Word on Earth, they call themselves.'

'If so, and it's a religious group, doesn't it have religious protections – certainly on the Norwegian side? Not sure what happens in Russia.'

Sam and Tom didn't like that at all, and The Owl turned back to me, his face a thundercloud. 'You're not listening, Nick. It's a cult, right? We need to get Mary out of there.'

I nodded that I understood, just to stop him throwing another one at me. But after eleven hours of reading, I now knew there were tens of thousands of cults around the world, and Russia had more than its fair share. I'd made a mental note of two things.

First, that not all cults were religious. Some were political. Some were all about therapy, focusing on things like self-improvement. Some were just about having enough of technology, moving off the grid and dropping out of the rat race. Mary was certainly in the rat race, living in this neck of the woods.

Second, that not all new religions are cults. It was just that old religions don't like new religions. They don't like the competition. Even the Romans labelled Christianity a cult and killed its leader in the hope this dangerous new idea wouldn't catch on. Religion is a business, and in business you have to protect your copyright.

Until I was proven wrong, it seemed to me from what I'd read that a cult was a group, a movement, a commitment to extreme ideology – believing the end of the world was nigh, rich people should be eaten, or they should all kill themselves to go and join a higher being. Typically, they were led by a charismatic leader who coerces and controls.

I looked at Tom via the rear-view. 'God's Word on Earth – it has a leader?'

22

'Matvey Sokolov, pronounced math-vyay. He's brainwashing people.'

Tom was agitated, and Sam's jaw was clenched. It was clear to me that they both had religion, and they didn't like the fact that somebody was out there claiming to be their Lord and Saviour.

I found it funny, all the different religious groups arguing about who had the best imaginary friend. The only time the different groups seemed to agree was when they had a common enemy, so they would come together to denounce Scientology and its belief in aliens as fantasy – as if it wasn't in the land of make-believe that a virgin has a bunk-up with God and then the son walks on water, heals the sick, and is able to raise himself from the dead. I was going to keep out of it.

'What do you know about Matvey?'

'He's in Russia, used to be a ship engineer in Vladivostok. Get this, his name means "God has rewarded". Can you believe that shit? It's a joke.'

The eastern seaport and home of the USSR's Pacific fleet until the collapse of Communism in the early nineties. That was when, Sam said, like the rest of the country's population, Matvey lost his job as the system unravelled. 'Russia had a surge of communes and new cults, religions and sects rising out of the post-Communist debris. People were looking for something to hold onto, to help make sense of all the chaos.'

I nodded. 'And, like anything else, it's just the cream and the scum that float to the top and survive. I think I can guess which one you think he is.'

They looked at each other, expressionless, but it was Tom who broke the link. 'Damn right.'

The mission was simple: to lift Mary Gaskell and hand her over to an American team who would de-cult her, or whatever the word was. These interventions were big business, and so was the next stage, deprogramming. Specialists used the same methods as they did to de-radicalize Muslim and right-wing extremists, but they involved a bit more than sitting in a circle and talking about themselves.

The American team would take Mary from us and get her to a clinic, where the psychiatrists would be waiting with drugs, hypnotherapy and, above all, credit-card machines. The intervention was going to be more like a rendition than anything else.

Mary was going to be gripped, lifted and locked up to prevent her escaping or being rescued, then shaped back into whatever she once was.

23

'Her folks and I can't understand how this Gedi guy influenced her so easily.'

Sam obviously hadn't mentioned what he'd said angrily to me in London, that if you know you're smart, and you're confident you're not going to get dragged into one of these things, then you're really easy prey. You think they can't touch you, but these cults, if she was in one, were also smart and intelligent. They're skilled at knowing who to target. They focus on newcomers to an area, or those who have recently undergone some personal or professional loss.

I shrugged. 'I don't know Mary yet, but she might have been lonely, searching for meaning, that sort of thing? It makes you susceptible to a friendly shoulder, somebody like the Austrian offering something it's possible she felt she didn't have – a community of like minds, maybe. She could be the brightest person on earth, but recruiting can be really subtle. It might have taken months to establish this relationship.'

Sam had been nodding. 'We thought about that, and we're

still wondering. More than two-thirds of cult members are recruited by friends, family members, work colleagues. That kind of invitation is really hard to refuse, because you trust the person. It's only once you're in their grip that the indoctrination starts. Maybe we won't know for sure until she's back here with us.'

Tom took over. 'We have this natural inclination to mimic social behaviours or even follow orders within a group – so once they've got you there, they know they can work on you.'

I'd read that in many cases members can willingly submit out of the desire to belong because there's some promised reward, like a place in Heaven, or space travel with aliens. If there's a promised reward they believe in, they'll stay.

Tom's face clouded, and I knew he'd be thinking about the less friendly forms of coercion. It could get very ugly. Cults use guilt, shame, fear, all kinds of negative emotions. They will totally discourage critical thinking, getting everybody modelled into absolute faith. They bank heavily on internal conflict, cognitive dissonance, to keep you trapped – the mental discomfort that comes from holding two conflicting beliefs, values or attitudes. People tend to seek consistency in their attitudes and perceptions, so this conflict causes feelings of unease or discomfort, and cults exploit it.

The inconsistency, apparently, between what people believe and how they behave motivates them to engage in actions that will help minimize feelings of discomfort. People attempt to relieve the tension in different ways, such as by rejecting, explaining away or avoiding new information. The brighter the victim, I guessed, the deeper cognitive dissonance would have to be to get them hooked.

I also guessed that, whoever they were, the deprogrammers were going to have their work cut out.

24

The dazzle of Santa Monica was behind us as we rolled on past beaches and billboards, the Tesla never getting up to the speed limit. Sheer weight of traffic was something the Hoff and Pamela never had to contend with.

The terrain on the right was steepening, with habitation lights dotted above us in the darkness. Sam swivelled in his seat, his face illuminated by oncoming headlights. 'Nearly there.'

'So, how old is she? She got all her arms and legs working?'

They might have sounded strange questions to Tom, but not to The Owl. It would be a waste of time getting to her with a plan of dragging her cross-country, only to discover she relied on a wheelchair.

'Twenty-three and in working condition, apart from the fact she has focal seizures, epilepsy. But it's under control, has been for years.'

I knew of epilepsy, but no idea what focal seizures were. Something else to take in as part of the planning and prep.

The indicator started to click: we were going to turn right. Seconds later we were heading uphill, on a narrow road lined with rock and scrubland. Gates were set back from the road, light spilling from real estate, which would be getting more and more expensive the higher we climbed. Malibu was the land of the rich and famous, and then some.

Tom cleared his throat and ran a hand over what hair hadn't been cut. If it was because he was feeling apprehensive, I couldn't think why. This was a good thing we were doing, right?

We pulled up outside a pair of fancy cast-iron gates and they parted. Tom took a deeper than normal breath and Sam was supportive. 'No problem. All will be good.' He reached out his left hand and laid it on Tom's on the wheel. I found it strange to be in a domestic setting with The Owl, especially as these two were suddenly acting like I wasn't there, like I was the worker, like they were giving the cleaning lady a lift home.

He finally looked back at me. 'Any last questions?'

I shook my head. I just wanted to get into the house, get my information and, of course, find out if they were willing to meet the asking price. Only then, maybe, would there be questions to ask.

At the end of the drive sat a huge multi-roofed, glass-sided house that could easily have starred in *Selling Sunset* or *Million Dollar Listing LA*, two of the favourite shows for ganja-fuelled deadbeats in Tulse Hill.

Tom parked the Tesla between a Lexus SUV and a soft-top Mini. I spotted the Gaskells behind the glass, not exactly arguing, but there was a lot of finger-pointing and arms being flung around.

We got out. The long rectangular pool was lit below the

surface, and strips of blue LED lighting shot upwards to make it look like a UFO landing strip.

There was no need to ring the bell. As we approached the door, it opened, and Tom took the lead. 'Michelle, Tripp, this is Nick.'

I smiled and stepped forward. 'Good evening.'

And they both completely blanked me.

25

Clearly Michelle wasn't someone who wasted her breath on the hired help. She looked straight past me to Tom and Sam. 'She's emailed us.' The harsh tone made it sound like a personal bollocking, or maybe that was just a Malibu thing. 'She's fucking graced us with her presence.' With that, she turned and stormed back into the house, her heels clacking on the wooden floor.

Tripp glanced at Tom and Sam before he followed her. 'You gotta read this shit – you've just gotta read it. Unbelievable.'

The Gaskells were in their mid-forties, glamorous and good-looking, and as a mixed-race marriage, they would have been a shoo-in for any rich and beautiful TV show. The only sticking point for the producers would have been that she was a little taller than him. They would have loved everything else about her, from the coordinated blue heels below the designer jeans, to the perfect relaxed hair held in a ponytail, the unblemished skin, sculpted eyebrows and gym-toned arms. As if to accessorize her, Tripp was in his showing-multi-million-dollar-homes clothing, which could be turned instantly into smart casual just by taking off his blue suit jacket and tie. His cuffs were down, held together by gold links, which glinted next to a very chunky gold watch. His styled and producted light brown hair looked like it hadn't moved off his forehead all day, and he was so tanned it was difficult to see where the hair ended and the neck started.

I brought up the rear as they trooped in. Tripp concentrated on The Owl and didn't bother to check that I was behind them all. 'Sam, I just want to say how sad it was to hear about your mother. Fucking pandemic and hospitals' systems down, what can you do?'

The Owl had been thinking about that. 'Don't just depend on a screen to save lives, use people. That's what you can do.'

Tripp wasn't expecting a real answer and tried not to get into anything too deep. He didn't seem the type who ever did. 'We tried to make it to the funeral but what with work, getting to the east coast and back, you know?'

The Owl nodded understanding. 'At least she was in your thoughts, thank you for that. '

Even I knew that was the biggest fuck-off, but not Tripp. He was too concerned with himself. 'You know this Norway business? You got to sort it, Sam. We look stupid. People think we didn't know what our own fucking kid was doing. I mean, it's her who should be taking the heat, not us.'

He hadn't finished. 'I'm under a lot of stress. It makes my job harder, all this shit. How am I supposed to concentrate? She's ruining business.'

They were well ahead of me as I stopped to close the front door, but then I decided against it. Childish, I knew, but I was starting to feel like one of the domestics from *The Crown*. Then I saw the picture mounted in a silver frame: Tripp with

Trump, both with orange hard hats on, a construction site as background.

The inside of the glass house was exactly how I'd expected it to be, a perfect bling show home, every item staged. Their interior designer had even matched the shade of green in the picture frames with the sofas. I couldn't see a MAGA ball cap and now I knew why. It would have clashed.

No wonder the parents were so angry about this business, rather than worried and concerned. Mary had burst the perfect family bubble and rearranged the cushions.

Still not including me in her field of view, Michelle picked up a sheet of paper from the coffee-table, which held half a florist's shop of multicoloured flowers. She thrust it at Tom. 'Read it!'

The Owl went to Tom and joined in the reading. Michelle didn't go and stand by Tripp: she stayed where she was as she continued in bollocking mode. 'She's weak, she's fucking weak.' And now it was clear why she didn't want to get too near to Tripp: it was so she could distance herself and gesture more dramatically. 'You've let her run rings around us for years. You never listen.' And then another idea suddenly happened in her head, like a car crash. 'I told you there was something wrong with that fucking Kraut.'

I was just a spectator. I decided I might as well sit down on the sofa, as no one was going to notice I was there anyway.

Tripp bared his teeth. 'Austrian!'

'What? What the fuck?'

'He's Austrian.'

'Who gives a fuck? They're all fucking Nazis.' She windmilled a hand. 'Go get some wine. Be useful.'

Tripp finally hit host mode, maybe to defuse the tension.

Who knew? Nobody here seemed to give a fuck about anyone but themselves. His estate-agent smile came on full beam, giving Tom and The Owl the benefit of a few thousand dollars' worth of snow-white veneers. He and Tom must have shared the same dental plan. 'I'm gonna hit you with a great Napa Merlot. We got a case of it today. It's so much smoother than the one we had on Michelle's birthday.'

He headed out in the direction of what I guessed was the kitchen, his voice trailing behind him. 'You're gonna love it, really.'

No, I wasn't. First of all because I didn't drink. And even if I did, I wasn't even sure if I was included in the offer. Neither of them had set eyes on me so far, let alone acknowledged my presence. But so what? I was here to make money, not friends.

Maybe he'd read my mind, but Tom finally handed me the printout, just as Tripp appeared with the wine and five glasses that went down in a small gap in the flower display.

I read Mary's email as Michelle interrogated The Owl. 'What the fuck is she on, Sam?'

It sounded like she was on uncut happiness:

Mom, Dad, I'm devoting myself to living in perfect harmony in a place where children run free, where the earth provides everything you need, and where money is meaningless. I needed to change my life to a new and more fulfilling one, and the way to change is to repent my old life. My devotion to repentance is deepening and cleansing me. Love, Mary

One of the things that had jumped out at me on the flight over was that you can do whatever you want if you wrap it in devotion, but this email sounded okay to me: no mention of a great leader telling her to cut herself off from the world, or to isolate because the aliens were about to land, or they were all getting ready to die in a mass suicide, or for her to give up all of her possessions so she could be cleansed of the great evil.

Tripp's thoughts about the email were at the other end of the scale, and off it. 'Repent her life? What does she mean? She telling us she's had a shit life? She fucking with us because she thinks we're bad parents? Look around you, man. Repent? I'll tell you one thing. She'll be repenting even more in her new Wonderland soon. We've cancelled her cards. And after all we've done for her . . .'

I looked up, but I still wasn't being involved in the conversation. Michelle jumped in, arms swinging. 'She'll be coming back for money, you'll see. Cash, that's all these fucking cults want, they want your cash. But we're not bankrolling no one. No one.'

The two of them nodded but Michelle wanted a bigger response. 'Don't you get it? We're the fucking victims here!'

Tom realized this was going in a totally wrong direction. 'Yep, sure, sure, I get it. But I think we should work out what needs to be done to keep her safe.'

The Owl looked down at me. At last, apparently, I was in the room. 'What do you think?'

I still had the printout in my hand, and as I leant forward to place it back on the coffee-table, my hand brushed against the flowers. They were fake.

'It's bland.' I sat back and focused on the Gaskells. 'Is there anything in this email that you can say for sure proves it's from Mary? Any word, spelling, writing style, anything that indicates that she wrote it?'

They exchanged a glance and it looked like they both

realized they wouldn't have had a clue as to what might confirm it was their daughter.

Tripp was the one to cut their embarrassment. 'Nick, right?'

Give him a sweet.

'Sam says you're the guy to get her out.'

It would have been nice if he'd phrased that as 'bring our daughter home safe'.

I nodded. 'Me and my team.'

I didn't say what I was thinking, which was that I had suddenly changed my mind.

I knew next to nothing about Mary, but I pitied her having these two as parents. If I asked a high enough price, might it make them value her? Make them value her as highly as Rio valued his two girls, and Gabe had valued his two boys? Those four didn't have a swimming-pool or a soft-top Mini between them, let alone a set of cushions that matched. They had fuck-all, but at the same time they also had everything. They were loved.

So, I was going to have fun hitting the Gaskells where it hurt them most, in the wallet, and The Owl couldn't say a thing. He'd done the sales pitch on me. Now he'd have to stand there and suck it up.

I wanted to make absolutely sure that the two in front of me were bled dry, and that we three were beneficiaries of the transfusion to the very last drop. International wealth redistribution at its finest. I was Robin Hood at last.

Unless I was very much mistaken, I finally had a win-win.

26

'Okay, let's get to it.' Tripp squared up to me, crossing his arms over his chest in full negotiator mode. 'How much?'

A mate of mine had once been bodyguard for a family in a smart part of London. The doorbell went one day and the owner answered, his BG hovering. 'Don't shut the door on me,' said the guy on the doorstep. 'I'm an estate agent. I don't normally do this, but my clients were very insistent. They're Chinese, and they want to relocate to London. Not just London, but right here, in this street. In fact, in your house.'

The owner shook his head. 'This is my family home, I'd never sell.'

'Don't lose me my commission, sir. Let's try it this way. Think of a number, the price you'd be prepared to relinquish your family home for. Okay, don't tell me that number, but double it. Done that? Okay, now round it up to something easy to grasp. Done that?'

'Yes.'

'How soon would you like to move out?'

I'd been thinking twenty thousand per day, per man, but Tripp was an estate agent. Time to use estate agents' tactics.

'Three men, fifty thousand per day, per man.'

I hadn't even finished the sentence and Michelle's head looked set to explode. I needed to spell it out so there would never be any misunderstanding. 'With a floor of four days, upfront, and a ceiling of seven. The day count starts as a full day on arrival at the camp, compound, whatever you want to call it, and ends as a full day when we hand her over, not when she arrives in Oslo. We have no control over that. If we go over seven days, it's on our time, but we will deliver your child and safely. She has a condition, right?'

Tripp's nostrils flared. If he'd been a cartoon, there would have been thunderbolts erupting from his head. Not even my calling Mary their child seemed to put her to the forefront of his concerns. 'That's a million fifty to pick a kid up and put her in a cab – you fucking joking me?'

I shrugged, but I was aware that this could go wrong. 'Only if it takes the full term to save Mary. Is she on any medication?'

Michelle had a bad case of the thunderbolts herself. She leant forward and down at me theatrically, hands on hips, eyes wide. 'Oh, I'm sure it'll be the full fucking term, all right.' She twisted sideways to Tripp, who had parked his wine on the coffee-table in shock. 'A million – it's a joke, right?' It was probably the first time they'd ever agreed on anything. 'You want us to pay a million dollars with no fucking guarantees?' She swung back to Sam, eyes blazing.

The Owl had stayed far too quiet for my liking, and still nothing from the caring parents about Mary's focal seizures.

Finally, Tripp punched one hand into the other. 'No fucking way.'

I was quite enjoying myself. 'Just to clarify, it's not a million dollars US, it's a million pounds sterling.'

Michelle had finished with me. Why would she confer with the pool-boy? She took a couple of angry steps to Tom and Sam, heels clacking. 'What the fuck is sterling? Is that cheaper money, or what?'

I cut in. I wanted to be the one who was the bearer of bad news. 'It's more expensive. That's just over one point two five million in your money.'

Fuck 'em both. They hadn't once said they didn't have the money. Their problem wasn't cash. It was their priorities.

Tripp clearly hated numbers rising, unless he was the vendor. He spat back at Sam and Tom: 'Why did you bring this joker into our house? Mary's an adult. We've already told you we'll wait, let's see how this plays out. If she wants to dance with the fairies, or whatever the fuck they're doing, then let her. She'll be back as soon as she needs her nails done.'

I stood up as if to leave, but really I just wanted to be at the same level as the masters of the house. The Owl looked as if he knew I'd had enough and was about to walk out. 'Listen, Tripp, I've told you so many times, it isn't as simple as that. She hasn't gone hugging trees and weaving raffia up in Santa Cruz. She's five thousand miles away. In danger. Everything says that place isn't good news for anyone. Are you really willing to take that chance? She's your daughter, for God's sake.'

I enjoyed watching the Gaskells' frustration as they both put their hands on their hips and avoided eye contact with anyone, let alone each other. They knew he was right. Michelle's heels clacked heavily out of the room, her hands waving away any responsibility as she disappeared. Tom followed to comfort his sister, and it was in that moment that I knew what this was all about, and that the job was on. They couldn't accept losing. The Gaskells were winners, and Mary had fucked all that up.

Tripp wasn't giving up. He must have thought he was in a negotiation here. He had to have the last word, or at least feel he had. The truth would come to him when he woke in the early hours of the morning with his head buzzing, and then he'd know he hadn't won anything. Right now, he really ought to be thinking of his daughter instead of himself, but the problem was, the Gaskells' front-of-house was every bit as fake as their flowers. All he could do was come back with the same thing said a different way.

'How are you going to do it? What exactly am I paying for? I want approval of what my cash is getting me.'

Hang on, what the cash was getting him was his daughter back, wasn't it? I didn't say that. Instead, I came out with an answer he was going to like even less. 'I don't know yet. You haven't even told me what medication Mary is on, and if she took it with her. Does she have enough? Do I need to get some to her?'

Tripp couldn't control all the pent-up anger he had to keep pushed down inside him as he spent the day pirate-smiling while sucking up to clients. 'Jesus, what the fuck with this drug thing! Yes, she's got months of that shit.'

'Good. I'll need to know exactly what medication, and the dosage. That will be part of the plan to keep her safe. But where, when and how – you're not going to know. Operational security.'

Then it came: the sharp intake of breath, the tightening of the jaw, the narrowing of the eyes as he prepared to deliver his it's-my-money-I'll-call-the-shots lecture. I put up a palm and looked as hard as I could into his eyes. I had to nip this nonsense in the bud.

'I know how to get Mary out, and I know how to do it safely. And why I know all that is because I'm going to be saving Mary from people who are just like me.' I jerked my head. 'Ask him.'

The Owl hadn't used his salesman smile once all evening, and he wasn't going to start now. He stared at his brother-in-law tight-lipped. 'This thing isn't going to end well unless you listen.' With the look of a sad puppy, he clamped a hand on his shoulder. 'Tripp, just pay the damn money. There's no such thing as a replacement daughter. They don't sell them.'

But still it looked like the deal was more important. His teeth clenched as he tried to find a way to be the top dog. It pissed him off, and made me happy.

I now had a question. How was The Owl planning on getting me back to the UK?

PART FIVE

27

Barents Sea
Day One: Friday, 8 October 2021

Freezing spray blasted my face, and my knees and thighs gripped the jockey seat, like I was riding a mechanical bull, as Grisha barrelled the RIB across the Barents Sea at warp speed. Then the engine revs got quieter and the bow dipped. We were entering an inlet maybe a kilometre wide. Grisha had told us the plan: to head inland from there until we reached Grense Jakobselv harbour.

It had been a well-organized journey so far. I'd applied to join the cult online, filling in all the boxes about who and why, my background and issues, how I thought they would be able to help me with them.

The website was more like a spreadsheet. There were no glossy pictures or flowery paragraphs selling you the dream, just plain text explaining that if you needed to be sucked in by hype then maybe this wasn't the place for you.

From the moment I signed up, they took over. All I had to

do was make sure I had my jabs. They paid for return flights from London to Tromsø to give me confidence that all was good up north, and I could leave whenever I wanted.

I knew Tromsø from my winter-warfare training a lifetime ago when I was young and keen. It was a tourist centre in the far north of Norway, where people from all over the planet came to witness the Northern Lights, meet a reindeer, drive a husky sled, and generally have fun in the snow. But for me, it was where I had met up with two couples, and we were put aboard a private six-seater Beechcraft dual prop and flown six hundred kilometres further to a small airport, Vardø, which in turn served an even smaller community, a declining fishing port on the Barents coast. My first impression was of fish, or at least the lingering smell of it that easily penetrated my cold-weather face mask. The harbour wasn't so filled with fishing boats any more, and the old processing sheds were now derelict, rotting and covered with graffiti.

But there, all five of us were decked out up to the neck in Gore-Tex and life-jackets, then taken further along the coast in a RIB by Grisha, our shoulder-length-haired and big-bearded cox from Russia. He couldn't stop smiling when he briefed us that our trip would have been more than two hundred kilometres by not-too-good roads, but the beeline he'd be taking by sea was only sixty-five. What was more, today we were going to be in luck. The sea was calm, he could rev the engines, so strap into your seats.

As we left the harbour I spotted more graffiti on the sea-wall, and the words 'SEA FEVER', two metres high, filling a section of the concrete sea defence.

'It's a poem from an Englishman, John Masefield. He loved the sea and so will you all. Please, enjoy the crisp, clean air!'

Our masks were off now, and the air might have been

cleaner than Vardø's for sure, but it certainly wasn't crisp. It was sub-zero. We were nearly three hundred and fifty kilometres north of the Arctic Circle, and it wasn't going to get warm up here any time soon. I'd be dead by the time climate change had bananas hanging from the local trees. But at least today was one of the few dry days for this time of year. It rained a lot up there, then dumped another few billion freezing gallons for luck.

The two couples released their grip on their jockey seats as the RIB swung further into the inlet and slowed more, then pulled down their hoods. The French couple, Madeleine and Mathulla, were in their mid-twenties and very much in love. Even in the Beechcraft he couldn't help but keep turning in his seat and holding out a hand for her, cooing and laughing all the while, which turned out to be infectious to the other couple, who were old enough to be their grandparents. Cameron and Elaine, from Edinburgh, had to have been in their seventies, but full of it themselves when it came to exchanging loving looks. To me, the two couples seemed to represent the circle of life. Madeleine was returning to what she called 'the village', and bringing Mathulla with her – just as Gedi had done with Mary. I wondered if those two had had as much fun on the RIB as these guys as they set out on their new quest. Or maybe Gedi and Mary had gone the two-hundred-kilometre route and had even more of an adventure.

What really completed the circle was Cameron coming here to die. He was suffering from Parkinson's. He couldn't control his head movements and his left arm had a constant life of its own. But his brain was there, and that must have been a fucker.

They were both retired teachers and committed Christians. Elaine told me on the flight from Tromsø that she had been providing palliative care for almost a year. But she was no spring chicken and was finding difficult the physical strain of caring for her husband. The decision to come here had been easy. They wanted to stay together and be close to God, and at the same time improve Cameron's quality of life – physically, psychologically and socially, as well as spiritually. Elaine had explained that the love and care Cameron would receive would be much better than any nursing home could have offered, where he'd be wheelchaired into a cubicle and left to wait an hour to have his arse wiped. 'And all for just two thousand pounds a week,' Cameron had chipped in. 'But Matvey, he doesn't want a penny.'

So far, none of this felt like I was being sucked into a cult, and maybe that was a problem. I felt too confident that I wouldn't be. What I did know for sure was that I envied Cameron, sharing the last of his time with somebody he loved and who loved him, and his life ending the way they both wanted it to happen, with their faith and love intact. Which wasn't a bad shout at all, I thought, compared with how things might turn out for me. Unless things changed dramatically, I'd die on the toilet and spend a day or two lying on the floor covered with my own shit before having my wallet nicked by a burglar.

28

By the time the inlet had narrowed noticeably to about four hundred metres, I'd got back to wondering about something that had been playing with me the last couple of days: how The Owl had managed to get the Kennan imagery, my AMC flights to and from the US without any immigration or Covid restrictions, and on top of that all of the normal cover docs, for a job that was in effect a bit of freelance. It wasn't that easy: there were hoops to jump through to get hold of workable passports, driving licences, even National Insurance and NHS numbers that would stand up to scrutiny – let alone a credit card. It looked like The Owl's backroom with a big lock on it was a lot bigger than I thought it was.

Grisha pointed energetically, arm straight with the other on the wheel. 'Who would guess? To the right is Norway and the beautiful King Oscar the Second's chapel. To the left is my beautiful Motherland. This water has been welcoming pilgrims and peace for over one hundred years. You who are returning, and you who are arriving, are following a long tradition. I welcome you.'

There were smiles and hugs all around between the two couples, but I kept my distance. We were heading to a small granite harbour, above which stood a very traditional church with a spire. I'd known what it would look like. I'd studied the area on Google Maps. The harbour was big enough for about four boats on a good day, and beyond that was a gravelled parking area. This was where we would RV with the cult deprogrammers who'd flown in from the US.

There were going to be two distinct groups waiting for Mary. The deprogrammers, social-worker types in socks and sandals, and bouncers in sixteen-hole combat boots. The latter guys were needed for three reasons. First, to keep the team safe. It wasn't unknown for deprogrammers to be killed by the cult member they'd come to rescue. They also needed to control the cult member for his or her own safety. The cult member mustn't have the opportunity to hurt themselves. It could be anything from trying to jump out of a moving vehicle to escape, possibly so high on drugs they didn't know they were throwing themselves out of a vehicle, or straightforwardly attempting to kill themselves. To keep them safe they must be gripped – which is why prison staff use overwhelming numbers to control prisoners who are kicking off, first and foremost to keep them from harming themselves. The last reason was in case there was any follow-up from the cult trying to rescue one of their own.

We would also have to grip her for our own safety and hers. But the moment Mary had been handed over our job was done, and she'd be on her way to Oslo to be deprogrammed by the social-worker crew while the bouncers protected the building and the cult member.

But for Mary it would be the start of something she was not going to like. After we in effect had kidnapped her, the deprogramming process would involve her being locked up in a safe-house run by a charity that dealt with this kind of situation, while receiving hours of intense debriefing from the socked-and-sandalled social-worker types. She'd be a prisoner, and the team of deprogrammers would use the same psychological techniques as the cult to bring her back to the world where she belonged. It would be like reverse engineering as they tried to get her to experience the same emotional connection to her former life that she now had with the cult. It could take weeks or even months for her past emotions to reconnect, and that was assuming the debriefing was successful enough for Mary to head back to LA.

At least one in three deprogrammings eventually failed, and even if they were successful with Mary, she'd be floating back and forth from cult to non-cult views of the world. Basically, once she got home, she was fucked, and Mr and Mrs Gaskell and their millions would be of no help to her at all.

They hadn't been in the Google photos, but today the parking area was filled with RVs and a group of motorcycles. The chapel was a popular stop for all the adventure travellers this far north before snowfall – and as far as they were allowed. No one was going into Russia, not even the bikers clumping about in big bike boots, leathers or padded Gore-Tex. The RV owners were in more casual gear, duvet jackets and jeans, and all of them were taking photos on their phones. The thing that stood out for me among the grimy, slush-stained vehicles was a gleaming black Merc MPV. The driver was feverishly wiping splash marks off the wheel arches while a group of six were taking bags out of the tailgate.

Grisha slowly and skilfully manoeuvred the RIB alongside the harbour wall. He could see my curiosity. 'Ah, they're from the village. They're on their way to spread God's Word on Earth – in Asia, I think.'

The side of the RIB bounced gently against a set of granite steps, and Grisha would accept no help as he tied up and controlled the RIB at the same time. He jumped onto a step and held out a hand for Cameron. 'Please leave your bags. I will take care of them. Please leave your boat gear on the quay.'

We dutifully started donning our Covid masks but Grisha would have none of it. 'Don't need those up here.'

The driver came running over, gesturing us to the Merc. 'Please, please.'

After pulling off the wet-wear, we all did as he asked. We met the missionaries halfway as they headed for the RIB, and there were lots of welcomes and smiles and contentment. I smiled back and watched as Madeleine hugged two of the women, wishing them luck and adventure. So far, it felt like a day trip off a cruise liner. I got myself past the sliding door on the Merc and took a seat. The rear bench looked big enough for the two couples to sit and continue their love fest together.

Two six-wheel-drive Polaris bikes roared past, each carrying two Norwegian soldiers in the new tri-Nordic countries' green combat gear, with their new HK416 assault rifles slung over their backs. The all-terrain vehicles pulled up at the RIB and their riders dismounted, where Grisha and the driver were now ferrying our bags landside. What were they going to do? Arrest the Russian? Check our bags?

The scrub-covered land and rock jutting out on our side of the border was replicated in Russia on the other side of the narrow inlet. And beyond that, just over the rise and no more than a hundred and twenty-five kilometres away, was

Murmansk, which had been the home of the mighty Soviet northern fleet until the 1990s. Then, just like in Matvey's hometown Vladivostok and its Pacific fleet, everything had collapsed and their attack submarines were abandoned, along with rusting warships that were eventually sold as scrap or simply stolen.

But now, just like their Pacific fleet, the Russian Federation's northern fleet was an even mightier nuclear-powered war machine, with its own ground and air support. No wonder the countries bordering Putinland up here were always a little nervous.

To my amazement, it was smiles and handshakes all round down at the RIB. I was even more amazed when the patrol men seemed to offer to move the bags on the backs of their six-wheelers.

We were all seated on warm and comfy Mercedes leather, the heat was on, and we were packed up and ready to go. Through the window, I watched the RIB finish being loaded with its new cargo, and Grisha and the now Gore-Tex-clad missionaries waved us off.

29

The road was graded, which didn't surprise me. There weren't going to be that many metalled motorways up here. It was a single carriageway, but maybe a third wider to allow vehicles to pass if one hugged the verge and the other moved out. That explained the ten-centimetre ruts in the middle of the road, and why the roadside drainage had started to decay. Not that any of that mattered to a Mercedes' suspension.

The two couples were in their own worlds, hands in hands, enjoying the scenery as we moved the eighteen or so kilometres to the village. Rock and stone competed with low scrub vegetation and stunted trees that in the short summer would be very lush and green, as they would with about twenty-two days of rain a month. By the end of this particular month that rain would be falling as snow, and it would carry on until the spring.

The Jakobselv river twisted and turned to our left as we followed it on the straighter road. It was wide, maybe thirty-five to forty metres, because we were still close to the coast. The low trees made it disappear now and then, but a constant was the large yellow posts positioned every kilometre or so, with multilingual signs warning anyone on the Norwegian side that the river was the border.

Now and again I caught glimpses of the corresponding red posts on the Russian bank with their signs probably saying the same. I'd spent a lot of time in Russia over the years, most of it a nightmare, but some of it happy. I liked the average working Russian and could get by with my schoolboy-level basics to buy and ask for things. Even though they were today's bad guys, to me real Russians were just like real people anywhere else, whether Basra or New York. All they wanted to do was eat, pay the rent and take their kids to school safely.

The driver hadn't introduced himself, but was just as happy a bunny as Grisha as he waved at a couple of SUVs that passed us on their way towards the coast. His mobile rang. Good – there was a signal. But why wouldn't there be, in one of the top five most technically advanced countries on the planet? He waffled away on his Bluetooth headset and checked his watch. The tone was social. Maybe he was local and had the best job in town, driving around in this posh Merc. That made sense to me, because if the border patrols were friendly with the village, why wouldn't the locals be – especially if it was providing jobs?

After about twenty minutes we turned left off the graded road and onto a track of well-worn gravel that looked more like compacted earth. It took us on a gentle downhill gradient towards the river. I pulled out my iPhone – the new one, the 13.

I messaged the team, as they would be tracking me on Find My.

Now left off the main. ERV.

This junction was now our Emergency RendezVous. The

one point that we all knew was where we would meet, especially if it all went to shit and I was running for my life.

The Owl had never issued us with mobiles before, let alone insisted we use them. He was throwing out of the window everything I'd told Tripp about operational security, and we weren't happy about it. I played the game and nodded when he explained the phones were just part of the package. We needed secure comms, he said, because he wanted sitreps every twenty-four hours. These three iPhones were at the same time mystery boxes because The Owl would have had them filled with surveillance software. Now he'd know exactly where we were, and exactly what we were messaging and talking about. Even if we turned the things off, The Owl would still be able to listen to everything within the mobiles' mic range, along with activating the cameras on both sides. But none of that mattered, because we were going to do exactly what was expected of us to keep him thinking he had the upper hand, then do what we really needed to do that he wouldn't know about.

I got a smiley emoji back from Rio, and was relieved. Had Jack replied, he would have written me a two-page letter.

Hitting Google Maps, I could see we were about five hundred metres line-of-sight until the river. The Merc driver was taking his time, snaking left and right as we contoured the track down the gradient. Trees blocked any view we might have had apart from directly ahead, and their branches grazed the windows and sides. No wonder the driver was taking it carefully. He'd probably die of hyperventilation if his paintwork got scratched.

Madeleine knew it wouldn't be long now and turned back to reassure us. 'Almost there. Don't worry, the road gets much better nearer the village.' She and Mathulla celebrated with a kiss and the other couple hugged and smiled in anticipation.

Madeleine was right. Maybe two hundred metres further down the slope the Merc's wheels crunched over well-laid gravel, and the sound coming into the cabin was the same as if we'd been driving up to a stately manor house. There had been no gates, fences or keep-out-private-land type signs to give the impression this was a compound.

The first building I saw was a long log cabin, windows double-glazed, a green alloy roof in very good order. Outside it stood a small woman with fragile facial features, maybe Somalian or Eritrean. She was overwhelmed by the kind of big chunky polo-neck jumper they wear in Scandi murder mysteries. It looked more like a coat on her, the hem reaching her knees. Just the tips of her fingers were exposed under the sleeves as she waved to us and bounced on the balls of her feet.

The driver spoke at last as he hit the sliding-door button. 'Welcome! Welcome!'

I looked beyond the waving woman and into my new world, while the other four readied themselves to step into it. It wasn't what I'd been expecting, as the imagery I'd been looking at couldn't give this real-time detail. Beyond the log cabin were other neat buildings of different shapes and sizes, linked by concrete walkways. Even the ground around the buildings had been cultivated. Out were scrub vegetation, rock and stone, and in was level-cut grass. There was no smell of smoke in the air; in fact, the buildings didn't have chimneys. There were no scrappy dogs on string being held by moody New Agers with long greasy hair, smoking roll-ups as they sat around an open fire waiting for a cauldron of lentil soup to boil. The people still had the whites in their eyes and didn't look like burnt-out cult zombies. If anything, they could have been city dwellers dressed for a country weekend in high-end outdoor labels. If this was The Owl and Tom's idea of a compound, they needed to get out more. Or at least download a dictionary app.

As I jumped out to join the others, Madeleine was already hugging away at the greeter. I couldn't see the woman's lips move because the wall of the polo-neck came up to just below her nose, but that didn't matter. She was clearly full of welcoming happiness. 'I'm so glad to see you all,' came from under the polo-neck. 'My name is Saynab, and I know in my heart that God is just as happy as I am to welcome you to our village.'

The Merc did a three-point turn and disappeared back uphill, no doubt heading for a three-hour wash-down.

30

Out of the blue, a go-faster carbon racing type wheelchair appeared for Cameron, which he was very happy to collapse into. Elaine pushed him towards the outer weather doors of the long log cabin, where Saynab beckoned us with a very cheerful 'Come, let's get warm.' Once through those, I opened the actual frame doors of the cabin and we were inside.

It was a massive dining room with six trestle tables, each maybe ten metres long, covered with white linen tablecloths and sets of condiments. Lining each table were trendy wooden Nordic-style chairs that you could easily spend an evening in – and maybe that was the plan. Interestingly, the trestles were placed widthways across the room, which meant there was no top table at either gable end for somebody to dominate from. There wasn't even an elevated area or stage.

To the left of the door, rows of coat-hooks hung on the wall over wooden pigeon-holes. The owner's name was attached under each, making up a mail-drop, along with a post-box to send out.

This wasn't exactly how I pictured a cult. They were supposed to be insular with just one voice of influence.

On the table closest to the door were hotel-style Thermoses labelled 'Coffee' and 'Hot Water', and boxes of different herbal teas. Alongside them were trays of pastries for the five weary travellers, and several grey Scandi no-handle mugs stacked on top of each other.

Three children stepped forward and picked up the trays of pastries. They were maybe nine or ten years old, shiny-haired and well groomed, and all dressed in a uniform of red pullover, red gilet and matching red trousers.

They might have been dressed as clones but they certainly weren't robots. They were very excited to be in the room with us, and all three beamed hello. It had clearly been rehearsed and they'd been told what to do and how to do it, but they couldn't have been more enthusiastic as they passed round the food and we tucked in.

Saynab explained the plan. 'As you can see, this is our dining room. Feel free to come in at any time after six this evening and learn how we enjoy our meals together, and meet our village. They're all very excited to meet you and want to help you settle in, in any way they can.'

As Saynab was talking, she stood behind one of the girls and rested a hand on each of her shoulders. 'This is my daughter, Poppy, and she and her friends, Michael and Andreas, were allowed to leave school a little earlier today to come and welcome you and show you to your rooms. This is their first time helping me during a reception, and I think they're doing a wonderful job, don't you?'

We all nodded and agreed, of course, and then Elaine initiated a round of applause for the three very embarrassed kids. We finished off our coffees and teas as Saynab gave her final notes. 'If you need anything, if you need to ask anything, or just want to talk, I'm here twenty-four/seven. Just ask anyone for me and I'll be with you. But please can I remind you that our village is a mobile-phone-free zone. We like having the time to talk to our friends, our children, and reflect on our thoughts and spend time with God.'

We nodded and agreed again, as you would do.

She pointed me out to Poppy, and the two boys to the other two couples. As the girl approached, I held out my hand to shake, not sure what to do or say. 'Hello, I'm Nick.'

'Hello, Nick. I'm Poppy. I'm ten years old and want to become a doctor, and I'm going to take you to your room.'

I already knew who she was and what she wanted to be from TikTok. She was the first person I'd come across when I'd hit God's Word on Earth's social media. She was celebrating spring with the rest of the village as the sun was high enough to shine into the whole valley. She was with her mates, their faces painted sun-yellow as they danced to 'Here Comes The Sun'.

Their website had already explained that the primary language in the village was English, but I hadn't expected everyone to be so fluent. All the kids sounded like they were born and bred in the Surrey Hills.

As we said our goodbyes to the others and she led the way to the double doors, Saynab had the final word. 'Once you have settled in, please feel free to explore the village. You're sure to have questions, so please go ahead and ask. The natives won't bite.'

31

It wasn't so much a cabin as a five-star suite. The moment I took my boots off at the door to the open-plan kitchen-diner-living area I felt the warmth pumping up through the tiles. The kitchen was kitted out with a Nespresso machine and the whole range of pods, and the fridge held every kind of milk from semi-skimmed to almond via oat and soy.

Back in the living area, all the furniture was high-end Scandinavian, including a Bang & Olufsen wall-mounted TV. Even the remote was sleek solid steel. Their website had explained that the village wasn't about being cut off from the world: it was about being a better part of it. Next to the internal phone on the solid glass coffee-table was a list of numbers for the admin offices, housekeepers, school, medical centre, restaurant. Every service a village required.

Through the door past the living area were the bedroom and en-suite. The decor was the same, a few thousand pounds' worth of minimalist oak bed with a memory-foam mattress, matching oak nightstands, chest of drawers and wardrobe.

Norway's answer to Lulu Lytle had made a fortune there. I could have been in a loft apartment in Shoreditch.

Laid out on the crisp white duvet, among a hundred luxury cushions, was the clothing I'd pre-ordered on the website: a black Columbia Gore-Tex jacket, black Canada Goose parka, and a pair of Sorel boots. I checked and they were size 44.5, just what I'd asked for. I had to smile. This was stuff I would never have bought for myself. I might talk myself into thinking of buying it, but baulk at the last minute when I saw the total figure in the basket. I'd never thought I deserved to own anything expensive or good, something Rio had thought about a lot – probably too much. He reckoned it was to do with my childhood: having jack shit and constantly being told I was Jack Shit meant I found it hard to think of myself as worthy. Unfortunately, and annoyingly, he might have had a point.

I plugged in the charger and opened the iPhone, checking the selfie headshot of Mary and Gedi on the beach to ensure their images never left my head. Then I put the iPhone on the bedside cabinet, camera down and screen lens next to the lamp, so that all The Owl would see was the inside of the lampshade – and, with luck, enough shock light to give him a headache when the bulb was illuminated.

I put on my new parka and boots, pulled up the hood with its wild coyote fur trim, and went to explore. I needed to find my bearings and, of course, Mary. I wouldn't go straight up to her and tell her what was what. I would play the newbie and work out the best way to make contact, which shouldn't be hard. Everybody I passed on the concrete walkways smiled and nodded a welcome.

I had passed more cabins with their owners' personal

touches outside, the sort of things you would expect anywhere else, BBQs, cycles, that sort of thing. The cabins, layout and immaculate appearance of this place should be the blueprint for Center Parcs 2040: there was money in it.

I eventually found the supermarket and decided to have a look inside. I had been expecting CCTV cameras on buildings or towers doing a Big Brother cult thing, but I hadn't seen any so far.

The store seemed to stock everything except alcohol and tobacco, and that suited me fine. There was no counter, no assistant, not even an honesty book – but why would there be? Just like Mary had told the Gaskells, money was meaningless.

There was a mixture of Western and Russian brands, but all the labels were in Cyrillic. You just helped yourself to pasta or stuff to make sandwiches, then took it back to your cabin. I grabbed a bar of Alenka and a carton of banana milkshake, my go-to flavour for most things full of additives. Alenka chocolate was one of the few luxuries available during the Soviet era, and was still a Russian favourite – mine too. Connoisseurs might gag at the cheap cooking-chocolate taste, but I'd really got to like it over the years. It sort of felt right to have it on the shelves so near to Russia – and, besides, there were some bad tastes I was about to want to disguise.

Low-level lighting now illuminated the pathways as I walked. I swallowed my Rasagiline, and washed it down with chocolate and banana. Munching and swigging, I next passed the laundry, where villagers worked away, folding sheets and piling them into wicker baskets. Another plus: no laundry to do. I supposed I'd be allocated a job at some time and quite fancied cabin services: they had a couple of golf carts plugged in outside that must be fun to ride around in.

Steel shutters slowly rolled up to reveal two women in

green overalls working on three or four snow blowers and their other machines for when the snow came, three All-Terrain Vehicles. These weren't six-wheelers, like the ones the Norwegian Army were using up here. The ATVs were Russian Phantom quads and, like anything else Russian-built to tackle the wilderness, they were military green, big, chunky, and with oversized wheels that could tackle any terrain. These things could even swim, and would have been a must-have garden plaything in every oligarch's garage.

It would soon be that time of year and the snowploughs that could be attached up front were laid out in preparation. The two-week forecast had mentioned some flurries but nothing serious, but this was the Arctic. Maybe the women, now giving me a wave and a smile, knew something no one else did.

32

All this place needed was a blacksmith for it to be the perfect chocolate-box village. Interestingly, there were no crucifixes, either outside or in the buildings, or images of Jesus hanging from a cross or Matvey smiling down lovingly on us. There was nothing new in that for religions. Islam doesn't use any kind of religious symbolism. But I was hoping there would be one or two of the leader as we hadn't been able to find any pictures online. The only image I'd seen stuck on a wall had been of a large red teddy bear telling me, in case I hadn't worked it out from the shouts and screams of fun coming out of the building, that this was Snuggly Bear Day-care Centre.

Parents were going home with their kids in red uniforms, school daysacks full of homework, but still no Mary. I continued my wander, and found myself down at the river. The Jakobselv was twenty-five to thirty metres wide, flowing gently from my right to my left, heading north to the inlet. An impressive, new-looking truss bridge spanned to the Russian side of the village. It was a bit of engineering overkill, as I hadn't seen any vehicles calling for such a heavy-duty structure. The paving on our side wasn't wide enough anyway. Maybe the golf carts or the Phantom quads used it for now, and they were planning ahead. What I did notice were the two thick black power cords securely fastened to the side of the bridge. Power coming from Norway to Russia, or the other way round? Yet again, the set-up screamed money. Why not have lots of power and a serious steel bridge just for people to walk over? The framework had been painted: our half of it up to mid-river was yellow, and the other half, of course, was red.

Pedestrians crossed in both directions and a couple of bicycles made their way to Russia, but still no Mary. Maybe she was working, perhaps on the other side of the bridge. Maybe they didn't all live on the Norwegian side. No problem. The other side was for later.

I checked the watch I'd bought at Heathrow. It had been years since I'd needed one as my mobile took over my life, but as the website explained, and Saynab reinforced, this was a mobile-free zone, even though it had a signal to tempt newbies like me. It was seven minutes before dinner started, so I turned and headed for the dining hall. I was going to be there at dead on six – and, hopefully, meet Mary.

As soon as I opened the double doors the air was filled with a wall of excited chat, kids jabbering about whatever kids jabber about, cutlery and glasses clinking, adults laughing. I hung my coat on the spare rack, and went in. No doubt I'd get my own hook and pigeon-hole soon. The fresh linen had menus and cutlery laid out at each place setting, and servers rushed around to complete the orders of what was probably the first wave. Parents would be wanting to get their kids fed, homework finished, baths done and bedtime stories told, ready to start the whole cycle again in a few hours' time.

My initial plan had been to go and sit so I could watch everybody come into the hall, but the perfect table to view from at the far end of the dining room was empty. A couple, maybe mid-thirties, about three-quarters of the way up the second trestle, made the decision for me. The guy, a man mountain, far too big and muscled to look comfortable in the chairs, waved a tattooed hand for me to come and join them. 'Hello! Welcome!' There had to be a gym I had missed.

I smiled and went and sat next to him, facing the woman and two kids sat either side of her, their legs too short to make the floor so they were just swinging.

'Hello, I'm Nick.'

The woman knew – they all knew the newbies' names. 'I'm Esther and this is my husband Kirill, and our boys George and Uwe.'

They all shook my hand, even the children, and sensed my confusion about the seating plan. I tried to work out where Esther came from, as it was clear she wasn't Russian, unlike her husband.

Kirill explained through his neatly trimmed beard how food worked here. 'When you arrive you simply go to the table that is being filled, and you and your partner sit opposite each other. Then more people arrive and do the same until that table is full. That way we always get to sit with different neighbours and talk about different things – you know, have more community.'

'Right.' I nodded. The fact I was on my own had clearly messed up the system, but Kirill was there before me.

'People just fill the next gap. We know you're alone, but soon . . .' he touched his heart, which looked strange with his hand covered in violent tattoos '. . . you won't be. Matvey will show you the way to open the door inside you into a better world.'

33

The tattoos on Kirill's hands screamed that he wasn't your normal man of love. In Russian Mafia organizations, your service history is inked on your body, and this boy's was pretty much an open book, even fully clothed. The blue and blurred patterns left no doubt to those who knew that these were visible signs of authority and prestige. I didn't know what they all meant, but the wrist bracelets, probably etched with ink improvised from soot and piss, were really manacles, signifying Kirill had spent more than five years in prison. The middle-finger ring tattoos were to show he'd served his whole sentence: no parole for this guy. His third finger, left hand, displayed a skull with fangs, making sure everyone knew he fought authority. Yet here he sat, a family man, a wide wedding ring on his third finger, right hand, covering yet another tattoo, to show that, just like Mary had written in her email, he, too, had repented and changed his life.

Two servers arrived with a tray full of spaghetti Bolognese, and served the family. I checked the menu. It looked like a city bistro's. I waited till they had finished their grace before ordering the *shchi* to start, then going Western with steak, chips and all the trimmings – and water would be fine, thanks.

Esther had read my mind. Her family was originally from Egypt, she said, but emigrated to Germany, where she had met Kirill and produced the multicultural family I saw in front of me. The kids' accents sounded like they were Surrey Hills neighbours with Poppy.

More diners trooped in and sat next to the family and opposite me. They knew who I was. They welcomed me and ordered, just as my cabbage soup arrived. It was becoming a bit of a Russian food fest for me on top of the Alenka bars.

Checking out the arrivals between spoonfuls, I saw another newbie couple, Madeleine and Mathulla. Madeleine knew the system, of course, and she organized for chairs to be moved when Cameron and Elaine arrived, so Cameron could be treated just like everybody else. I liked that.

Everyone wanted to know about me and how they could help me feel at home. I joined in the conversation because I wanted to know more, I wanted to blend in, and I wanted to stay there as long as I could and check out the arrivals. I found myself quite enjoying it: the people were happy.

In answer to my questions, they said they were free to come and go as they pleased, either to the Russian side or to leave altogether. The main village this side of the Jakobselv comprised all the accommodation and services. Across the river was Matvey, God's Word on Earth's church, and the Spiritual Centre. They must have been the larger buildings I'd seen on the imagery. Apparently, the Spiritual Centre was where God would get in touch with me.

For the first few days, I'd be staying in the village to ensure I'd made the right choice. It wasn't that they were deciding whether they would have me, it was whether I would decide to have them.

The village was going to guide me and help me make my choice. I wouldn't want to leave the village, they said, which now, with the newbies, had a population of 424. But the big deal was that at the end of the week, on Sunday, we would all go to church together. I, and the other newbies, would be the guests of honour.

Kirill had an idea. 'Would you like to join us this evening for yoga at the gym? It's at eight thirty. We could pick you up – maybe eight fifteen? Would that work?'

It would, but not tonight.

'That is so kind of you but I'm exhausted. It's been quite a journey. I think I'd fall asleep as soon as I lay on the mat, so an early night would be best.'

I was getting stuck into my steak and chips when Mary appeared by the coat racks, accompanied by Gedi. He had also hit the gym, something I hadn't been able to tell from the headshot on the beach. He was about a foot taller than Mary, and that was saying something, as she was the same height as her mother. Apart from Gedi's physicality, they looked the same as they did in the selfie. Mary's shoulder-length light brown hair, somewhere between wavy and Afro-textured, was flatter due to the beanie now shoved into her coat pocket. She wore jeans tucked into Sorels, the boot of choice round here, and a jumper that Saynab would have been proud of. She was full of joy and smiles for Gedi, who looked even more like a male model as he pulled back his wavy blond locks and rubbed down his beard. They were just as radiant as Madeleine and Mathulla as they made their way to the far trestle.

As I watched them, and Kirill and Gedi waved at each

other, Saynab appeared and leant over my shoulder. 'Good evening, Nick. Is everything okay? The clothing was the correct size?'

I nodded, everything was good, and I gave her a thank-you.

'Good, good. And the cabin – it's okay? Everything you need?'

'Tired, but absolutely fine, thank you.'

Mary and Gedi were now ordering; they were going to be here for a while.

Saynab had something else to explain. 'This evening is all about making friends. They'll answer any questions you have, but then we start tomorrow to see if we can help you – if you can find your way with the help of God. What do you think of that?'

I said I thought it was a very good idea indeed and, yes, I would be adventurous and find my own way to the Spiritual Centre for 10 a.m. It was a very kind thought, but there was no need for Saynab to pick me up. She left just as Mary's food was delivered, and I made my own farewells to my neighbours.

I collected my parka, and exited, not to go back to my cabin for an early night, but into the shadows between the building opposite and the dining-hall entrance. Establishing contact and making friends with Mary in the dining hall would be difficult: the seating system simply didn't lend itself to it. I was going to have to sort something out and try to get next to her and Gedi. Yoga might have been an opportunity, but I had other things that needed doing. You don't just dive into an abduction. I needed to find out whether she was on any new medication, voluntarily or not. If so, I needed to make sure I had it with me when I lifted her for her medical continuity. I also needed to find out her state of mind. Maybe she was so absorbed in the village, so much a part of it, that there would be screams, kicks and shouts while she tried to stab me with a kitchen knife. So the only way out was the bare-nuts way: with a head-butt and dragging her by the hair. But move-fast-and-break-things wouldn't work here and, besides, I didn't want to do it to someone from the real world. She'd be traumatized enough when she got back to LA, where the two fuck-ups would make her pay with enough guilt to get her running into the sea and her body being found on the longshore drift. Becoming friendly with her, talking to her, her getting to know me was the better option. It was a fucker, but you sometimes have to take the hard route.

Naturally, it started to rain. My Canada Goose did a good job: with the hood up, I was completely warm and dry for the next thirty-odd minutes until Mary and Gedi emerged from the dining hall, along with two other couples and some kids. I followed as the group broke off and walked to their respective homes. None of them unlocked their doors to enter. Soon Mary and Gedi were on their own. They headed arm in arm towards a cabin and pulled down the handle without unlocking it. Just like my door, there was only the lever lock, and its lone key would probably be hanging from a hook on the frame.

At least I knew where one of them lived, or maybe they lived together, something I wasn't expecting. But maybe God was quite liberal in that respect, and so he should be. After all, he'd got someone else's wife pregnant, though that didn't seem to be a problem to his followers.

As I turned and walked back to my cabin, I felt surprisingly upbeat. I wasn't too sure what I'd say to God when he contacted me, but the rest of the people in the village were fine by me.

34

It was only 20:00, and though Mary and Gedi were in their cabin and might be tucked up in bed for all I knew, it was still early doors. Even so, there wasn't much foot traffic about the village, and unless there was a curfew Saynab hadn't told me about, it was probably because of the rain. I got a couple of hellos and you-must-be-Nicks through white teeth from under parka hoods, and I nodded and replied and pressed on. I needed to get back to the cabin.

Retrieving my iPhone from under the lamp, I plugged in my earphones. They were old-school, wired sports style; if I needed to run, a fancy bud falling out of a sweaty ear wasn't going to help me.

The Owl's sitrep was due at 15:00 east coast time – if he was on the east coast. Wherever he was, it was alien having to check in with and send a situation report to somebody each day. I'd never liked it in the army, I hadn't liked it working outside, and I certainly didn't like it now. Maybe I should get a ring tattoo like Kirill's.

Normally The Owl wouldn't want any contact in case he

was going to be told there'd been a cock-up. He just wanted results. All I'd normally do was receive the brief and we'd meet up a couple of weeks later or whenever the job was over. Plausible Deniability were probably The Owl's middle names. This time, though, the job was personal. He had opened an eager eye for it, which made me feel like he was looking over my shoulder with the mystery box as he followed me outside.

Constant hovering always created problems. The one who wanted to direct from the back seat didn't see, didn't hear, didn't feel what you, the operator, felt on the ground. Worse still, it conveyed the impression that they, the decision-maker, either didn't have confidence in the operator or didn't trust them. The Owl had been around long enough to know he probably couldn't even trust his husband.

It wasn't one-way traffic. The chances of a fuck-up were increased when the operator didn't trust the decision-maker, and I certainly didn't trust The Owl.

Phone in hand, hood back up again, I stepped into the shadows outside just in case the rooms were bugged. Maybe Matvey wanted to know what the newbies were up to or, come to that, what everybody was up to.

Rainwater dripped from one of the gutters and tapped on my hood. The Owl answered in three rings. 'Tell me.'

What I had to report would be equally short, sharp and concise, giving him just what he needed to know.

'Situation: I've sighted her on the Norwegian side of the village, but no contact. She and Gedi are still together, possibly live together.'

The Owl knew not to interrupt me, just to take the information. Anything specific he wanted to know about, he'd ask when it was time for him to talk. That was why there was a sitrep template.

'Summary: we all live in Norway. On Sunday the main church service takes place over the bridge. That's where Matvey and the Spiritual Centre are – don't know what that is yet, but both are in Russia.

'Action to date: I've recced the Norwegian side of the village.

'Actions to do: sitrep the team, and make contact with Mary.

'Issues: I can't stick by this sitrep time as I'm expected to socialize. I'll call each twenty-four-hour period when it's safe. Questions?'

Now was his time. 'None. But you'll recce the other side before tomorrow's sitrep. Find out what you can about the cult, whatever is going on over there. Have a look at this Spiritual Centre and get pictures of Matvey.'

There was no point in discussion. There was more important work to do. 'Okay. Closing down.'

Why did The Owl want pictures? Maybe the parents or Tom wanted one to throw darts at. Who knew? Actually, who cared?

I hit Find My. Both their phones were a couple of hundred metres off the main, further south than where the Merc had turned off. I called Rio instead of Jack as I didn't have all night.

He answered, straight into it: 'We're thirty minutes' rain time from the ERV.' As if there was any chance of it being drier, and therefore faster.

I needed to know how long it would take them to get to the junction where the Merc had turned left going down towards the river. If it all went wrong for me in the village and I had to get out quickly, with or without Mary, I had thirty minutes before Jack and Rio would reach the emergency rendezvous.

They had flown separately to Oslo, met up, and rented a campervan before driving the six hundred kilometres north to be on standby for my arrival at the harbour. Maybe they'd already been there when we landed, watching us from the car park. I didn't know, because I didn't need to. All I knew was that they would be up there on time and ready to kick off at a moment's notice, and that's loyalty – that's trust at work. Whatever they told me, I trusted; whatever I told them, I knew they'd do the same.

I gave Jack and Rio the same sitrep as The Owl, and just as formally. That was all right; Jack liked formal and Rio would be bored but he'd be listening. Rio finished it off: 'Okay, closing down.'

I did the same. All of us knew The Owl would have been listening but that was okay. We had done what he expected of us.

Back in the cabin the iPhone went back on the charger cable and under the lamp. I turned on the light and hoped The Owl's reaction was as I imagined. Even a little win is a win. Another was not having Saynab coming to pick me up tomorrow.

All I wanted was for The Owl to hear the coffee machine buzzing and me rustling around in a very comfortable duvet. Now was the time to pull out a Samsung from my backpack and do what we really needed to do, and which The Owl wouldn't know about. We had one Samsung each. The iPhones and Samsungs were manually logged onto the aptly named Norwegian cell network, ICE. There was to be no risk of us roaming onto anything Russian.

I rustled about taking my parka off, filling the kettle for some hot chocolate and making general living-life noises while the mobile powered up and I WhatsApped them both. It was a simple message.

RV tonight - I'll give 30 mins notice - rolling pickup

Job looks simple no restrictions so far no security unless I fuck up we give it the full 7 days

Thankfully, Rio was the first to reply, with a short and sharp GIF of a cat twerking. Jack would have sent a PowerPoint explanation of how they had spent their day. But now they'd be doing their maths together and realizing they had three hundred and fifty grand each coming their way for being on a one-week camping trip – because the job would last the full week. Happy days. All I had to do was keep those days rolling on to keep the cash coming in.

I closed down the mobile and shoved it inside a Sorel. What was the point of having a help-me phone if I was out there and it was in a drawer? All the while I was smiling to myself, savouring the moment, but not because of the cash. It was the GIF. That, and turning the lamp on, had really made my day.

After the hot chocolate and then an extra rustle around I got my parka back on for my walk to Russia. There were even fewer people out and about now. Passing Snuggly Bear, I found the gym and looked through the window at the high-end shiny steel equipment and the yoga class in the stretching area. If she was there, maybe it was a way of meeting her. So, if she went, so would I. And as I saw immediately, she was there, along with Gedi. There were maybe twenty-five others lying on mats, stretching out, doing yoga stuff. The only one who wasn't on the floor was Cameron, still in his go-faster wheelchair. Elaine was lying next to him, and as the rest of the class did big moves, he grabbed his shaky arm and dragged it across his body, grinning from ear to ear. He was absolutely loving it.

As the walkway's low-level lighting took me towards Russia I thought about Kirill. Maybe I could learn something from him that would help me once I'd binned my present existence and stepped into the real world.

35

I stood in the darkness to hide my breath cloud. At least the rain had stopped. The imagery had shown me three large buildings over there on the Russian side. About fifty metres further along from the bridge stood the first two-storey building I'd seen in the village. It was well-lit. People emerged. Two groups came in my direction, crossing the bridge back into Norway, heads down, hoods up. There was no flow of foot traffic in the other direction. I waited a couple of minutes and then moved towards the bridge to change that. Hands dug into the chest pockets of my parka, my hood up tight, I was going to play the excited but stupid newbie if challenged. If I was doing something I shouldn't, I'd be sorry, I hadn't been told. I'd turn around.

To add to the bridge's over-construction, its deck had been laid to concrete. It could easily take the golf carts, snow blowers, ATVs and much more besides. It would hardly have registered my weight. The main pathway on the Russian side was wider, and the power cables disappeared underground to the left. It was also more brightly lit. I continued on the path until I hit the two-storey. Same as on the Norwegian side, it was a log-cabin construction, but with windows only on the first floor. Bright light pushed through them and around the edges of the outer door. I closed my hand round the handle, ready to play stupid. I pulled it open, and was hit by a wall of pure blinding white. There were no stained-glass windows, no pulpit, no Stations of the Cross or anything religious up on the brilliant white walls, but this was without a doubt the church. White wooden benches faced the far gable end, where there was a raised stage. On it sat a drum set and several music stands, with speakers stacked up and wires trailing like spaghetti. Other speakers were set high into the walls. Front and centre stood a small table, a bottle of water, just one lone glass, upturned. The windows were set high in the walls, maybe so the congregation was never distracted by looking out at the rain or snow or trees. The preacher would have a captive audience.

Why was the church unlocked? Why were the lights on? Maybe all churches in Russia were open twenty-four/seven – I didn't have a clue.

I exited, and as I headed for the group of buildings beyond the church, it started to drizzle. These were another set of Center Parcs 2040 cabins, linked together to form one wide and low building. Going by the absence of light and sound, they were all empty. Low-voltage external lights illuminated the thresholds at ground level, but there was no activity inside. Ready to do my dickhead act if someone threw a switch or an alarm was tripped, I opened the first door. The room was open-plan, with sofas around the perimeter, the same sort of high-end interior decorations and Nespresso machines as on the Norwegian side. My guess was, this was the Spiritual Centre. I'd seen enough.

The drizzle was coming down heavier as I went back onto the main path and followed it maybe sixty or seventy metres deeper into Russia. The path was still wider than on the Norwegian side. To my right and set back thirty or forty metres was another two-storey building. The lights were on this time, on both floors. I stepped off the path and moved through wet grass into a group of trees for cover. I got close enough to hear the rain bouncing off the alloy roof, and stopped, looked, listened. Without a doubt this was living accommodation. The kitchen looked very much like mine but bigger, a minimalist dream. Two lights were on upstairs. Bedrooms? There was no movement, no sound.

Was this Matvey's house? Maybe he preferred to live in Russia for whatever reason, maybe security, or he wanted to let the villagers live a normal life with their families. Maybe he just liked being near God's HQ. If he did live here, no pictures would be taken today. I couldn't know for sure it was him, so why run the risk of fucking it all up taking a picture of someone The Owl didn't even want to see? That would have to wait for Sunday when I could identify him, know what I had to take imagery of, then get on with it. I had all week.

Voices drifted from the dead ground on the other side of the house. One was female, for sure, a higher-pitched laugh and a bit of talk – I couldn't make out exactly what it was – and then two shapes were on their way towards me. I stood still, holding my breath, trying to listen to their conversation over the patter of rain on my hood. The voices were happy, upbeat, and they were, it sounded to me, French. They passed me and turned right, away from the bridge. Their voices receded into the darkness.

I left them to it, because what I wanted to know was where

they had come from. I moved forward, as far to the right of the house into the grass and trees as I could for a bit more of an angle on what was going on behind it. Passing the house on my left, I came to a collection of log cabins, all one-level like the village. I'd seen enough. I turned and headed back towards the main drag. Now I knew where they had come from, I wanted to know where they were going. Still in cover, I retraced my steps to the path and turned right, away from the bridge.

It took about ten minutes, but eventually I found where I guessed they had gone. The path widened to the size of a single carriageway, and disappeared into the darkness and Russia. The road fed into shutters set midway into a very long building, but it wasn't a log cabin this time. It was the third of the large structures, a wide, low steel-structured warehouse affair, the sort of thing found in trading estates. I couldn't tell the colour in the dark. The building sort of made sense: supplies for the village couldn't come in every day because of the unpredictable weather, so they had to be stored somewhere.

As I got closer, I could hear an electrical hum. I got to the gable end nearest to me and it was clear that, whatever else the building was, it housed a small power substation. Power from this side of the bridge must be feeding and heating us. As for the goods coming in, I couldn't see any trucks, but the road was substantial enough to take a six-wheeler, that was for sure. There was nothing on the Norwegian side strong enough to support a big vehicle, which meant the village was probably condemned to truckloads of Alenka bars and banana-effect milkshakes from Murmansk, six hours away. Then again, maybe some stuff came in by boat and was taxied up; it was only about ten kilometres line-of-sight from here to the Russian coastline of the Barents Sea.

How the fuck was all this financed? The cost of the road alone would have broken a small bank, but all this besides? Maybe Matvey was one of Putin's oligarchs who had stolen the Soviet Pacific fleet when the country collapsed, then simply marked it up and sold it on. Or maybe a billionaire had found God in the village and got out his wallet.

More voices came from the far end of the warehouse. I stopped again and pulled back the hood. With my mouth open to stop any internal noises disrupting my hearing, I tilted an ear towards the sound. The rain had softened to a mist, and that was probably why I'd been able to hear those voices. They were Russian, male, talking in a low monotone. Their voices were getting louder: they must be heading for the pathway that led back to the bridge.

Shadowy shapes materialized. I stood stock still by the power station, holding my breath as the two figures sauntered past, hoods up. I didn't budge or exhale again until they'd faded away.

I headed along the side of the warehouse in the direction they'd come from, the dead ground at the other gable end. I passed the big shutters that took up the centre of the long structure, and I saw I was in an area of concrete hard-standing. This must be where the trucks unloaded. Putting my hood up, my hands into my pockets, I got back to playing the excited dumb newbie.

I turned the corner of the opposite gable end and was immediately confronted by a doorway set into the steel. It was solid, no illumination. Admin access for the warehouse's office?

And then two things happened within the space of a second and I knew I was in trouble.

The dull red LEDs of the first CCTV camera I had seen

illuminated the area for the lens's night vision to film the area I'd just wandered into.

And then, before I could turn and walk away playing stupid, the door swung open. Light spilt out and was then blocked. It came from a large bank of computer screens, and the block came from a body standing in the doorway.

36

'Hello, I think I got lost down by the . . .'

A lifetime of bad experience had me braced for aggression.

'Welcome.' He smiled warmly. 'And how are you?' The accent was Russian but Americanized, the voice very clear.

'I'm sorry, my name's Nick. I arrived today.' I pointed into the darkness. 'I thought the village was back that way but . . .'

He stepped up closer. He was about the same height as me, skinnier, with a groomed beard and geeky rectangular glasses. He was dressed in a dark fleece and jeans. Behind him, the room was in semi-darkness, apart from a long bank of monitors and corresponding workstations. It looked like an underground war-room bunker. Two faces were behind their screens, keys being hit.

'Nick, no problem. Welcome to the village.' He held out a fist for me to pump.

I shrugged apologetically and reciprocated. 'Saynab said to explore and I followed the road and, well . . .'

'No problem at all.' He could see me taking an interest in the scene behind him. 'You want some coffee? Come, I'll show you around.'

'Thank you, yes, please.' With my over-ingratiating tones, we stepped into the heat and he closed the door.

Mathulla sat at a workstation with Madeleine beside him. Both wore headphones. Madeleine seemed to be mentoring as he entered lines of code. She looked up and gave me a smile, tapping Mathulla's shoulder. He turned, smiled, and added a thumbs-up.

To the right of the door was a table and some cabinets with drinks, bread, and bags of Kopobka. Someone round here had the taste for Russia's answer to chocolate-covered wafers. The Nespresso machine got humming as he threw in a pod and pressed the button. He selected two mugs – even on the Russian side they had their stylish Scandi stack.

There were eight workstations. They were set up on trestle tables with wires running all over the floor and wall sockets overloaded with plugs, but only two stations were operating. They looked like they were in a hardcore telesales department, where the different stations were personalized by the users' pictures of dogs, cats, families, and Hands-Off-It's-Mine type mugs. One even had a small red bear stuck on the top right corner of her screen.

He motioned to ask if I wanted any extras. 'Just black, thanks.' I tried to look noticeably impressed.

He beamed. 'This . . .' he turned from the table and waved his arm '. . . is where we, God's clicky people, hang out.'

I nodded thanks as I took my coffee and the machine hummed again over the noise of Mathulla still clicking away for God. He came up and stood beside me, admiring the view just like me. The screens reflected off his lenses, obscuring his eyes. I was sure he had some in there, but I didn't need to see them. The expression on the rest of his face said it all. 'This is where you sent your application to, and from where we send God's Word on Earth out to the world. We've also got our ambassadors spreading God's Word on Earth in Africa, Europe, Indonesia, Taiwan, and next year, Australia and New Zealand. But we don't just promote faith, we provide health care, social justice and, most importantly, education. Inspiring, don't you think, Nick?'

What I thought was that I'd seen many NGOs operating in many countries and become very jaded with them. However much a lot of these groups were offering, it came with a price tag. I nodded approval and got down some of the coffee as he retrieved his mug and came back to me.

'It's from here we support our villagers, both their physical and spiritual needs. It lets them know that we're always thinking of them, always sending our love and, more importantly, God's love.' He let me take it all in. 'Pretty cool, don't you think?'

'Very. The building, it's the food and equipment storage for the village?'

'Everything we need is here, enough for the complete winter if the road can't be cleared – which often it can't. Impressive, don't you think?'

I had to agree it was. 'Is there only the one village? Are there any others out there, say in America? I didn't see any on the website.'

'No, no, just this one. People like yourself, you've chosen to come here and see if you wish to take our path. Then, when you feel you're ready, you too could go out on one of the adventures, spreading God's Word on Earth. Perhaps you will one day, Nick. One of the new destinations, maybe.'

I nodded away with excitement at the prospect, and actually, a trip like that wouldn't be too bad. I could hardly remember the last time I'd been on a flight that wasn't to go on a job. The only out-and-out pleasure trip I could think of was as a nineteen-year-old squaddie: a group of us booked an all-in holiday in Alicante, a hundred quid for the week, only to discover we'd booked it with Saga. We had breakfast with pensioners who'd brought their own brown sauce with them.

I nodded at the workstations, still suitably impressed. 'Looks like you get really busy spreading the word.'

'We sure do.'

I still couldn't see behind the glint, but the smile was there, so I supposed it was in his eyes too. I finished the coffee and turned back to the table. His hand came out for the mug. 'Let me take that, Nick. Have you been to our church? You must have passed it as you came over the bridge.' He placed the mug on a cleaning tray alongside some plates.

'Yes, I did.'

'On Sunday, you're going to be one of our guests of honour.'

'I'm really looking forward to it. Will you be there?'

'Of course.'

As we said our goodbyes at the door I nodded an acknowledgement to Mathulla and Madeleine. 'How do I get back?'

'Let me show you.'

We stepped out into the cold and damp and he pointed back the way I had come. 'Nick, I really hope you like our village and what we do here, and that you'll stay.'

'I hope so too.'

We fist-pumped once more.

'Until Sunday.'

The door closed and I was back on the concrete track to the bridge and the RV.

37

I wanted to carry out two more recces before I got up the hill and RV'd with the other two. The first stop was Gedi's cabin – or was it Mary's, or both of theirs? I broke a twig off a tree and looked around, feeling a little guilty in case I'd been seen. Were we allowed to do that in the village, damage a living thing? I pinched the leaves and pulled back until I had maybe ten centimetres of fairly straight, not too thin and flimsy wood. Then I clamped it between my front teeth and pulled it through a couple of times to strip off the bark.

Following the path into Norway, I had my hood up, hands in my pockets, as you would with the drizzle and the cold, breath trailing behind me. I looked at any buildings with lights on, especially any windows without blinds. As I passed the dining hall, there still wasn't anything to worry about. Most lights were off. The villagers were tucked up warm for the night. Those lights that were on were finding it hard to penetrate their blinds. Third-party eyes were going to be non-existent.

The only body I saw was from behind. I heard it first: the

gym doors opened about twenty metres ahead, 1960s beat music leaked out, and a guy emerged, facing away from me. He threw on his hoodie and broke into a steady jog, no doubt heading home to beat the cold. The doors closed again, and as I got up closer the lights were still on. From inside came the faint thump of bass, and through the window I caught a glimpse of a couple of big guys still working out. I walked on.

This first job was going to be short and sharp, which was how I was going to approach it and walk away from it. It's pointless hovering around, waiting for the right moment, because there never is one. Just get on and do it. The only certainties are what you see, hear, and smell at that very moment.

There were no lights on in the cabin, and the three senses were telling me all was good. Standing straight and keeping as close as I could to the cabin wall to minimize my profile, I walked up to the green door, bent just enough to reach the lever lock's keyhole, and gently inserted the twig. As I'd expected, it didn't encounter any resistance. There wasn't a key in the lock on the other side. Slowly withdrawing the twig again to avoid leaving any traces, I headed on the path towards cabin services. Having no key in the lock didn't mean the cabin hadn't been locked, but it seemed unlikely. No one I'd seen so far had had to unlock their doors when they got home: they'd all gone straight in. The shop had been open, everything had been open – so why would anyone here lock their door at night?

So far, I didn't know anything for sure, but the lack of a blocked key-well was at least a little information to start building on, even if it didn't tell me whether or not Mary slept there. That was a job for tomorrow, and if it turned out she didn't, it would mean hours of surveillance to find out what her sleeping habits actually were. I wanted to avoid that if I could: it would mean getting wet and cold, and there was a big chance of compromise.

There were no problems accessing the workshop through the side door. It was unlocked: why wouldn't it be? First thing that struck me, there certainly wasn't any energy conservation in this village, even on the Russian side. The workshop lights blazed, and the heating didn't seem to have an off switch. It was great. Hood off, I unzipped and enjoyed the heat. Before I went any further, I stayed by the door, listened, and looked around to get a mental picture of what was in front of me.

It seemed the two women I'd seen in the workshop earlier had had an extreme case of OCD. The tools were hung perfectly over their corresponding painted shapes. There wasn't a drop of oil on the polished concrete flooring, and it was swept spotless. Waste bins were empty. Even the workers' mugs were clean and hanging from a tree – no handleless Scandi nonsense for these two. Rio needed to see this: maybe it would shame him into getting a grip. Maybe not.

When I was sure I knew where everything was, I pulled out my Samsung and took a slow sweeping video of what I was about to go into. Everything had to be left exactly as it was at this moment. It was more subtle than just making sure I didn't knock things over. In the morning they could come to work and maybe not even consciously register that a bin, say, was a centimetre out of place. But their unconscious just might, and that could give them an uneasy sense that something wasn't right – and, in turn, that could produce drama. It wasn't as if the two women would decide that the new guy Nick had been in during the night and then ask why. But if they ended up thinking they had strangers coming into the village trying to steal kit, would they then lock up? People know a lot more about their environments than they think they do.

I took my boots off so as not to leave any sign on the concrete, and socked it into the workshop with two objectives. As I moved, I checked. Was I leaving feet-shaped moisture marks? No, it was far too warm in here for that.

First objective was to check out the ATVs, the Phantom quads. They had been configured with two padded bench seats that could just about squeeze three bodies plus the driver on board, with the loading platform taking up two-thirds of the vehicle behind them.

Were the keys available? I checked. Yes, they were all in the ignition. I took pictures to ensure the key tags lay exactly as they were before I turned each one to its first click to make sure the batteries were attached, and they were. The instruments and voltage meters lit up.

What about fuel? The gauges said zero. That wasn't a problem. I would have expected the fuel to be emptied if they'd been stored over the summer. Same as with a motorbike, there's nothing worse than having a machine standing for months and months with fuel in the tank. Today's ethanol blended fuels can start to go bad in as little as thirty days. Leaving fuel in the tank for an extended period allows for dirt, rust, sediment and other pollutants to build up and mix with it. When you fire up again at the start of the biking or, in this case, Phantom-ing season, this debris can then flow into your fuel lines, straight up to your engine.

The anal-retentives running this place would have emptied the tanks completely and allowed the inside to dry out to avoid any damage from fuel going bad. I bet they'd drained every drop of fuel and stored the ATVs in this pristine dry environment with the caps off for a couple of days to allow any residue to evaporate completely. Then they would have replaced the caps – and, sure enough, they had. They'd even placed stickers on the tanks with the date they'd emptied them and what fuel to refill with, E10.

I studied one of the fuel tanks for greasy fingerprints or marks, which would have to stay. There weren't any, of course: this thing had been polished. I took a picture of the cap position before twisting it off to smell that the fuel tag was correct, then went looking for E10.

I finally found what I was looking for. The row of four twenty-litre red steel jerry-cans was next to the two big lawn mowers in a millimetre-perfect line. I pictured the cap before I unscrewed, looked, and sniffed. You have to inspect, not expect. It was E10.

The second objective was to check that the shutters would open when I needed them to. The little red LED on the motor in the top left-hand corner told me that the power was on. I also wanted to make sure there was a manual that could be used as an override, and there was. It wasn't the usual chain that was pulled, like on a set of blinds, but a steel rod with an angled handle at the bottom and a hook at the top that fitted into the motor. When twisted, it raised the steel.

All was good. I would continue to check out the workshop whenever it felt safe, to ensure what I needed would be in here on the day.

Once back with my boots I checked out the video with what I could see in front of me, and all was good. As I got my boots back on, I checked my watch. I'd text the other two to be at the RV for 00:30. That gave me forty-five minutes to get up the hill.

38

The vehicle creeping closer along the main towards the ERV from my right was on full beam. As I lowered my hood to catch the engine note, water bounced from leaf to leaf and onto my head. It was starting to rain harder. I wasn't going to move to the edge of the road just yet – just in case.

The Samsung vibrated in my hand. I'd set the brightness as low as it would go, and glancing at it quickly, I made out the thumbs-up emoji. This set of lights was theirs.

Still in the treeline, I soon heard the engine and the churn of tyres over wet gravel, no doubt pushing up more mud to cover the van. This system for pickup was a standard operating procedure. Whoever was driving would not use the brakes to stop. Instead, he'd be relying on the gears and handbrake to ensure the brake lights didn't come on. Had it been a proper ops vehicle, there would have been a switch to override them when you hit the pedal. The side door would already be open, which was why I was on the junction side of the main. I'd simply step into the van, ensuring I crossed none of the vehicle's light-beams, and the van would continue. At a distance, even a very short one, if a vehicle is on full beam and there are no other interior or exterior lights, it's very hard to establish if it has stopped. In a wooded area like this, where the headlights would be flickering between the trees, it would be almost impossible. As far as anyone could tell, it would be a vehicle that was travelling without stopping. They probably wouldn't even recognize it as a campervan.

And that was exactly what happened. The van slowly approached the junction, no brake lights, no lights in the interior, apart from the instrument panel that caught the hair mass of Rio at the wheel. As I slipped inside, the camper clunked into gear and moved off. Jack was still holding the door open, and he'd keep it like that until we'd got up enough speed to cover the sound of it being closed. And even then, it was only onto the first click. A harder shut would come further down the road.

It was boiling hot in there, and it stank. I unzipped my coat and tossed it on top of their sleeping bags on the fold-out bed. It should have been converted back into a bench and a table in daytime, but not today. Probably never, while these two were aboard.

I lay with my soles hanging over the mattress edge, one eye on the timer on my Samsung. 'To the harbour, Rio, but take it slow time.'

'Mate, as if!' He waved his hand at the windscreen, shouting like I was miles away instead of just behind him. 'I mean, for fuck's sake!'

The full beam cut through what was becoming torrential rain, creating a tunnel effect as it got contained by the treeline. 'Never mind the pointing, mate, get that hand on the wheel.'

I turned to Jack as he put on the roof light. 'You get the kit?'

Their job had been to buy everything we'd need to lift Mary – ideally, catering for any drama. His expression told me they'd failed.

'Tasers, pepper spray – they're illegal here. We've had to go old school. Handcuffs, doorstops, and duct tape, plenty of it.'

It was better than nothing.

No wonder it stank in here. The van looked like squatters had taken up residence for the last month then bailed out because it was too messy. There were paper cups and sandwich wrappers strewn all over the place, among glasses, supplied with the van, now full of old teabags. A couple of carriers overflowed with junk food. They must have emptied entire service stations of their supplies of crisps, chocolate and Fanta. Basically, Coburg Crescent had been squeezed into a van in Norway.

I scrunched up a sandwich wrapper I'd been sitting on and tossed it to one side. 'Fuck sake, lads, even Gabe would be having a word about this.'

Rio was still in shouting mode, but he kept his hand on the wheel and his eyes forward. 'Shut up honking! He would have loved it: happy campers!'

His grin wasn't shared by Jack as he handed me a Thermos mug and reached back to pick up another of his own. They seemed to have come from the sink, where they'd been wedged among what looked like the van's complete array of crockery, used and unwashed. His face was a picture of resignation. 'Rio is an even worse domestic hand grenade in a confined space. It's a nightmare.'

I ferreted in my parka pocket and threw an Alenka bar at each of them. 'See what you get if you turn up on time?'

Jack put his chocolate away for later, whereas Rio was already opening his as he drove, the bar wedged between his hand and the wheel as he strained to use his teeth to rip at the wrapper. 'These are shit, but do we love 'em?' He wasn't looking for an answer. The chocolate was already in his mouth.

I turned back to Mr Sensible sitting on the edge of the bed. Sometimes it was better to have answers from a walking Alexa. 'Where did you leave your iPhones?'

The van juddered from side to side, either Rio avoiding potholes or his hand not controlling the wheel as he bent to get at the chocolate. Our heads jerked in rhythm with the crockery in the sink. I really missed the Merc.

Rio threw his scrunched-up foil back over his shoulder and it hit Jack's head. He kept calm. 'They're back at the site, wrapped up in the treeline. The Owl thinks we're all tucked up for the night, I'm sure. We did the whole thing about getting our heads down early, et cetera, et cetera. We're staying there in a campervan lodge until the morning, doing the adventure thing up north before the winter sets in. We got a hook-up, which was great, so we got power, but the site closes tomorrow, end of season. We're out on our arse first thing, but no problem, we'll just float about.'

I took a sip of the brew. It was horrible and stewed. Jack was full of apologies. 'It's UHT. This one broke the fridge on day one.'

Rio didn't like the accusation. 'That's bollocks. It was already bust.'

I believed Jack's version. The tea was bad, but it was wet and warm, so I drank it, and got out my Alenka to improve the taste. We'd all had worse, but I now knew how to improve our lives when it came to brews. 'Listen, lads, when we get back we need to get ourselves a Nespresso machine.'

Rio laughed. 'Buy any fucking thing for my house you feel

the need to. One of those Quooker taps would be handy and all.'

We rattled our way towards the harbour and Jack was really interested about what we'd left behind. 'So, what's it like down in the village?'

'Better than Tulse Hill, that's for sure. There's good living accommodation, it's clean, it's warm, good food, lots of facilities. They've got it well squared away.'

'But what about the people? They all in robes or praying every five minutes? What goes on?'

'There's none of that. Well, there's God, but the people themselves seem okay. I reckon Mary won't want to go back to LA – and she certainly won't want us lifting her. I reckon she'll be back here ASAP.'

Jack didn't seem that convinced. 'Freezing her arse off tree-hugging here rather than cocktails poolside LA? Seriously?'

'Really, I like it. It's all right, down there, and she's still with Gedi. We'll do our bit, the Oslo deprogramming lads will do theirs, but it won't matter to her. She'll be back.'

Rio couldn't help jumping in. 'Oi, Your Holiness. The only reason you like it is because everything's free.'

I laughed. 'It's more than that. It's like being with real people who want to look after each other, rather than being with you two twats, trashing and farting your way across northern Europe. And you know what? They do their washing-up.'

The van slowed and rumbled over rougher ground. Rio was immediately business-like. 'We're here.'

39

I checked the timer. It had taken us just over twenty-seven minutes: slower than the Merc had been, and definitely not as smooth.

Rio swept the van round the parking area to face back the way we had come. The whole area was quiet. The headlights played across an empty harbour, which Rio seemed to think called for a bad pirate impression. 'Arrrr, matey – we saw you, Cap'n Birdseye. Getting off the RIB. There were a couple of women there who got back on that would make very nice crewmates, you know what I mean? They from the village?'

Jack sighed. 'He hasn't stopped going on about them. He thinks he's the one who should have gone down to the village.'

We moved off again, heading back onto the main to retrace our route. We now had a timing. I put a hand on his shoulder. 'Ignore him, they would have loved you. Okay, so – first thing.' I kicked out and hit Jack's prosthetic. 'Have you driven this thing yet? At least you'll change gear without letting the van do its own thing.'

Rio knew what was coming and laughed. Jack shook his head. 'No. The deal was that he drove, and I cooked and cleaned. But you know what? I've given up. He's like a gorilla with the shits in here.'

Rio liked that one. 'I'm on me holidays!'

We had to get into work mode. 'Jack needs to drive because you'll be with me in the village. But there's not going to be time to chat anyone up.'

Jack grinned.

'This is what I have for you two so far. We lift Mary on day six, that's Wednesday, and we deliver her soon as possible after midnight, that's Thursday, making it seven full days, for the maximum payday.'

I knew both would like that, which clearly they did. 'So – the general outline. Rio, you with me in the village to lift Mary. Jack, you stay with the van, and hold off ready to be called to the ERV to pick up the three of us. Any questions?'

There was nothing from either of them. Even Rio knew this wasn't the time for jokes. 'The village dies down early. There are no bars down there, so by 23:00 on day six, Rio needs to have been dropped off by Jack and walked down the track from the ERV to make sure it's clear, and to be stood off the entrance to the village. Be there by 23:00, day six.

'Jack will never be more than five minutes from the ERV and facing towards the harbour so there's no fucking about with three-point turns. Rio and Jack, ready to kick off 23:00, day six. Any questions?'

There were none.

'At 23:00 I'll prepare an ATV for Mary's exfil.' I showed Jack the picture of the Phantom on my phone, and he leant to one side for me to move forward behind Rio so he could take a look without taking his eyes off the road.

Jack couldn't resist a dig. 'See that germ-breeder? Even an off-roader is cleaner than this shit-hole.'

Rio wasn't biting. He wanted to, but he knew now wasn't his time. It was mine.

'The ATV will still be in the shed, less than a minute away from Mary's cabin, where me and Rio will make entry and lift her. This could change, as I'm trying to check if she and Gedi live together. I'm not one hundred per cent sure I've got the right cabin. But I will confirm, and I'll also confirm if the cabin stays unlocked. Any questions?'

Rio had one very loaded one. 'Why wouldn't they lock the door? Wouldn't they if they're shagging?'

'Like I said, it's all right down there. They all trust each other – but if it's locked, I'll just knock.'

Rio knew this wasn't the time for a funny come-back but I sensed he had one and was gagging to deliver it.

'So, at 23:00 on day six we will all be prepared to cross the start line. I will call Rio and RV with him. We head straight to Mary's cabin, open the door or knock, and grip Mary – Gedi too, if they're together.

'Rio will stay and control them while I go and get the ATV. I ride it back to the cabin, we get her on board, and head up the track to the ERV with Jack. Into the van, and away to the harbour. That's just under thirty minutes in this thing, so we should get there after midnight on day seven. If we're going to be early, we slow down until we cross into day seven. Any questions?'

This time there was one from Jack. 'What happens if the track's obstructed?'

It was a good point. 'Once the ATV is out of the shed, we've got to keep moving, no matter what.' I hadn't seen any gates, but if we hit an obstacle, we'd have to defeat it first, and we could do that once I'd RV'd with Rio. 'Whatever is blocking the track, we'll try to move it. If we can't, we'll have to move up the track on foot to the ERV. We've got to make as much distance as possible from the village as soon as it goes noisy, so we'll drag her if we have to. No matter, on wheels or on foot, we've got to keep moving.'

Rio needed to have the last word on that. 'Caveman style, yeah? Sweet.'

'No, that's the fucker. If we stress her out too much, she could go into seizure. But that doesn't take away from the fact that, from the moment the Phantom revs up, we're against the clock. There's no telling what'll happen when they hear a vehicle at that time of night. It could be something that happens all the time, I just don't know. So it's up the hill, as far as we can, as quickly as we can, dragging, running, on the Phantom, whatever it takes to get to the ERV. We've got to get to the van, get her in, and go. We'll have about five hours of darkness left to drop her off and get out of the area.

'I don't care what happens at the harbour, whether they go by boat or they have to drive. That isn't our problem. We hand her over, with seven days on the meter, and that's the end of our job. We use those hours of darkness to get the fuck out of here and then the day or so's drive to Oslo. We'll get Rentokil to fumigate the van before handing it back, then dump the Samsungs, split up, and head home. There's no telling how the village will react to having her lifted. There's a lot of money down there, and that means power. They could have contacts in the police, border force or even Interpol – who knows? We don't want anything linking us to her, including text messages.'

It was just like after the French job: no one would know how the others were getting back to the UK, but my plan was to train it through Denmark to Hamburg, then a flight to Stansted.

Rio slowed. 'Two minutes.'

Jack pulled the door back and kept his hand on it, making sure it didn't slide back on me or make a noise, and I waited till the handbrake was gently applied and the van was almost rolling to a stop. I stepped out onto the junction, and the van continued on its way back to the campsite and The Owl's iPhones.

Back in the cabin I hit the Nespresso machine. I wouldn't be sleeping afterwards, but I liked them. While the coffee smell invaded the kitchen area, I powered down the Samsung before it got a charge.

The door was bugging me. I just couldn't help myself. I went back over, locked it, and hung the key on its hook.

Old habits, and all that.

40

Day Two: Saturday, 9 October 2021

Perched on a stool in my kitchen area, I peered through a chink in the blinds just wide enough to see out and onto the path leading to the dining hall. Mary would have to walk past here if she was going for breakfast – that was if she ate breakfast. Maybe she just had a protein bar while saluting the sun or whatever. After all, she did come from LA.

I'd been sitting there, door unlocked, Samsung down my boot, coat on, ready to jump outside since 06:20. The morning meal service started at 06:30, but Mary might be an early bird. It was now 08:21 and still no Mary – and not as many families this morning as there had been eating together last night. Mornings here were probably like they were in the rest of the world's households with young children, a busy and anxious time of getting the kids up, getting them fed, getting them dressed. Not much time left for a leisurely walk over to the dining hall.

I'd wanted coffee since the start of my vigil, but I couldn't afford the toilet visit that would go with it. No matter, it would taste all the better when I finally got one.

I watched the steady stream of people who chatted and smiled at each other and I genuinely liked them, and it seemed they genuinely liked me. I really liked being there. It was going to be a bit of a fucker wrenching this place apart.

Almost on cue, to make me feel even worse, Mary and Gedi passed my little crack in the blinds, arm in arm, heading for the dining hall. I was off the stool and straight out into the cold, doing a little jog to get behind them as I zipped up the parka.

Gedi heard my footsteps and turned. 'Ah, good morning, you're Nick, right? You were at dinner with Esther and Kirill last night?'

As well as being built like Schwarzenegger, he also sounded like him.

They stopped, waiting for me to catch up the four or five remaining paces. She smiled. 'Good morning, Nick – nice to meet you.'

I gave my nods and smiles. 'Nice to meet you, too.' We carried on walking. 'Everyone's so nice around here.'

'Of course, yeah – makes a change, right?'

She and Gedi were dressed in identical coats and beanies.

'Yeah, and Esther, Kirill and the kids, they were so welcoming last night.'

They agreed. Mary said they'd been really welcoming to her when she came along. She turned to me without breaking step. 'What do you think of it so far?'

I didn't have to lie on this one. In fact, I hadn't lied at all this morning yet. Which was a fucker, because I'd have liked to lie to myself and believe these two weren't the people I was going to fuck up the most. 'I like it a lot. How long have you two been here?'

They gave each other the kind of smile a couple shares when they're saying more than words can, but it was Gedi who came out with some. 'Nearly two years for me, and Mary joined just over two months ago.'

I focused on Mary. 'How do you like it? He does, clearly.'

She nodded. 'What's not to like?'

The dining room looked half empty. We unloaded our coats and their beanies before going and taking the next vacant spots at the middle trestle table. Everything was going as I'd been hoping. So far, so good. We all sat together, Gedi and I next to each other, facing Mary. All the others on the table did the 'Hello, Nick, welcome' stuff and the server came over. I asked for fried eggs on toast with extra toast and a jug of coffee.

'Good choice, Nick. They're from our own free-range hens.' Mary pulled up her sleeves before eating, and a medic-alert bracelet fell to her wrist from further up her forearm. Made of blue silicone, with a rose-gold steel clasp engraved with the medic-alert emblem, it would have contained her personal details, including, of course, that she suffered from focal seizures.

I'd checked online, and about 60 per cent of people with this type of seizure can live a normal life. I watched a YouTube video posted by a US first responder with the condition. She described the experience as like having a laptop crash, and then, when it rebooted, the laptop taking ages to work out where it had left off. Mary had been lucky with her drug regime, keeping her condition under control, which was just as well: Michelle and Tripp didn't even know the name of the drug she had been prescribed, Oxtellar XR. They just complained that because it was new, the insurance wouldn't pay for it.

I went into happy-smiley-inquisitive mode. 'Have you got any pointers for me today? I'm meeting Saynab at ten, and at the moment it feels like my first day at school.'

They laughed and I joined in. It was Mary who had the closest memory of her first day. 'It's great. It's all about letting you know that you're welcome – and that God welcomes you. And it's kind of "How would you like to see your life here working out? We're not rushing you, it's just to get your mind in shape to think." That make sense?'

I nodded and agreed. It did make sense, and I noted that, interestingly, as she was already into this place, it was all about 'we', not 'they'. My prediction about her rebounding like a boomerang would probably come true.

There was a weird duality going on, because I wanted to ask these questions to get to the point where I extracted information, yet at the same time I really did want to know the answers. 'So how does it work here? What do you do?'

Whatever it was, Gedi was very proud of it. 'I'm training to become a teacher for when we go out there and spread God's Word on Earth. Maybe next year we'll go, depends on Mary's choice.'

She was eager to jump in, her eyes doing that couples' mutual-confirmation thing again before speaking. I presumed this was love.

She was full of enthusiasm. 'I'm working in child development at Snuggly Bear, and I'm also going to train as a field medical assistant in the spring. Then we can go together, spreading God's Word on Earth. We'll have good skills.'

I nodded energetically to mirror her. It still wasn't a lie. 'Australia or New Zealand could be happening for you guys by then?'

'Yeah, but we want to go to Africa.' Gedi glanced at Mary

and she smiled. 'We feel that the work there would be more fulfilling.'

They'd certainly be getting more experience there than in Sydney or Auckland. I found myself going off-track now, wanting to know more about their overseas work. Were they an NGO with an agenda?

Disaster and war were the playgrounds for NGOs. The NGO thing had always seemed to me to be about looking good rather than doing good. Over the years, I'd seen NGOs running around in places like Africa and I never really liked what I saw. They were businesses, busy competing for a slice of the disaster pie. Often the locals didn't just need protection from the disaster, they needed protection from NGOs.

The MONGOs – My Own NGO – were even worse. They were the guys who thought they could get things sorted more cheaply and effectively than anyone else. Most of them arrived under their own steam. Tourist visa in hand – if there was anyone around to issue one – they rented a vehicle, bunged on an ID sticker and, bingo, they were in business. Some of them, of course, were scams for cash, the slave trade and, of course, sex.

The God Squad NGOs and MONGOs were the worst. I'd seen, first-hand, Christian hippies with guitars in Africa, rounding up patients for what they called their 'mercy ship'. It turned out to be an old cruise liner that had been converted into a floating hospital to bring 'hope and healing' to the poor heathen. But because the thing was only in place for a week, they could only conduct operations that didn't need aftercare. The place was crawling with people dying of gunshot wounds and machete amputations, and all the mercy ship could deal with were cataracts and a dose of the shits. But that didn't matter to them because what the 'mercy ship' was all about was sitting the patients in front of screens to watch films about Jesus over and over. And that was even before groups like the Scientologists were on the loose: no guitars for them, but plenty of high-tech mind-over-matter techniques to show the light – otherwise, no treatment. This was nothing new: the old empires spread Christianity in much the same way and it was just as fucked up then as it was now.

'So how does it work? If you teach, if you give medical care, do all the good stuff, does it come with a price? Do you have to recruit people to God's Word on Earth? That how it works?'

Gedi knew what I was getting at. 'No, Nick, no. There's a lot of noise out there about our type of work, but all we are doing is spreading God's Word on Earth – and that word is . . .' He let Mary finish it off.

'Peace.' She beamed. 'There's no deal but peace.'

Our food came and the conversation dropped as people sorted themselves out. I dunked a corner of toast in the yolk and got some coffee down my neck at last. The lull was a good thing: it made my question sound like I was just picking up the threads of the conversation. 'So how did you both meet? Was it here?'

Gedi took this one, as Mary went to fetch a jug of water and some glasses. 'I was travelling in the US. Matvey wants us to travel to meet people, experience things outside the village, so it makes your conviction stronger, more committed to God and the village. I went to Los Angeles to check out the bodybuilding scene and found something so much better.' He and I both nodded our thanks as she returned and started to pour water for us. Gedi continued: 'Mary wanted to come back with me, to have a new and better life with God.'

She'd finished pouring and sat down. 'And so here we both are.'

It wasn't just that I wanted to keep the conversation going to get where I needed to be – I was still genuinely interested. 'Why leave LA? I mean, people have everything they need there.'

She was very clear in her answer. Clear, because her commitment to where she was now shone through. 'That was the problem. I had everything, but nothing – life was about me and stuff, there was no substance. I was becoming a husk, just like my parents. And that I will not become.' She sighed. 'There's just one driver for my parents and that's ego . . . so unbridled.'

That I had no doubt about.

'They're always looking for Heaven – well, what they think it is, right?'

I shrugged but guessed what their versions would be and was correct. She numbered them on her fingers.

'So, it was money. They chased it, they got it, but still no Heaven. So, then it was sex. My mother is still banging her personal trainer, my dad got his assistant pregnant and made the poor woman have an abortion. Yet still no Heaven. So now they're chasing power. Dad is on the ballot for the Republicans. But not because he believes – he believes in nothing. It's because he's thinking they'll win.'

What impressed me about her was that she spoke without anger, without malice. She oozed confidence in what she knew was the truth. If you're angry about shit and people you're still part of the story. But not her.

'They were always jumping onto the next big thing, whether it's socially, politically, financially. Anything else just doesn't exist. It was all front-of-house. There was no trust, there was no love, it's just gimme-gimme-gimme. Look at me. They just don't get that reality minus expectations equals happiness.' She took a sip from her glass. 'And that's here – this, with Gedi, this is real. Because God and the village are real. This is Heaven.'

The glass went down. 'So, tell us. Why are you here, Nick?'

Again, no need to lie. 'I guess I'm looking for something. Not sure what it is yet, but early days, yeah?'

Gedi leant over and gripped my arm, like a vice. 'You'll get there, Nick. All of us will make that happen for you.'

I thanked both of them and realized that I was still telling the truth. *Shit!* I had to cut away from my own stuff and get back to Mary. 'So how do partnerships work here? You two live together? Is that allowed? I was thinking if I had a partner would she—'

They burst out laughing and I joined in, for no other reason than that I'd obviously said something funny. I didn't know why. Mary reached over for Gedi's hand. 'Of course we live together – Nick, this isn't some creepy sect. We're not the Branch Davidians or Heaven's Gate. There's no dogma here. That's just words from weird guys pretending they represent God, but they don't. That stuff's all about their power. And that's not Matvey. He gives you the power, because he gives you God with just one word.'

I knew what she was on about and I liked the idea, so I put my finger up to stop everybody. 'And that's peace, yeah?'

They were both impressed and very happy for me, and Mary touched her heart. 'You've got it, Nick. Peace, right?'

41

There are so many bad things about starting out life in the army, and timing is one of them. Saynab wanted me there at 10:00 hours; in army time that was 09:55 hours, because you must be five minutes early. However, the army's five-minute logic dictated that you needed to be there five minutes before that, so I had to be there at 09:50 hours, five minutes early for the five minutes early. I knew it was mad, but I couldn't help myself. Old habits.

Not that being early put Saynab out in any way. As I came through the door she was in the corridor, ready and waiting. She was wearing the same jumper, the neck of it still covering half of her face. She'd keep it on until the spring, probably.

'Good morning, Nick. You're keen! Come on, let's go and get comfortable.'

I nodded my hellos and followed her down the corridor. It felt more like an office block than somewhere you went to talk about God. There were fire extinguishers and evacuation notices, along with boards with admin printouts and ads for social events and courses to attend. From the number of signatures, Russian lessons and traditional Sami needlecraft looked popular.

She opened the last door on the right at the far end of the corridor and ushered me in. The tourist-hotel-sized room was dominated by two high-end brown leather chairs, the sort with a footrest that popped up and a back that reclined. An A5 notebook and a pen lay on one. Next to them were a couple of light-wood side tables, with bottled water and a glass on each. I knew this look: it was therapist decor, but Scandi style. A box of tissues sat on her table, ready to be offered. But for now, Saynab showed me the seat without the notebook on it. 'Would you like some coffee, Nick? Tea? We have a wonderful selection. I'm having the new one we've just got, liquorice and mint. Would you like one?'

'That would be very nice. Thanks.' I sat down while Saynab picked up a digital Bang & Olufsen phone on her side table and called the order in before picking up the notebook and sitting down, facing me.

It was straight to business. 'So, Nick, welcome to the village, and I so hope this will be the first day of your new life with us.'

'Thank you. I'm looking forward to it.' It was part of the process of blending in as part of the cover to get the job done, but at the same time I was quite looking forward to it.

'There are a few things we have to cover. Unfortunately, even at God's Word on Earth we need a few housekeeping details. Some of it is of a personal nature, so that's why we don't ask you during the online process. Is that okay with you?'

'No problem at all.' I smiled, but wasn't that happy with it. It was nothing to do with the questioning: it was because I'd be back to lying again, just when I was feeling quite enlightened for not having had to lie this morning to Gedi and Mary.

There was a gentle tap on the door and Saynab welcomed in the tea. A young guy appeared, early twenties, just finishing off those teenage acne years. He came in with a tray full of white crockery, cups and saucers instead of mugs, a white teapot, and a plate of biscuits. It was more of an afternoon-tea affair, which was fine by me.

Saynab introduced us. 'Nick, this is Joshua. He is our administration mainstay here in the Spiritual Centre. Any questions, anything you need, Joshua is your man.'

I thanked him for the tea as he laid it out on Saynab's table. She began to play Mum as Joshua took the steps over to me and extended a hand. I half stood up and shook.

'So nice to meet you, Nick. I'll see you this afternoon. We have so much to talk about.'

I smiled as he left, not having a clue what that meant but I was sure I'd be finding out. Saynab presented me with a cup and saucer and the strong smell of liquorice wafted up.

'Now, Nick, if these questions make you feel uncomfortable, that's fine. You don't have to answer. We can come back to them whenever you feel happy answering. Today, maybe tomorrow, whenever it feels right for you.'

I took a little sip and liked it. It reminded me of the liquorice wheels I used to nick from the corner shop when I was a kid.

'First of all, is there anyone you would like us to contact in the event of an emergency? A family member?'

I shook my head. 'There's no one.'

'Okay . . . Are there any friends, maybe, that you'd want to know if you needed help in any way?'

I made a face of considering, but there was no way Rio or

Jack was going to be part of this. They had a job to do outside, making a mess of the campervan. There was no one else. My having no next of kin or friends didn't faze her. There had to be many people like me who had no ties, or people like Mary, who had cut away from theirs.

She scribbled a note. 'Okay. So do you have any dependencies? I'm thinking drugs, alcohol, gambling, anything that we could help you control?'

'None. I've got a drug for my condition, but you already know about that, right?'

'Yes.' She gave a big smile that was easy to see now that she'd pulled her jumper's woolly neck under her chin. 'Maybe it won't be long before you have no need for any drugs. Your life will light up when we take you out of the dark. That's a promise.'

I gave her a happy looking-forward-to-it type of smile.

'Allergies? Any underlying illnesses that we need to be aware of? Our doctors here can give you a complete medical if you wish. They might be able to assist you with your diagnosis if things progress, give any information you need to help settle your head and your heart.'

'Yep, thank you, I'll be having some of that if I can, but I feel fine. I've got no underlying problems. I had broken bones and tissue damage in a big bike accident years ago, but all that's healed now.'

And there it was, the first real lie. I'd known they'd have to start soon.

'Okay, then, Nick, let me organize that for you. We have four very good doctors here, and if any treatment is required that the village cannot provide, we will fly you to Tromsø to receive the care there. We'll look after you, Nick, no matter what you need.'

My first thought was about Mary, and that she wouldn't have any problem accessing her Oxtellar XR. I hoped the drug was as good as the marketing material I'd read because one potential trigger for Mary's type of seizure was stress – and she was going to get a big dump of that no matter how we lifted her.

'That sounds very good to me, Saynab, thank you.' I took another swig of liquorice as she jotted down a few notes.

'Nick, let me tell you about my family, and then if you feel comfortable, why not you tell me about yours? Is that okay?'

I kept a mild smile going.

'I came to the village nearly five years ago with my daughter, Poppy. You met her.'

'Yep, very bright girl.'

Saynab liked that. 'We come from Yemen. Do you know it?'

I shook my head. 'I sort of know where it is, but that's about it.'

Another lie.

Nearly a quarter of a million men, women and children had died in the war since 2014. Not that the media or anyone else gave a shit, maybe because they were so far away and expensive to report on, but more likely because they weren't white, or because the people dropping the ordnance on the Yemenis were oil-rich Saudis, friends of the West. Probably all four. We tended to care more about conflicts closer to home and fought by people who looked the same and wore the same chain-store clothes. That made it easy for people like me to fuck people over in countries that most in the West couldn't find on the map.

'The fighting . . . the war . . . in Hodeidah was terrible. My husband, he was an artist, not a fighter . . .' Her voice tailed off mid-sentence and she looked at the floor suddenly, as if she was searching for something. When she looked up again, her eyes were distant, but her voice was firm. 'We went onto the street to find something special for Poppy's birthday. She likes milkshakes, you know?' She did a hand gesture of whisking something in a cup. 'The powder mix? Strawberry. Poppy loved that. She still does.' Her eyes told me she was reliving a nightmare, but there was no sadness in them, or even in her voice. In both just a steely resolve. 'You see, Nick, women are taken from the streets for sex in Yemen, sold as slaves. They attacked my husband, grabbed me and tried to haul me away. We fought them off with stones, sticks. I even had to bite into the neck of a man beating my husband. But I was too late. He died.'

'I'm so sorry, Saynab. It must have been awful.'

She gave a small smile. 'We were alone for a long time, struggling, and then we found Matvey – well, we were found by his villagers, who had come to our country to help people just like us. So, here we are, both of us. We were the first to come here in 2017. Matvey wanted us to be the first to live in his new village. The church, even most of the cabins, were still being built. We're loved, we're cared for, and now we want to pay forward and do the same for others. Well – that's our story. What's yours, Nick?'

I emptied my cup. Saynab offered me more, and stood to pour. 'Thank you.' I shrugged. 'There's not much to say, really. I was brought up by a single parent, my mother, until I was about eleven. Then she remarried. We had no money, living in social housing, on welfare benefits. My stepdad was violent to me, basically because he and eventually she didn't want me there. I took three years of it and left home when I was about fourteen. I never saw my mother again.

'Since then, I've floated from job to job, place to place.

Good times, bad times, no plan, no marriage, no children, nothing basically, just a no one who didn't make it up the ladder. Now I'd have trouble climbing the first rung if I wanted to.' I held up my neoprene hand, and as I did, I realized I was doing a Jack, lying about my life. He did it to try to attract women, and I was doing it to try to get this one on my side. But, then, what else could I have said? That since leaving home all I'd done was run around fucking people over, including in her own country?

'So there it is, Saynab. No life, really.'

Still she showed no signs of sadness or concern. Maybe this wasn't the first time she'd heard a story like that, or maybe she was much more switched on than I thought and could see right through my lies. Yeah, most likely the second.

'Thank you for that, Nick. It was very helpful, and I hope it wasn't too painful. But, you know, life is about the sensation of living, not the story we tell ourselves.' She took a sip of tea and I did the same, but I didn't feel up for biscuits. For me, that meant something was wrong.

Saynab continued: 'Nick, we know that everybody has a past. Out there in the world they are thought of as good, bad, boring, selfish, violent, super-stressed – those types of labels.'

I had to agree. 'People can judge without knowing the facts, that's for sure.'

Saynab had the answer, of course. 'Nick, I'm here to tell you that in our village we do not do labels. What we do in this place is the here and now. All that matters is the present, not letting ourselves be consumed by thoughts about the past or even the future. No past, no future – just now.'

She paused to let that sink in. If it had, I would have had a question. But that didn't matter: it sounded good to me. 'I like it.'

Saynab liked the idea of me liking it. 'That's so good to hear, Nick, because the purpose of us, of God's Word on Earth, of our village, is not religion but the people who practise it. Too often, in religious communities, they withhold healing and peace instead of offering it. Those with power grasp for more rather than giving it away – claims to perfect truth are always bent to serve their lies. People are hurt in such unimaginable ways. But not here, Nick.' Her eyes and smile radiated total sincerity. 'You see, a healthy religious community like ours exists with a simple idea: we invite anyone to join us, and then, together, we become a tiny bit more whole – an even healthier religious community that can exist to bring peace to those who aren't so fortunate. You like that idea too, Nick?'

I nodded. I was still processing what I knew I liked the sound of.

She'd thought I would. 'You see, what we do here is people, and because we do people so well, they, in turn, do the same to others. And that is how we do God. Make sense?'

I nodded. 'Sort of.'

Then I thought of Kirill's tattoos and his long stretches in prison: it seemed to have worked on him.

42

'Nick, would you like to come along to a mindfulness meditation this evening? It really helps us to focus on the here and now, to stop that constant noise in our minds that niggles away at us. I'm sure you know the one – it's that noise we all try to repress, sometimes suppress, but at the same time we all know it just makes the noise worse. What we learn in the village is to welcome the noise with a smile.' She did, and raised an index finger to match. 'Ah, there you are again. And when we greet it with a smile, a very, very curious thing happens, Nick. The noise goes away, and we live in the present. And you know what?'

Not really. I was still getting my head around it.

'There's tea afterwards and you will get to meet even more of our wonderful people.'

'Okay, I'm in.' In for what, I wasn't sure. Smiling at noise?

We agreed to meet at the gym at eight thirty for her to introduce me round, but she was soon back to business. 'How does your condition make you feel in this very moment,

Nick? Here, remember, that is all that matters.' She sat back and clearly it was my turn to expand.

I knew I didn't have to, but I wanted to. I wanted to get back to telling the truth. 'I don't think about it all that much, really. It's not avoidance or denial, I just accept it.' I'd never thought I was close to saying that, but I was now. I wanted her to know that I wasn't lying. 'Dying doesn't matter. I won't know I'm dead because I'll be dead. That's it, the end. I don't think there's a heaven or reincarnation. Once you're dead, you're dead. But it's the way of getting dead that's my concern. That make sense?'

She didn't have to think about an answer. Maybe I wasn't as unique in my thoughts as I kidded myself I was. But I was frustrated: I couldn't and wouldn't tell her that most of my concern was that I had put two friends' lives at even more risk than was necessary, and promised them it would never happen again. Yet still they wanted to operate with me. At least I hadn't lied. I just hadn't told.

'Totally. I get it – because that is what we believe. When you die, Nick, that is the end. You've been dying since you were born. But for us, you can't die until you've done what God put you here to do – and that is to live. When you die, you need to know in your heart that you have lived rather than simply won or lost at life. Do you think you have lived, Nick?'

Fuck, she had me on that one. I sat back as if I was thinking about it, then realized I had always known the answer. 'No, I haven't.'

'Well, that's what you can do with us, Nick, in the village. What we're all here for is to live our life so we can die. God put us here to live our lives in love and peace. That's all – nothing more. Our lives are not about earning points for an upgraded ticket to Heaven, because there isn't a heaven up there. It's down here, now, this very moment – that's what we believe, Nick. Do you like the sound of that?'

I did. I really did. I felt a bit of a lifting into the light, as she put it. 'So how does it work? How do I live a life?'

She shifted in her chair, making herself a little taller so she could check my cup. She saw it was half full, and nodded at the teapot. I shook my head. I didn't need it, but I did look at the biscuits. She offered me the plate and I took three of the digestive fingers.

'You could live your life through the arts, Nick. Or it could be through educating people, or discovering a hidden talent and passing it on. Some serve the community in a more practical way, forestry work, trades to be learnt. Or if you already have a talent, we will use that – why wouldn't we? You pass that knowledge on. Many learn how to teach in school, or medical skills. We want you to discover what it is that lets you live a life, Nick – but it's not all about having a life list. It's not just the work. It's the satisfaction of serving others in the village and allowing them to serve you. It's not just the practical, it's the peace between us all. And then who knows? If your condition allows it and you want to, you could go out into the world spreading God's Word on Earth.'

There it was again. 'What – peace?'

She smiled. 'It's the only word that matters in Heaven. The Chinese have a saying: "When trade stops, war starts."' She leant over, picked up a biscuit and took a bite. 'I know it to be true.'

43

I lay stretched out on what last night had turned out to be a very comfortable duvet, so much so that I'd missed lunch. Well, I blamed the bed, but the reality was that Saynab had jumped the electric fence protecting my brain – and the even truer reality was that I'd let her do it.

It had taken a lot of avoidance, but I'd finally got there. The problem with her, it hit me, was that everything she said was rational and made sense. The God stuff hadn't bothered me, and it didn't really seem to bother her. It was very clear to her what he'd already done and what he expected of us, and that he was leaving us to get on with it.

We're born, she said, we live a life, then we die. It was the middle bit, obviously, that I was having problems with. In fact, I wished there'd been more God stuff, so all the ideas and concepts she came out with would have been easy enough to cast aside. I wished I could have sat there thinking, This is all part of the cover story. I've just got to sit here. But her explanation struck a chord. It felt more real than the real world I'd been trying to avoid all my life, and which the real-life people like her were clearly trying to change. Most of all, I wished that she'd been speaking a year ago, and the other three were in the room with me to hear her. Maybe Gabe would have had second thoughts and spent the last days of his life living to the full. But enough. I had to force myself off the bed: I still had stuff to do. I took the iPhone from under the lamp and called The Owl.

It brought me back to my world in an instant. The only plus was going to be if he was on the east coast, and I'd be disturbing his breakfast. Hopefully another little win. I wondered if he and Tom had matching Princess Di coffee mugs.

I wasn't worried about the cabin being bugged by Matvey because I felt confident now that it wasn't. Possibly a big mistake, but I couldn't cut away from the thought that I really didn't care if the job got compromised or not. It would mean me running up the hill after the compromise to get to the ERV as quickly as I could, yet at the same time Mary would stay in the village, and all that would remain for me to do was to explain to the other two why I'd lost them three days' money.

Sadly, he was already awake. It took only two rings this time and there was no grogginess coming from the phone speaker, just the high-pitched screeching of gulls fucking about.

'Yes?'

The Owl was probably at the wheel of their superior wooden sailing boat with his captain's hat on while Tom manned the cafetière. I liked to think that besides the mugs they'd also named the boat after her.

He sounded his normal new cold, so I got straight into it.

'Situation: I confirmed that Mary and Gedi live together.

'Summary: I have had casual contact with Mary to help with planning and prep for the lift.

'Actions today: I have recced the Russian side. There's the church, the Spiritual Centre – it's a learning centre – then accommodation, a store facility for the village, a power sub-station, and an IT centre.

'Actions to do: continue with my cover story, with my introduction sessions at the Spiritual Centre this afternoon, and make contact with Mary this evening to confirm exactly where they live. Imagery of Matvey: there's an opportunity for it tomorrow. Questions?'

Straight to the point. 'Where exactly is the IT centre?'

'On the eastern side of the storage facility. It's a part of the building.'

There was a pause. He had a thought. 'You need to confirm it.'

'I can. I was invited in.'

'What did you see?'

I described the dark, intensive telesales room, and what it did.

'Okay. How long before you lift her?'

'Not sure yet.'

We were here for seven days regardless, so I might as well get that sorted out now. 'I need to know exactly where she is, and how Gedi is going to affect the lift. It's going to take time finding out her routine to decide where and how.'

The Owl was helpful with that. 'You have seven days, so use them. You stay there. You go back to the IT centre, find out what you can about what exactly they do there. I want to know their contacts, who they're talking to, what information they hold. I want everything and anything you can get about that IT centre. I also want the same detail on Matvey. I want to know about the man, I want to know about his circles in the village and out. Use your team, do it yourself, I don't care. Whatever, you just get it done. Repeat: you have seven days. Use them, then out with Mary.'

Ever the opportunist, I was straight back at him. 'Who's going to be paying for these extras? We're here for just one job.'

The temperature dropped to sub-zero. 'Listen good. No one is paying extra. You are there, you're on day rates, and you belong to me. Do the job. You understand?'

Yep, I understood. That was The Owl talking about loose ends. He might as well have ended it with: 'Or else I'll fuck you all up.'

'Get it. Closing down.'

The next job was to give the sitrep to the team. I phoned Jack, and gave it to him word for word, both of us knowing The Owl would be listening. I included the news that we were going to be taking the full seven days.

'Warning order: we've got to recce the Russian side of the village, the IT centre and do a full discovery of Matvey. Stand by for an RV once I've planned.'

'Roger that.' Jack closed down. Like me, he knew not to query the matter of no extra pay for a lot of extra work. But that didn't mean I wouldn't be hearing about it the next time we were together.

I closed down. The phone went back in its normal position and I turned the light on to get a burst of light into his retinas if he was looking. Why not?

Pulling on my coat and boots, I headed back towards the Spiritual Centre for my meeting with Joshua, via, of course, the shop for some Alenka and milkshake. I waited until I was getting closer to the bridge, and out of the accommodation area, before the earphones that had been folded inside my parka went under my hood. I tucked myself under a tree and reached inside the coat to call the team from the Samsung.

It was Rio who answered. 'Mate, what the fuck?'

'Look, I don't know. I don't know what he wants, I don't know why. But he's got a thing up his arse about the IT centre and Matvey.'

'Okay. Then has the daily rate gone up, or what?'

'No. But we might not get paid the remaining three days if we turn it down and just bring out Mary. Who knows with him? Who knows what the fuck's going on?'

Rio wasn't impressed, but it was better than the other option, me and Jack trying to calm him down as he plotted and schemed to kill The Owl – and, even worse, trying to get him to understand that he'd never get away with that without all three of us being severely fucked over.

'Listen, mate, the upside: it's still a full seven days. He wants us to be on the ground and get as much int as possible. The reality of the situation is that we have to get this shit done. If we find stuff out for him, all good. If not, then we've tried, and we see what he says. I'll just make sure the sitreps demonstrate that we're trying. We're fucked either way, mate. Both jobs have got to go on.'

Fortunately, Rio was much smarter than to force his point. 'You know what, mate? This feels a wrong 'un. All of a sudden this new shit is more important than getting Mary out – I reckon he planned it, you know what I mean? Otherwise, he'd want us the fuck out of there with her, soon as.'

I agreed. 'Just stand off until I've worked out how we're going to do this. Then I'll be on the iPhone for an RV so he knows what's happening and he thinks he's still in the loop. That'll keep him out of the way while we work out what the fuck to do.'

I powered down the Samsung and pushed the earphones into the pocket alongside it. Rio was right. Mary was sounding like second fiddle all of a sudden. I wasn't sure if The Owl cared or not, if Mary was the main job or not, but that didn't matter. What would matter was screwing up these recces he wanted. It would mean there was no chance of getting Mary out, and also no control over what would happen to a bunch of Brits if we were caught lurking about in Russia.

As I stepped off the bridge onto the Russian bank I could see the church lights blazing in the gloom to my left, and beyond, those of the Spiritual Centre. Apart from the latest dramas The Owl had delivered I was surprisingly upbeat. Not only had I just had a late lunch of Alenka and a strawberry yoghurt – a breakout for me from the norm – but I would be spending time with Joshua. He was going to show me the world of options Saynab had spoken about, which I could learn or work at in the village as part of living a life. It wasn't just good for the cover story, it felt good for me personally.

As I carried on along the path, I had a weird fantasy of being a teacher somewhere in the world, doing my shaking Elvis impersonation in front of my class as I popped handfuls of Rasagiline down my neck.

44

There was no funky music bouncing off the gym walls this time, just a general chatter and hubbub from the groups hovering round their mats and laying out their pillows ready for the mindfulness thing I had agreed to. Mary was up front and I started towards her, but Saynab was lying in wait. She ambushed me with her daughter, who looked very excited to see me again.

Poppy came bounding up. 'Hello, Nick! I saved you a mat next to me!' She pointed to the far left-hand corner where three mats were laid out, each with a small pillow. No problem, I'd make sure I said hi to Mary after the class. If they did lock their door and I had to knock to make entry, I needed them to feel comfortable when I did so.

'That's great, Poppy, thank you very much. Is this your first time as well?'

She thought that was very funny. 'No, silly.' I was secretly hoping it was, so I wouldn't be the only one cocking up whatever was about to happen. 'I come here with my mum. It's fun.'

Saynab joined us and immediately introduced me to more villagers. Naturally they knew who I was, and I found myself liking chatting away about how nice everyone was, how good it all was. I was hit by that strange duality again: I could justify to myself joining in, so it looked natural and helped support my cover story, but at the same time I actually enjoyed it.

Elaine and Cameron appeared, and his mood looked as buoyant as Poppy's, even though he was in his wheelchair and shaking a bit more than normal.

'Hi, Nick – this your first shot at mindfulness?'

I nodded and bent down to get to eye level. 'Yeah. First one ever.'

'Think of it as Mr Muscle drain unblocker for the mind.'

Soon I heard the gentle Spanish or South American tones of Catalina, ushering us onto our mats. One side of her head was shaved, and the rest of her hair trailed down her back. With that and her Popeye arms, she could easily have been taken for a champion cage-fighter, but her voice was the sort that calms hyperactive kittens.

Poppy lay with her mother on one side and me on the other. Cameron was two rows forward, but tonight he was on a mat like the rest of us. The back of my head resting on the pillow, I began taking deep breaths just as Catalina was telling us. She explained that we were going to use the body's natural sedative to slow us all down for the session. The rest of the group knew what was going on, and I went with the flow.

Soon I was breathing what Catalina called 'the 4-7-8'. She guided us into inhaling deeply for four seconds, holding that breath for seven seconds, then breathing out for eight, with a big whoosh at the end to expel any remaining oxygen. We repeated the cycle over and over. I tried hard to follow her instruction to focus on the air coming into my nostrils and out again through my mouth, but my mind was all over the place. I couldn't keep my eyes closed and enjoy the experience, because they were fixed on Cameron. He was still doing his Elvis impersonation, but I couldn't stop asking myself if that was my future, too. If it was, I hoped I looked as happy and content as he did. He had his eyes closed and a big smile on his face as he performed the perfect 4-7-8.

My breathing wasn't so under control, but it was beginning to have an effect. I felt myself relaxing, my limbs going weak just as she said they would, sinking into the mat, my feet flopping out sideways.

'That's right, deep breath for one, two, three, four . . .' She wanted us to lie there with our eyes closed, and I could hear her voice wafting closer, then fading as she moved among us. I convinced myself she was South American: there was a hint of that Americanized accent I'd got to know when I operated in Colombia. 'Now let us be mindful of our thoughts. When I ring the bell, I want you to notice the thoughts that are passing through your mind.

'Just one or two, that's right. For some of you there might be lots of thoughts, and others might have just one, maybe two. But it's okay. There's no right or wrong. It's just thoughts. The practice is to acknowledge those thoughts that pass through your mind, whatever they may be, and now I want you to describe them factually to yourself. They might be thoughts about what you have done today, or thoughts about your breathing: you're thinking about how you're breathing, trying to physically think about that breath. Or think about somebody here in the group and about them doing the same exercise. Now if you notice your mind just wandering to the content of the thought, just notice it and gently bring your attention back to the experience of thoughts passing through your mind . . . not the thoughts themselves.'

A bell tinkled. All I could think about was that after the deep breathing and all the calming down, everything felt really good – so much so that the next thing I knew Poppy was prodding my shoulder and trying not to laugh too much. The session had ended. I looked around me to see mats being rolled up and people heading to the table in the corner. There was a grin on Saynab's face to match her daughter's. 'You certainly enjoyed that, didn't you?'

I wiped my eyes before getting on my knees. 'How long was I out?' I rolled up my mat and joined Saynab and Poppy as they went to drop them off.

'Well, over thirty minutes. But that's fine – in fact it's better because it means you truly relaxed. Everything is good.'

I was happy with that.

Saynab led us to a table laden with Thermoses. 'Tea?'

Mary was already chatting with those nearby, most with trendy no-handled mugs in hand.

We put our mats on the pile and joined the group, chatting over what turned out to be camomile tea and digestive fingers. Saynab introduced me to yet more people who welcomed me to the village with smiles. I carried on enjoying it, but what I really wanted to do was make contact with Mary. Then I saw Cameron sitting in his wheelchair, and she dropped to second priority. I manoeuvred myself until I could break away and take a few steps in his direction.

He looked pleased to see me. 'So what do you think? Not bad, eh?'

I squatted lower, and as I took a sip of tea, he lifted a drink from the cup-holder of his wheelchair and put the straw to his lips.

What did I think?

I didn't know what he meant, Catalina's session or my whole stay so far. I decided to go with the session. 'I probably liked it too much. I fell asleep. What about that?'

His lips released the straw so he could have a bit of a chuckle. 'Do you know what happened to me once? Years ago, I fell asleep and I woke myself up farting!'

We both laughed. For all I knew that could have happened to me. Poppy would have been raised too polite to mention it.

I fixed his gaze. 'Cam, I've got a question.'

He nodded – or I thought he did.

'I had a talk with Saynab this morning. She was explaining about not being able to die until you've lived. I sort of understood it, and by the look of you, I think you've got this live-to-die thing squared away. So what's it all about?'

He knew, which was good. I needed an answer to stop it spinning around in my head.

'Look, son. All of this – the village, even this meditation – it's all the physical side of it. It's what Saynab was talking about this morning. Have you had a look at all the facilities here, and all the jobs and training you can do?'

I nodded.

'That's all the physical stuff, and that's important. That helps you live the real life, the full life, so you can die. That fullness is completed with love. That's all there is to it – it fulfils your life, and brings peace to those around you.'

He allowed a second or two of silence, but I wasn't about to fill it. I didn't have anything to fill it with.

45

'Do you have anyone you love, Nick?'

Cameron rescued me from my very long pause. He got the straw back to his mouth, and as he took a suck, Elaine made as if to come over to join us. She must have sensed this was more than a chit-chat and went back to her group.

He wiped some drops of tea from his chin with a gloved hand and stared at me with one of those confident, seen-it-done-it I-know-what-I'm-on-about smiles.

'I haven't got God, Cam, or anyone like Elaine, but I have three – well, now two – people I'm close to.'

He nodded. 'That's good, but it doesn't cut it. It's got to be love, Nick, that's the thing. I'm lucky. I love Elaine, I love my family, I love God – but love, *my* love, goes both ways. I give it, and I get it back. It doesn't have to be like that for everyone, of course. It's what *you* feel that's important, because it is *you* that is giving love and so living a full life so you can die. Love, give love. Your life is full so you can die – it's not about this thing.' His good hand moved about his body before coming to rest on his heart. 'It's about this.'

'Why didn't she just tell me that in the first place?'

I got a raised eyebrow in response, and probably deserved it. He shook his head. 'Saynab, she's not a teacher. She's a coach. Her job is to show you the door, but you have to open it and discover for yourself what's in the room. That discovery then remains solid within you – not because somebody told you but because it has to come from you.'

I gave it some thought, but I wasn't sure it sank in completely. 'Cam, I know what you're saying is right . . . not sure why yet . . . and it's given me a lot more questions. But that's good, isn't it?'

'Absolutely. But, Nick, do me a favour. Don't tell Saynab we've had this chat, okay?' He smiled. 'She'll want to get to you clean.'

I nodded. Between-mates sort of stuff.

'Thanks, Nick. But it has to be said, you do seem a little dim with this life stuff. I thought I'd give you a shove in the right direction, or Saynab is going to have her hands full working with you for weeks to come, and she has enough on her plate running the village.'

'Isn't Matvey the boss?'

'He is, but she's the power behind the throne. Someone has to make sure the bins get emptied.'

Elaine joined us and took the handles of Cameron's wheelchair. 'Exactly. It takes a woman or it would be a disaster.'

He erupted into laughter and so did I as Elaine wheeled him towards the door.

'Come on, let's get you home.'

I was brought crashing back to the real reason I was in the village. Kirill had emerged from the workstation area and joined the others at the tea stand. His T-shirt was wet with sweat and the ink on his massive chest showed through the cotton to give me another couple of chapters of backstory to add to what I had already learnt from his hands. His chest was covered with a bull. He was a killer, an enforcer for the only employer in Russia that would use that skill and like his labelling: the Mafia. The rest would have to be read some other time because he was on his way towards me. Not that it mattered: the bull said it all.

'Good, isn't it?'

I nodded in agreement, presuming he was on about the mindfulness session.

He sipped his tea as if he was at one of the Queen's garden parties. More of his hand revealed itself as he tilted his mug. 'You like them?' He wiggled his fingers around the cup. 'Can you read them?'

I shook my head, checking them out once more now that I'd been given permission, but he didn't believe me. 'People fear them, and then they fear me. But last night, you were reading.'

He smiled; he knew.

'I know a little.'

Kirill was happy with himself and with the answer. He didn't dig any deeper but I wanted to. He had managed to break away from his cult. If he could change, why not me?

'So how did you land up here with a beautiful wife and kids? I mean, it's not what you might call a normal career move for someone with your past, is it?'

He rolled the mug between his palms, staring into the tea as if it was going to give him the answer. 'No, it's not, but Esther, she changed everything.'

Kirill explained that he was lying low after 'answering a request'. The plan was for him to keep a low profile in Munich for two years and then return home to Novosibirsk, an industrial city in Siberia. For him to leave Russia it had to have been a multiple killing, something big – and by Russian standards it would have been very big. The US used to have the Wild West; Russia had the Wild East. Even Russians stayed clear.

It was in Munich where he met Esther while he sat, bored, drinking coffee in a shopping mall. Instead of keeping a wide berth because everything about him said trouble, she asked if he was okay because he looked sad.

'It was love, Nick, for both of us. So quick and so simple.'

Shit, there it was again, that giving-and-receiving-love thing.

'So why here?'

'We just wanted to be somewhere safe and full of love. Matvey married us. Our family was born here. This is Heaven.'

I had to agree with him. He might just have this life thing squared away.

'There're no labels here, no past. There's no such thing as a monster, just people doing what they think is right at the time. So don't worry, you'll feel safe and loved here.'

Mary and Gedi joined us with hellos and smiles, and asked if I'd enjoyed the mindfulness session. It didn't look like Mary was a fan of camomile tea and digestive fingers. She had her own plastic bottle of yogurt with a goat on it and a protein bar she was getting into.

I was enjoying myself with these three but Gedi burst my bubble and got me back into the real world – well, my world. He had news for Kirill.

'The snow's definitely coming tomorrow. We should organize the run before we're locked down.'

Fuck the run. 'But I'd read the snow would come later in the month?'

Gedi nodded. 'Sure, usually, but it's early. It's happened before, maybe five years ago, but not as much as tomorrow's forecast. This is not going to be flurries, it could be enough to settle for the winter.' He had a thought. 'Nick, you run?'

'I have, but not for a long time.'

'I'm organizing for us to all go, while we still can. It could be our last chance before the route is blocked. We normally go up the hill to the road and down, and we do it two or three times. It's a bit of a thing we do in the village every year, because who knows when it's going to be possible again until the spring? Would you like to join us?'

'Thanks, but I'll wait for the spring, I think. I'll have to get in training because you lot are far too fit for me.'

He laughed, looking me up and down. 'No problem. But if the snow comes, you're going to be in the gym until the spring. We're training most nights, me and Kirill. Join us any time you wish.'

I nodded my thanks, but I needed to get away as fast as I could. No time even to talk with Mary. I said my goodbyes and headed back to my cabin as quickly as I could without busting into a run and drawing attention.

46

I went straight to my room and grabbed the iPhone from its lead. As soon as I was online, I checked time and date, then weather. The nearest location it gave conditions for was Vardø, and that was all I needed. The forecast had certainly changed its tune since we'd done our planning and prep a couple of days ago, and Gedi was right: snow was heading our way from about 22:00 tomorrow, getting heavier during the night and even worse in the days following. I hoped The Owl would get an alert that I was doing something, pick up his phone, check, and see for himself that the weather was deteriorating. It would be quicker to explain to him what had to happen.

I called him and it rang a little longer than usual.

When he eventually answered his tone was the new normal. 'Yes?'

'The plan's moved forward to Sunday, day three. I need the deprogrammers stood to from last light tomorrow. The weather's closing in. I won't be able to get Mary out via Norway after day three. And Russia's not an option.'

He didn't need any detail yet, just the facts. Not that it helped me avoid the other looming problem, which was clearly at the forefront of his mind.

'What's happening in the IT centre? Have you found out about Matvey? Where is his imagery?'

I'd been hoping it wasn't going to come up, but Rio was right: Mary had clearly slipped down the charts.

'Look, if I start the recces tonight there'll be no time to prepare Mary's lift. On top of that, if I get compromised, both jobs will be a failure. We're talking about Tom's niece here. There's no such thing as a replacement. They don't sell them.'

Would he remember his Malibu deal-closer line? I waited a couple of seconds and nothing was coming back at me. I had to move on. 'First things first. I get Mary out, then get on with the recces. That will have to be a different plan now, old school, because I won't be part of the village. One certainty: the lift must be tomorrow. The deprogrammers must be standing by from last light. I will give thirty minutes' notice for the pick-up.'

Still nothing back. All I got was the gulls squawking. Was he still there? I carried on: 'Tomorrow – repeat, it has to be tomorrow, day three, otherwise it's a no-go.'

'Wait.'

I next got The Owl's idea of 'Greensleeves', which was basically the gulls chattering about how their day had gone, ripping bin liners apart and scattering the contents over everyone's driveway.

Finally: 'Okay, tomorrow night.'

'Good. Closing down.' Which I did as quickly as I could before he continued about recces. I'd sort that stuff later.

As soon as I closed down, I called Jack.

'Everything okay down there?'

'No, it's not. Warning order. Weather's closing in. We lift Mary tomorrow night. Day three. Start moving now to the ERV and hold off until I give ten minutes' warning. I'm leaving now.'

I closed down, put the iPhone inside my parka, and pulled out the Samsung from my boot.

I texted Rio.

iPhone briefing

What that meant was that the Samsungs were not to be used, and we were to act as if The Owl was with us. I knew their reaction would be the same as mine – 'That's shit!' – and it was confirmed fifteen seconds later when a GIF of an owl chick being wrenched from its nest by an eagle's talons appeared on my screen.

As I headed for the shop, the shutters on the cabin-services building were up and bright light shone out. One of the overalled women was filling an ATV with fuel. I went over, all smiles. 'Hello, I'm Nick. I arrived yesterday.'

She looked up from the jerry-can, returning my smile. Her blonde hair was gathered up in a bun. 'Yes, I know. Hi, I'm Claire.' Yorkshire accent. She eased the nozzle out gently. 'It's so nice to meet you, Nick. I was going to say hello tomorrow at church.'

I looked admiringly at the Phantom. 'Getting ready for the snow?'

A little fuel gurgled up from the can and speckled the ATV's tank. A rag was immediately in her hand, wiping before any of it dripped onto the floor.

'It's come early this year, but that won't bother these big boys. They're used to collecting supplies from the storage warehouse, snowploughing, that sort of thing. We have more in Russia. They're our work horses for the winter.'

I stepped far enough into the workshop to see how many fuel cans had been moved. All of them, it looked like. 'Do you use them to go up the hill, or just over the bridge?'

'Over the bridge during the winter. We don't go up the hill when the snow's down.' She tapped one of the fuel tanks with a red fingernail. 'We have to be careful. Even these things, the snow's so deep, it collects underneath and they flip. People have been injured.'

Then there was a smile, as if she knew what I wanted to hear. 'But just before the final thaw of the spring, when the snow's reduced enough, we do have a race up the hill – so what do you think? Is it worth staying with us to have a go in the spring?'

I had to agree with her. It sounded fun. I left her to cuddle her machines and, after picking up some stuff from the shop, I worked my way as covertly as I could to the bottom of the hill, then broke into a fast walk.

47

The track snaked left and right as it contoured the hill, and I kept checking it as I climbed. The rain stopped, and it took me another fifteen minutes to reach the ERV. I was immediately on the iPhone to Rio.

10 minutes

Closing straight down again, I moved off the main and waited, eyes glued to the screen for the two-minute warning. My jacket was unzipped and the hood was down to help me stop sweating, but the parka still weighed heavy on my shoulders. Every pocket was rammed with items I'd grabbed off the shop shelves.

I'd been thinking about The Owl and his iPhone mystery boxes. It wasn't just that they let him be in the room that irked me. It was that they made it feel like he was biting into our lives, learning about our relationships and how we coped with each other. Until now I'd always been the buffer between The Owl and the team. He had enough of my life already, and these two were the only people close to me. The buffering felt like a good thing, because the team was a chunk of my life that he didn't know much about. But, far more important than that, there was the question of their safety. The Owl didn't like loose ends. By standing between them, I could kid myself I'd be a shield if ever the shit hit the fan.

I was jolted out of that train of thought. The Owl's mystery box pinged and the screen filled with a thumbs-up emoji. A second or two later, a set of full beams bounced up and down in the distance, cutting into the skyline. A few seconds more and they played against the foliage. Then came the scrunch of wheels on mud and gravel. The shape of the van slowly materialized and rolled to a stop.

I stepped in, and this time I went straight to the bed. As far as I could smell, not much in the van had changed. Rio was in the back this time, and he placed his mystery box on the drainer next to the sink full of debris before gently easing the door to its first latch.

Jack found first gear and set off towards the harbour, but Rio didn't put the cabin lights on, like last time. We'd decided we wanted The Owl to work hard trying to look at our faces to decipher whether or not we were play-acting – which we were going to be. We wanted him to feel this was all real, not just verbally but also visually. If he felt that he was in the room, then with luck that would make him feel in control.

I knew I might as well get straight into it. 'Okay, listen in.' I spoke up so Jack could hear while working the wheel to avoid potholes. As we swayed around, the crockery made exactly the same sound as last time, clinking together in the sink. I was sure not a single dirty cup or plate had been moved.

'There's a big snow dump late tomorrow night, and it's

going to settle – and it's going to continue. I can't guarantee we'll get Mary up that hill and away as quickly as we might have to. I have no idea what kind of follow-up there will be. The fact is, we might fuck up and even cause one when we're trying to lift her, but there are no options. We must go tomorrow, and we've got to move out of here as fast as we can and make distance.

'So, the plan: the deprogramming team will be stood to from last light tomorrow. We need to lift her as soon as I think it's safe to do so, in case the dump comes early. Questions so far?'

There were none – none that were actually expressed, anyway. I was sure they'd have many buzzing around in their heads, and top of the list would be that we weren't going to get the maximum payday but at least there was four days of it already in the bank.

'Listen, I obviously wanted more time to plan and prepare, but that's not going to happen. Yes, we're going to lose three days' money, but tough shit – that's where we are, so we just have to get on with it. Here's what we're going to do.'

I went through exactly the same plan as I'd given them before. The only difference this time was that, from last light, Rio had to be stood to at the bottom of the hill just outside the village.

'Rio, that means once you get dropped off, you just go for it. Avoid the track but check it out on the way down. I'll be checking it once more on the way down tonight. So far there are no obstructions, no gates, no chains, no fallen trees. If you find anything tomorrow, we will clear it. If we can't, we drag her. Any questions?'

Rio was straight in. 'The Matvey recce – that's binned now, yeah?'

'I don't know.'

Jack called back at us, his head silhouetted by the instrument lights and the full beams bouncing off the tunnel of the trees ahead. 'That absolutely has to be seen as a separate job now. It's going to be harder to carry out with you and Mary out of the village. They'll be hyper-alert once they put two and two together, surely.'

'I know.' I nodded and agreed with him while emptying my pockets. 'But let's get this over with first. Then I'll sort out what's happening.'

I threw Alenkas at the pair of them, but left the plastic bottles of goat's yoghurt and protein bars on the bed. Rio spotted them, picked up one of the bottles and tried his best to read the label. 'Mate, what the fuck? We having a vegan picnic or what?'

'It's for Mary. It could be hours before she gets anything. Something she can recognize, keep her calm.'

Rio threw the bottle back on the bed and ripped open his first bar of chocolate. 'Okay, that's good. That's her calmed down.' He might be playing a game, but his concern was real. 'But, mate, time to calm me down. The recce, if we get lifted the wrong side of the bridge, that's us with shaved heads digging holes in Siberia until we drop. That's if we're lucky.'

Jack jumped in. 'Exactly. He's right.'

'Lads, there's nothing I can do about that for now. I've already told you, we wait until this job is finished, and then I'll have to explain that it's a new situation, a new job, therefore it has to be a new deal.'

We all agreed, and hopefully The Owl would as well when the time came. Who knew? He might even be nodding in agreement as we spoke. But I wasn't holding my breath on that one.

Rio finished his bar and was already unwrapping the next when I kicked out and made contact with his half-arm. 'So – we've run out of tea, then?'

Even in the near darkness I could make out his grin. The stage was set for him. 'Mate, we got no fucking Thermos mugs. Soggy bollocks there threw them away. We're drinking out of cracked cups, spilling it all over the shop like you'll be doing in a couple of years.'

'Your own fucking fault.' Either Jack was playing along or he had finally reached the end of his tether with Rio's lack of domesticity. 'If you'd cleaned the mugs in the first place, we'd still have them.'

I let him get on with that, but only for long enough to be convincing. We'd done what was required, and I didn't want The Owl listening to any more than he had to, intruding on our lives. 'Right, if there's no tea, turn around. I've got hot chocolate waiting for me back at the village.'

They did a couple of theatrical 'Ooh, get you, then!' comments for effect. Jack did a five-point turn in the narrow main and we headed back to the ERV. They gave me the campsite story, why they were getting kicked out on Monday morning because it was the end of the season, why Jack was pissed off at Rio being a domestic hand grenade. It was filler for The Owl, but I still didn't like it one bit.

It wasn't long before Rio had his fingers on the door handle, ready to pull back just before Jack started to slow. I had one last thing to say: 'Remember, lads – last light, ready to go.'

But Rio had to finish. 'Can you get your hands on fuel? The van, mate, we want to keep driving south for as long as we can, yeah?'

The door slid back.

'I'll check.'

The van stopped, and I stepped out into the tree cover. I stayed there until the red glow of the rear lights had disappeared into the distance, then turned and ran back down the track.

48

Day Three: Sunday, 10 October 2021

It was nearly time for church, and I hadn't slept all night. When I got back from meeting the other two there'd been work to do. I hadn't gone to breakfast. I couldn't face sitting there with a big pirate smile, knowing I was about to turn people's worlds upside down. Not only Mary's, but the whole village's – and even my own.

Not that I had any other option. If I'd been working alone, maybe I could have lied and bluffed and sidestepped and, if he ever found out, taken whatever shit came back on me from The Owl. If only it could have been that simple, but I had the other two dickheads to think about. Me, I had nothing to lose. They had shedloads. Children. Relationships. Futures.

As soon as I'd come down from the hill last night, I'd gone and checked the Phantoms. Critically, did they all have full tanks? We couldn't end up running around trying to find one that had been topped up: we needed to know we could jump aboard any of them. I unscrewed each cap and, of course, they were all full to the brim, and the keys were in all of the ignitions. What about the jerry-cans, once more in their regimented line? I released the caps one by one, and a full load of E10 glistened near the top of each. Rio was absolutely right: we had to keep moving south without stopping, and that called for as much fuel as we could carry.

Checks done, I had walked the route from the cabin services to Mary and Gedi's door. We needed to load her up and be gone fast, and that meant driving as close as we could to their cabin and swinging the Phantom round so it faced up the hill. From there, I had gone back to my cabin and drunk far too much coffee. I ran out of pods but couldn't be bothered to go and collect more from the shop, so I hit what was left of the hot chocolate. I'd managed a smile as I thought about the other two out there, bickering like an old couple over the UHT milk and dirty cups, and not being able to drink as they drove because it spilt all over the place. I just hoped they hadn't touched the goat yoghurt.

There was a knock on the door.

'Coming!'

I pulled on my parka. The door wasn't locked – the key had been on the hook all night. I pulled it open to reveal Saynab and Poppy blowing vapour clouds on the doorstep. Saynab's chunky polo-neck jutted out from under a duvet coat, and Poppy was dressed more or less as a mini-me. The only difference was her big purple beanie with a bobble.

Saynab was all smiles. 'We saw you in the kitchen window. Poppy thought maybe you'd like some company.'

Poppy was beside herself with excitement. 'Come on, Nick, come on – it's your big day!'

She grabbed my hand and semi-dragged me outside. I

closed the door behind me, and we headed together in the direction of the bridge. It hit me that my only glimmer of hope in all this was that I knew Mary would boomerang straight back. And, who knew, I might even help her do that. These people were all about today, and nobody had a label, and I liked that.

Poppy's total happiness radiated out of her, and it was enough to make me smile – and it wasn't a pirate smile.

49

People were congregating near the bridge, ready to cross into Russia. As we got closer, it was almost like they'd been waiting for us. They greeted me with big smiles and happy shouts. 'It's your big day today, Nick!'

They were right, it was, for lots of reasons. And they weren't good ones.

I wasn't expecting too much out of the morning, and neither should The Owl when it came to pictures of Matvey. I hadn't brought the iPhone with me and certainly wouldn't be pulling the Samsung out of my boot. That job was on hold. Hopefully, it was binned. Why take the chance of compromise when there was work to do tonight? Lifting Mary was the priority, not trying to get pictures of a church leader. I hadn't even found the guy yet.

It was hard not to think of the consequences of ripping Mary away and messing up this happy environment for Gedi and all the others. And I dreaded that the happy village myth I'd enjoyed so far would be broken when the congregation turned into the Manson Family and suddenly began drinking babies' blood or whatever Matvey commanded them to do. If it did turn out that way, at least I'd be saving Mary instead of fucking her up.

Poppy was still tugging on my arm as we crossed the bridge. I nodded my hellos to well-wishers and began to hear live music coming from inside the church. It was rock, but not happy-clappy rock. Poppy knew who it was. 'Nickelback!'

Music was something I'd never really got my head around. I'd grown up sort of knowing the names of some of the bands, but I couldn't identify their songs. I didn't even know any nursery rhymes or bedtime-story-type stories – stuff like that didn't happen in our flat when I was a kid.

As we got closer to the church door she started singing along. We followed the group of families filing in and the music came at us full blast. The band were stage left, and the centre table with the upturned glass and water hadn't moved. The all-white interior looked full to capacity: 424, if Esther's calculations were correct. Smiles and waves came at us from all sides as Poppy dragged me across the aisle to the front row, where Cameron and Elaine were already in their positions, along with Madeleine and Mathulla. I hadn't seen them since the IT centre but maybe there was no need to cross into Norway if you were working this side of the river.

Saynab had gone ahead to bag us seats. She patted the empty one next to Cameron's wheelchair, which had been inserted into the line instead of just being tacked at the end. 'That's for you. Today you're our guest.' She moved to the side so I could sit down. 'Tomorrow, who knows, you might decide to become one of us. I hope so.'

Two other seats were empty, the other side of Elaine and Cameron. They were soon filled when Mary and Gedi turned up. They waved at someone on the other side of the aisle, trying to shout over the band. All in all, it was more like a very large, happy family get-together than the kind of regimented herding I remembered from Sunday parades in my squaddie days. Mary and Gedi stood hand in hand, very excited as they sang along to whatever the song was. Everyone else was also on their feet, singing and dancing like an evangelical group, except their hands weren't raised to the sky in prayer. Heaven wasn't up there for these people: it was under their boots, right here, right now.

Saynab tried to get me to join in with her and Poppy, but even if Heaven was where I was it wasn't going to get me to sing. Instead, I pretended I was embarrassed and swayed a bit to blend in. Maybe I should get into this music thing one day. People seemed to enjoy it.

It wasn't long before the band stopped and everybody immediately clapped and whooped, finally sitting down, full of excitement. It all started again as two of the lads in the band picked up trumpets. I thought they were going to herald the big guy onto the stage, but instead the drums started a long roll and the trumpets blared out the theme to *Hawaii Five-0*. I knew that one. It was a TV show tune. Everybody clapped and hummed or played air drums or trumpet. As the band built to a crescendo, so did the applause, finally erupting as the main act entered stage right.

Poppy shouted as loudly as anyone. 'Good morning, Matvey!' and then 'Matvey! Matvey!' like a football chant.

It was then that I realized I already knew who he was. He was dressed totally differently, in a white T-shirt and matching jeans that made him look even skinnier, but he was the same forty-something I'd met before, and his groomed beard and geeky rectangular glasses on top of all that whiteness made him even more imposing.

50

Matvey worked hard to quieten the crowd. He had a head mike that came round to his mouth, like a tech CEO at a conference raving about a new digital paper clip. The difference was, these people weren't getting excited because it was their job. They were doing it out of pure elation.

He put his hands up and gave us all that Russian but Americanized accent: 'Good morning, you wonderful people!' The reply was rapturous as he poured water into a glass and held it up to us all as a toast. He took a mouthful and put the glass down, addressing us in true motivational-speaker style as he strode up and down the stage and threw out his arms.

'Let's welcome our new members to the village.' For the first time there was silence, as they gave Matvey space. 'As you all know, we're honoured to be joined by new members who arrived on Friday. I know many of you have already met and said your hellos, but I want to give them a big warm welcome that is full of peace and love, from me . . . from you . . . from God.' He held out his arms in our direction, gesturing for us to stand.

Cameron was eager as Elaine helped him to his feet, and the whole congregation broke into a big round of applause and more whooping.

'Welcome, Elaine! Welcome, Cameron! Welcome, Mathulla! Welcome, Nick! Welcome back, Madeleine!'

We were encouraged to turn and face the congregation. I put a hand up to sort of acknowledge them, not really knowing what was expected. It was a new phenomenon for me. The last time I'd faced crowds I'd been a young squaddie in Northern Ireland, and the reaction I always got was raised fists or a volley of spit.

It eventually died down and we settled into our seats. Matvey had even more news. 'Today this is a double special day for us all here. I'm so happy to announce that we will not only be welcoming the spring with its renewal, new beginnings and rebirth but also with a marriage!'

Matvey turned to Mary and Gedi and got them to stand up to take the thunderous applause. People even stamped their feet on the wooden floor. I joined in. The happy couple stood hand in hand and smiled and mouthed their thank-yous to everybody. Esther and Kirill couldn't contain their delight as they came running up the aisle to hug them both, and their kids did the same from behind, cranking their arms around the adults' legs to join in the group hug. Even the trumpets sparked up with 'Here Comes The Bride' and I carried on clapping and looking happy, just like everybody else.

But I was thinking: Fuck this. I wished I'd never come here.

I sat down with the rest as the noise died away. It was clear the congregation wouldn't be drinking any babies' blood to make me feel better about lifting Mary tonight.

Matvey carried on, walking up and down the stage and peering into the crowd. 'I know, isn't it so great?'

No, not that great at all.

'To think, we'll be having a spring wedding – isn't that so cool?'

If there was a wedding, it would be because she'd be back here in the village. It was a weak consolation, but the only one I could think of. But then I had another, as the first hadn't helped me at all. Tonight's drama and separation of the couple could only strengthen their relationship and their marriage. It sort of sounded right and a little better than the first, but didn't feel it.

Saynab turned and looked at me. 'Isn't that good news?'

I agreed with her and smiled, but seeing everybody else's happiness didn't give me any.

Announcements over, Matvey started what I presumed was the service. Glancing around me, I could see that some people stood with their hands together down by their waists, while others faced straight ahead, eyes closed. Matvey commanded the stage, moving up and down, praying to God, generally thanking him for giving us life. In response, everyone promised to live their lives as he wanted them to, because that way there would always be God's word on earth, and that word was peace.

He ended it all with a big happy shout of 'Thank you, God, for listening!' Then he was straight back into his high-octane delivery. A large cinema screen unrolled at the back of the stage and the band members produced two cameras, positioning them left and right, facing the congregation. 'Okay, then, let's see who we have with us today.'

Filling the screen were five beaming faces, three of them European-looking and suntanned. There were claps and whistles this end.

Matvey had moved to the right of the screen so he didn't mess up the view. 'Hello, Hodeidah!'

There was a two-second delay before the smiles got even wider and they waved at us. It was a live feed from Yemen.

A young woman was their opening voice today. 'Good morning, Matvey! Good morning, everybody! And especially the newcomers. We can't wait to meet you once our work here is done – and, of course, a special congratulations to Mary and Gedi. We wish you peace and love.'

The congregation waved and there was a couple of minutes of people in the church shouting messages that everything was all right in the village, and the villagers in Hodeidah said everything was all right in their camp. It started to get serious as we listened to the work they'd been doing. She was giving us a sitrep. 'Things are really going well. The clean-water programme is working, the hygiene-education programme is working, the medical centre is working, the school is working.'

Loud claps, and the people on the screen nodded their appreciation after a two-second delay. Another of the group, an older man, just a hint of grey in his beard, got in front of the lens. 'We're so happy to say that this has now been the fourth month of peace in our area – no village attacks, no kidnapping, no violence against any woman. God's Word on Earth is here with us.'

There was a roar of approval and thumbs-ups everywhere, and then Matvey started to close down. 'Well done, Frank, we thank you all, and God thanks you all, and we'll see you back here soon.'

But Frank hadn't finished. 'No, no, no, no! One minute! We've got one more thing to say. We've got a special message for Saynab and Poppy.'

We could see one of the women waving for somebody to come on from off-screen. A twenty-something local lad appeared and everybody got him in position. He started shouting away in Arabic, as if that was going to help us hear better with the distance. Basically, he seemed to be saying hello to Saynab and Poppy, who jumped up and down and blew kisses at the screen, and then the guy blew even more back.

I watched all this love being shared between different parts of the world, and it flashed through my mind that I was one of the people who had helped fuck the world up in the first place. But despite all that, I still felt nothing but hope. Matvey wasn't the evil mastermind of some weird or Doomsday cult. He had said hardly anything. There had been no preaching, no dictatorial rules, no bollocking for not following any rules. He had let the people talk, and enjoy.

They were living their lives.

51

The service went on for another hour, with the video link extending to Ukraine and Pakistan, before it descended into a bit of a parish council meeting. The big topic was the snow coming early. Apparently a drainage ditch was blocked and needed clearing out that afternoon, but that was about it. Everything else seemed to have been squared away.

Ukraine was a strange one for me. I naturally thought that Matvey only had people in far-flung developing countries. But, then, why not Ukraine? They didn't need any water-wells sunk but they had been at war with Russia since 2014 when Putin had decided to invade and seize Crimea. The largest country in Europe, bordering the EU and NATO, and we had forgotten about the fourteen thousand people killed so far in their war against the Russians. The village hadn't, though, and was helping families reunite, and to construct new housing for them outside the conflict zones in the east of the country.

As we headed back towards Norway, Poppy was still

excited about seeing the lad on-screen, but she soon spotted her friends and ran to join them.

I turned to Saynab, and she could see the question coming. 'So, the young guy who said hello?'

Her pleasure was undisguised. 'My nephew. My sister's son. Both his parents were killed just over ten years ago. God's Word on Earth have looked after him ever since.'

'Why didn't he come here with you two? Wouldn't that have been better?'

We stepped onto the bridge. 'Not for Anwar. He wants to become an engineer and rebuild our country, but first there must be peace. He's a normal young man. He loves football, he loves riding his BMX. But he's strong-minded, he's driven. He wants to be able to do that in his own country. He's going to make it happen, Nick. He's going to bring peace to Yemen. The only way to do that is for him to stay with God's Word on Earth.'

I nodded. Fair one. The world needed to pay more attention to places like Yemen, not just those full of blond hair and blue eyes, Starbucks and Zara. I'd been in a lot of war zones and seen a lot of misery, and the ugly truth was that our humanity is skin deep. It's as if we identify whether or not a life is worth saving by where they were born, the colour of their skin, the language they speak, the religion they practise. The world needed to wake up to the fact that everybody has dreams, homes, careers, aspirations, passions, families. They just want to pay the rent and take their kids to school without mortar rounds fucking them up.

As if.

'So, Nick, what do you think? Did you like church? Did you like Matvey? Do you think staying with us would be a good thing?'

I pretended to think on it a second. 'Yes, yes and yes.'

We joined the rest of the village as they filed into the dining hall, for what was clearly a big affair after church on Sunday, villagers enjoying each other's company, chatting, laughing, eating biscuits, drinking tea and coffee, kids running around. I played my part as best I could with lots of pirate smiles and right answers to questions about whether I was enjoying myself and finding life here interesting. I wished I wasn't being asked. What made it worse was that Esther, Kirill, Elaine and Cameron all came up and chatted away as if we were long-lost friends. The thing was, I felt the same. I needed to get the fuck out of there and start switching on to things I understood properly, like the job in hand.

After another hour and a half of too much pirate smiling and lying, I made my excuses and said about a hundred goodbyes as I headed to the coat racks. Mary and Gedi were standing in a group at the rear of the hall, and she saw me. She waved and called, 'Hey, Nick!' She joined me as I pulled on my parka. 'What did you think about this morning? Pretty cool, yeah?'

I agreed as I zipped up, something I wished I could do with my head. 'Yeah, it was great. And congratulations! You two look so happy.'

She was, and she agreed. 'We've been bursting to tell everybody for days. But it was worth biting our tongues just to see everyone so happy for us. Now I can't wait for the spring.' Her excitement was as intense as Poppy's, and that made me feel even worse.

I made with my best Captain Hook. 'Yeah, I know, it's going to be a long cold winter, but no matter what happens, the spring will come, and you will be happy.'

She rubbed my arm and looked back at her group. 'That's a lovely thought, Nick. Thank you. I hope you stay with us.'

The cold punched my face, and I pulled my hood up tight. I used to know as a certainty that being a pirate was always better than being a coastguard. But even that belief had been fucked up since I'd come here.

52

I stood in the shadow created by the light at the gable end of the long log cabin, the one where Saynab had been waiting to greet us when we were dropped off by the Merc at Center Parcs 2040. Rio's shape emerged out of the darkness of the treeline just beyond the village. It had been only two days ago, but it felt like a month. The first snowflakes were now falling, the wind so gentle they fluttered down vertically, sparkling in the lights.

Everything that could have been done in preparation had been. Now, the wheels were turning.

I checked my iPhone was on aeroplane mode, and put it back into the inside pocket of my parka, zipped up with my cover documents, passport, drugs, and the Samsung. We'd all have to use The Owl's mystery boxes from now or he'd know he hadn't been in control as much as he thought he was. Nothing good would have come of that.

Since leaving the dining hall, I had spent the rest of the day in hiding, not wanting to see anybody, let alone talk to them. Never had I wanted a job over and done with so much as this one. My only hope was to switch off from everybody and everything, and focus totally on the job. I'd have preferred not to: I'd been so close, I thought, to getting my head straightened out and ready for the real life that awaited me. But, fuck it, I was better where I belonged, I supposed. Feelings of guilt and regret could be postponed until Mary was handed over and we were heading south.

As Rio got closer, I stepped onto the gravel, now thinly covered with snow, to meet him. I could make out the shape of his daypack hanging off his back, and he had his hood up. That meant I couldn't see his mouth moving, but it certainly was. 'Is His Holiness all right, then?'

'Just crack on.'

Our boots crunched in unison on the path as we turned towards the village. It was pointless trying to keep to the shadows any longer. The entrance to the village was our start line. Once you're committed to a start line, you might as well get on with it, get it over and done with fast, one way or another.

He passed me a length of paracord with the handcuffs' key, one end of which I threaded into my parka's buttonhole. The rest went into the outside pocket. Next came the handcuffs, which I shoved inside my parka. The restraint would be harsh, but temporary. I was hoping that the bouncers would release her at the harbour, but I doubted it. They, too, would have to keep her controlled in case she tried to fuck herself up.

They were rigid cuffs, with a moulded grip bar so we could easily control or drag the body that was wearing them. A sharp yank really fucked up the wearer and they'd soon shut up and calm down.

'You still got those bars and yoghurts for her?'

'Yeah, of course. But goat's milk. You taking the piss? You did that on purpose, didn't you?'

I didn't take the bait. 'She's alone. Gedi was in the gym five ago. We should be out of here in fifteen.'

The Gore-Tex rustled as Rio nodded under his hood.

'I'll try the door. If not, I knock. You stay out of sight until it's open and I make entry.'

We hit the pathway between the buildings and the low-level lighting glistened on the snow. It was that time of night. The weather had everyone inside, their blinds down. Now and again a TV screen flickered through a chink.

'I'll take the lead. Remember, we need her uninjured and not going into seizure. No matter what she does, we need to deliver her in good order.'

Another rustle. 'No problem.'

We passed the cabin services on our left. 'The Phantom is inside, fuel loaded. Once those shutters are open, I'm no more than forty-five seconds away.'

We were approaching the cabin. 'Two buildings ahead, thirty metres. All the lights are on, the blinds are down.'

Rio turned back to check the route from the cabin-services area. 'Got it.'

As the path curved towards the target building, we could see its gable end and the door. The kitchen window to the left of it was clear of its blind, but there was no sign of Mary.

We were four or five steps from the door, and no one had disturbed the snow.

Rio took up position on the side of the door frame furthest from the kitchen window. I placed my hand on the door handle and gripped. I pulled down. 'Hello, hello! Anyone in? It's me!'

The door opened into a wall of warmth and cinnamon. I

stuck my head through and put my foot over the threshold. 'Hello, hello! It's Nick! Hello, anyone at home?'

A couple of candles burnt on shelves. The TV was on mute, showing a current-affairs show to an empty room.

'Hello? Anyone home? It's Nick!'

She appeared from the bedroom in a dressing-gown, with a towel wrapped around her wet hair. Shit: we wouldn't be moving as quickly as I wanted.

She looked surprised, but not scared. 'Nick! Is something wrong? Can I help you? What's—'

Surprise turned to horror as Rio burst into the cabin, hood down, dreads flying. He waved his arm up and down in a calming motion and, ignoring us both, headed for the kitchen to pull down the blind.

53

As I grabbed the Bang & Olufsen remote from the coffee-table and hit the volume button to distract Mary, Rio pulled down the blind and turned back towards the door, unzipping his daysack. He retrieved a wooden doorstop, then kicked it under the door and turned the key.

Mary was still trying to internalize what was happening around her.

'That's to stop people coming in, not you going out. Everything is okay. You're safe.'

Her eyes narrowed as she saw the second wedge of wood go in two-thirds above the threshold.

'Mary?'

Her eyes bounced between me, Rio, even the TV. She was still trying hard to process the challenge to her reality.

'Mary, look at me.' I bobbed my head round to get into her eyeline. 'We're not here to hurt you. Do you understand that?'

No response. I couldn't be sure she'd even heard me.

'Mary, we're not here to hurt you, okay?'

She gulped a couple of sharp breaths. Tears welled and rolled.

At last, her head jerked an acknowledgement.

'That's really good, Mary. Now what I want you to—'

Her eyes drifted.

'Mary, look at me.' I had to get her back.

Rio passed us at that moment on his way to the bedroom. She flinched, wrapped her arms around herself, took a step away from him.

Rio didn't stop. He had things to do. He gave a brief smile. 'It's okay, Mary, yeah? It's all right. Calm.' He disappeared into the bedroom.

I needed her attention. 'Mary, look at me, nothing else. Can you do that?'

She trembled. No acknowledgement. 'Mary, look up. Look at me.'

She gave a shaky nod. 'Please, don't hurt me. Please.'

A pair of ski trousers more Gedi's size than hers flew through the bedroom doorway.

'Mary, I want you to get dressed. Where is your passport and where is your medication? The Oxtellar, where is it?'

She stared at the wall, trying to download.

Behind us, the TV panel were having a very serious debate and Rio was pulling open drawers. If this took any longer, I was going to up the ante.

Finally, a reaction. She looked at me.

'Get dressed.' I pointed. She turned and saw the clothes collecting on the floor.

All of a sudden, in the middle of a kidnapping, there was embarrassment. She looked first at me and then at the bedroom, like she was trying to work out which was the lesser of two evils.

'Go to the corner, face the wall, we're not watching. Mary, where is your passport? Where are your meds?'

I'd let her go to the wall, but no further. Once you have control, you don't let them out of your sight. It's not like in the films where the victim tricks them into letting him go to the toilet, then jumps out of a window. That just doesn't happen.

She shuddered.

'Mary, deep breaths. It's me, Nick. I'm going to help you. Come on, calm yourself, deep breaths, with me – ready? Four in, remember?'

I took an exaggerated breath. 'Two, three, four. All right, let's hold it for seven . . . three, four, five, six, seven. And let's push it all out. That's it, keep going.'

Rio appeared in the bedroom doorway clutching a blue passport. I nodded. 'Good news.' Now it was back to the owner. 'Keep breathing, Mary, deep breaths – but you must get dressed.'

She approached the pile of clothes, and seemed to be calming down. Her actions were quicker, a bit more in control. But then she started to talk. 'Nick, what are you doing?'

'We're here to take you home.'

She spun round, embarrassment gone, the ski trousers halfway up her thighs, the dressing-gown gaping wide open. 'Please, Nick, I don't want—'

'Stop. You have to stop. This is going to happen.'

'Why are you doing this? Please, let me stay, let me live my life. You know what we're about here. You know how happy I am. You even wished me luck for our marriage. Why did you lie to us? The village, we all opened our hearts to you. We welcomed you.'

I ignored it, like I had all the other bad thoughts I'd had

today. I had to crack on with this. 'Mary, it's money, that's it, but you must listen to me. You're an adult and you can do what you want. You will come back even stronger – you'll be back here soon, I know you will. But this has to be done. I'm sorry, but this is happening. Things are never as simple as we wish they were. Get some more layers on. We're going to be taking you, no matter how cold you are. Now, where are your meds?'

'The kitchen drawer.'

Good. Real life was coming to her.

'All of them?'

She nodded, pulling a long-sleeved thermal over her head and then a fleece.

I kept my voice just loud enough for Rio to hear me over the TV panel. 'Kitchen. One of the drawers.'

He started the search, and it didn't take long. I went to the front door, unhooked her coat, and passed it to her along with her boots. 'Remember, we're not going to harm you, but the weather could. Zip up.'

She wiped tears away with the palms of her hands as Rio passed her the blister packs of Oxtellar. 'Mary, love, put all the drugs in your pocket, zip them up so you don't lose them.'

Giving her control of the drugs hopefully gave her one less thing to be anxious about. On top of that, if it all went to rat-shit and we had to bug out, we didn't want to be stopping to hand over her meds.

'You'll get more when you need them, I promise.' He nodded down. 'Get your gloves out of your coat, and put them on.'

She sat on the sofa and complied. She tried to talk, but I closed it down. 'Not now, Mary. It will all come later. Get ready – and quickly.'

Rio had now moved behind the sofa and produced a black merino wool ski mask out of his daysack as he waited for me to take out the handcuffs. She instantly knew what was about to happen. 'Please, Nick – no! Please don't hurt me.'

She was louder than the TV, and I hit the volume button again. 'Mary, this is not to hurt you, but to keep you safe. This is to keep us all safe.'

There was no resistance, just resigned sobs as the cuffs went on over her gloves, but not as tight as they could have been. 'Mary.' I crouched down to her eye level, searching for contact before I spoke. 'We're going to put a ski mask on you.'

Her eyes widened and the begging in them was genuine. I'd seen enough of it over the years to know. Rio pulled the ski mask down over her head and I helped settle it round her neck, pushing my fingers around the face opening to get all the hair out of the way. 'This is to protect you.'

She heard duct tape being pulled from a roll behind her and her mouth moved under the merino. 'Nick, please, please.'

It was too late. Rio reached over her head and planted the first length of duct tape over her mouth and wrapped it completely around her head. The mask was only there so the tape wouldn't hurt her when it was ripped off again.

54

I had my hand on top of her head, keeping the merino static as Rio carried on wrapping the tape around her. 'This is all going to be over soon, Mary, I promise.'

The tape went round her head another three times before Rio bit the roll and it went back into his daysack. A sock should have been shoved into her mouth to ensure there was no mouth cavity to produce sound, but that might have pushed her over the edge. In any case, she only had to be quiet until we exited the village.

I stayed crouched down with her, holding her face in my hands as gently as I could yet keeping control. The mask was soon wet with her tears and snot. 'Just do as this man says and it'll all be over. Okay?'

She didn't or couldn't answer, I wasn't sure which. It didn't matter: I had to leave. This was taking too long.

Rio gave the thumbs-up from behind the sofa, then laid his hand firmly on her shoulder to add to the control as I went and pulled out the stops from the door and unlocked it. Turning off the lights, I checked outside and stepped out, closing the door gently behind me. So far, so good: it had gone slowly, but we were ready to move.

I reached the cabin-services store and made entry through the door, just as I had done an hour before meeting Rio. This time I didn't have to take my boots off, had got the iPhone out and aeroplane mode off.

Jack answered after the first ring. 'Standing by.'

'Wait.' I hit the shutter button and the steel gently rattled its way upwards. I jumped on the Phantom that had four jerry-cans strapped to its rear platform, and slapped my fucked hand against my thigh a couple of times as if that was going to ensure it would work, before turning the key, and hitting the ignition button. The ATV ticked over. 'Move now.'

'Moving.'

I closed down the iPhone and got my wheels turning, lying with my face almost touching the instruments so I cleared the still-rising shutter. These things were automatic and, just like a moped, controlled from the right handle. I hit my hand against my thigh again, before slowly moving out onto the snow-covered concrete and heading for Mary and Rio.

He would have his hand on the centre cuff-bar now, controlling and consoling her at the door, ready to move. It would be a fucker for her, but she had to be gripped. It was safer for all three of us. We didn't know how she'd react at any point. Even once we'd got her aboard the Phantom she could try to jump, either confused or trying to escape, and end up injured. A casualty would slow us down badly. When under pressure, people don't think straight. They have to be controlled.

I passed the cabin and did a wide U-turn to face back the way I had come, then drove as close as I could to the door.

Rio would have heard me, and he'd be waiting for me to open the door. He wouldn't come out with Mary while I manoeuvred: villagers could be out there, or something could be happening outside that wasn't safe for us. I would therefore physically open the door, then both of us would put her on the ATV. Rio would grip her, keep her safe, and I'd drive us up the track to the RV with Jack.

I stopped, kept the engine running, and jumped off. I took the two steps to the door and opened it.

I didn't see the hands that grabbed my jacket and hauled me into the wall, or the ones that rammed a plastic bag over my head and pulled it tight against my face.

55

Instinctively, I collapsed my weight to the floor and thrashed to twist myself free, but my attacker clung on. The bag was pulled tight against my nose and mouth with a huge grunt of exertion and I could feel the bristles of a beard against my neck.

The plastic rippled as I fought for breath. I brought my hands up to try to tear it away but whoever had me wasn't letting that happen. The bag moulded to my face like cling-film. My sweat was like glue. The pressure around my neck increased until my head felt as if it was about to explode.

All I could do was keep ramming my body backwards, getting my back into whoever was behind me, using my feet and legs to try to smash him against the wall, the breakfast bar, a door, anything. Still he held on, and I pushed and pushed. In response, he heaved harder and harder against my neck.

There was no sound from Mary. I couldn't see where she was, not that I could look. The bag had misted up. I could hear Rio, though, and he was in pain. That was exactly what

I wanted to do, but I had no air. I pushed again, but I knew I was weakening. Soon I would run out of air.

Then I realized: he didn't want me dead. If he had, I would have been by now. He wanted me to collapse, to asphyxiate. He didn't want to kill me. So, I complied. I gave myself up. I leant forward and stopped fighting, and this time he let me drop to the floor. As I went down, the bag loosened, and the hands controlling it shifted to my shoulders.

Before he had a chance to do anything more, I thrust up my hands and grabbed above me. I felt an ear, then wet hair. I gripped the back of his head as hard as I could and raised mine, ready to butt him and take the pain. He snarled with aggression, then screamed as our skulls made contact and I rolled aside, pulling the bag off my head, gasping for air. All I could see were bubbles of red light and starbursts of white. All I could hear was the rasp of air in tortured lungs, his or mine, I didn't know. The pain went as my adrenalin took over.

Scrambling to my feet, I grabbed the TV remote from the glass-topped coffee-table and, gripping it dagger-style, thumb over the top of the slim steel sheath, I brought it down onto Kirill's forehead. He staggered back but didn't fall, so I got right up close, grabbed hold of the back of his neck and rammed the remote again and again into his head and neck, three, maybe four times, before jamming it into his mouth, forcing it with both hands to the back of his throat. Kirill's eyes bulged as it cut off his oxygen supply and vomit forced its way between my fingers. His arms and legs flailed for a moment, then went limp.

I pulled the remote from Kirill's mouth and left him to sort out his own world of pain. I tried to focus on Rio, but my head was still pounding. He was on the floor by the TV, on his back, his legs bear-hugging Gedi, trying to control him, trying to stop him damaging him even more. The two of them must have come back from the gym together.

Clearly, he could see what was going on with me. 'Nick, fuck sake – Nick!'

I staggered over and kicked into Gedi, until finally I connected with his head. He rolled sideways off Rio, exposing his blood-covered face. I yelled, 'Keep him down, for fuck's sake, keep him down!'

I staggered back to Kirill. I had to make sure we didn't have any deaths on our hands. I grabbed his arm and pulled him over into the recovery position so that vomit could release, then crawled back to Rio.

'Don't kill him, just keep him down!'

But Rio wasn't moving. His face was a mess. I still couldn't see Mary, but she wasn't the priority just now. Controlling these two was. We could find Mary afterwards, and if we didn't, we'd have to bug out of here as fast as we could and make distance. I dropped my knees into Kirill's back, pinning him to the ground.

'The tape, mate – throw the tape!'

No reply came. As I looked back he was trying to use his feet to grip the daysack and pull it to him.

'I'm fucked, mate – my arm.'

I went back, unzipped it and pulled out the tape. With my knees on Kirill's back, I yanked his arms behind him and bound his wrists together, and on up his forearms.

Rio had shuffled himself on his arse until his back was against the wall. His face was a mess but I couldn't tell if it was his blood or Gedi's. His only arm dangled in his lap like a bird's broken wing. He couldn't even support it, just had to take the pain.

'Where is she?'

He jerked his head at the closed bedroom door.

I ran to it but stopped. She might be just the other side with a knife. I eased it open a fraction.

'Mary?' Through the crack I saw her curled up in a ball on the bed, holding a pillow over her head, as if that was going to stop the horror entering her brain. I closed the door and went to deal with Gedi. The parka kept all my body heat in and sweat now dripped from my face as I taped his hands and arms.

Rio was still struggling to get up as I dragged Gedi, the smaller of the two, by his ankles over to Kirill, and laid their legs on top of each other. Gedi stirred, his life coming back to him. He had to have another couple of kicks, this time very hard into his thighs, and he whimpered and jerked. It was pointless talking to him. Duct tape was the only thing that needed to be happening right now.

Rio had managed to haul himself onto his knees and then to his feet, but he couldn't unbutton his coat to check the damage. Gasping for breath, sweat streaming down me inside my parka, I knelt next to him so I could feel up inside his sleeve, and I didn't have to go far. The large bony bulge said it all.

'Mate, it's fractured. Good news – there's no blood, skin's still intact.'

I made my way to the kitchen, pulling out the drawers, and found what I was looking for, the same long wooden salad servers as in my cabin. Rio had followed me. He knew it was going to have to be a quick immobilization job. I positioned the servers over his coat sleeve. 'Deep breaths, mate – this is going to hurt.' One hand gripping the servers over his forearm, I used the other and my mouth to rip and pull the duct tape around the wood.

Rio didn't like it at all. 'You fucker!'

No option. It had to be stabilized.

I stood up and unbuttoned his coat halfway. 'Put it in there to support it. I'll get Mary.'

I was about to go back to the bedroom, but Kirill had started to come round. His face was in as bad a state as Gedi's and his beard covered in vomit. I crouched, knowing it was taking up precious time, but I wanted to explain. Instead, all I could say was *'Ya sozhaley.'* The formal apology in Russian was the only one I knew.

He didn't look at me; his eyes were down at the floor. He turned his head away to spit more vomit onto the tiles.

They had done what they had to do when they came back from the gym to find a stranger in the cabin and Mary quite clearly in distress. It was human nature to protect. Kirill understood there are no monsters, just people doing what they think is right at the time.

'She'll be back. Tell Gedi.'

I returned to the bedroom door.

'Mary?' I knocked again, opened it slowly to see the bed empty.

'Mary? Mary?'

She was on her feet, stumbling as if she were drunk, and her fingers were making a repetitive and compulsive movement, grabbing her coat alternately with both handcuffed hands. It was what I'd seen online. Stress had made her brain's nerve cells send out sudden excessive and uncontrolled electrical signals.

She was having a focal seizure.

56

Just as the advice online had said to, I kept my voice low and even and friendly. 'Mary, you're having a seizure. I'm here and you're safe. Don't worry.'

There was no flicker of recognition, no hint that she could even hear me. Glazed and lifeless, her eyes stared into the distance, her fingers manipulating the edge of her coat. Then her mouth moved under the duct tape in what looked like an attempt to swallow. I knew not to handle her unless she was walking into danger, which she was now: it was more like a shuffle, but she was going to bang into the bathroom wall. I slid in front of her, arms stretched out to the sides. 'Why don't you stop, Mary, maybe turn around?'

Gently, I redirected her and let her shuffle off into the middle of the room.

Rio appeared in the doorway, bristling with urgency. I put a hand up to silence him. 'No more movement.'

He wasn't happy. He wanted to get away. He wasn't the only one.

A glimmer of life came back into her face. These seizures

lasted two to four minutes, and the rebooting time was variable. At least she was blinking, where her eyes had been completely static and vacant. She tottered – her movements were a bit drunken. The compulsive swallowing hadn't stopped, but she was no longer doing the scrabbling thing with her fingers. One of her gloved hands flexed open and closed.

'Mary?' I pulled the length of paracord from my pocket. 'I'm going to take off the handcuffs, make you more comfortable. Is that okay?' I didn't expect an answer, and I didn't wait for one. I just pushed the key into its well and the cuff arms swung open. Her freed hands came up to her face and tried to touch it, but there were too many layers of glove, tape and wool. I peeled the tape from the back and past her mouth and pulled down on the mask. The tape still hung there but she would feel air on her skin, could breathe unimpeded, maybe feel a bit freer.

'That better, Mary, yeah?'

A small nod of recognition.

'Okay, just stay where you are for me. Will you do that?'

I grabbed the duvet off the bed and ran into the living area. Moments later, I was back. 'Okay, Mary?' I didn't expect an answer: it was more to do with comforting. 'Let's go.'

I didn't want to drag her. Instead, I sort of shepherded her through the bedroom door. The bodies I'd hidden under the duvet were stirring. I kept talking to distract her. The TV was still on, another round of adverts. 'That's it – well done, Mary. Let's keep going, yeah, you're doing really well. Nearly there.'

I motioned to Rio to get the door open, but that was a non-starter. He had no hand. I did it, and we all exited together. It was much colder, and the snow was dropping more heavily. There were too many other things to worry about than encountering anyone on the pathways. If it happened, I'd deal with it. We had to move now, and nothing else mattered.

'Mate, get on the back. You're gonna have to try and sit sideways, wrap your legs around her to stabilize both of you. She's still rebooting. There's fuck-all going on in her head.'

He struggled, taking a sharp breath to suppress the pain he'd just caused himself. His parka was a makeshift sling for his broken arm, but every movement must have been agony. It was about to get worse. When he was finally in position, I motioned Mary to join him on the rear bench. 'That's it, Mary. He's going to wrap his legs around you, keep you nice and safe. Come on, let's go.'

As Rio guided her into the seat with his only two functioning limbs, I climbed into the driving seat. 'Mary, why don't you lean forward a bit and wrap your arms around me? You'll feel more secure, like riding a motorbike.' I reached my right hand behind me and helped her. That was good enough. We had to get moving.

57

Negotiating the pathways carefully, I made a direct line for the exit from the village. The Phantom ate up the metres and soon we were contouring left and right up the hill. The freezing wind bit into my face and hands.

The track had had some snowfall but the bulk of it was held back by trees and foliage. A bit more weight and it would dump soon enough. I kept a steady pace going up the hill, taking the corners with care. It wasn't only Mary I had to think about keeping on board: it wouldn't take much to dislodge Rio too. I had no idea what actions were going on just behind me as she tried to reboot her brain, but Rio's voice was calm and reassuring. 'It's all right, Mary, love, no drama, yeah? I've got you, just take some of those deep breaths, eh? We're going to be there soon.'

I could have done with some of that deep breathing myself. Maybe leaving the village was as much of a wrench for me as it was for Mary. I did my best to ignore the thought, as I had done for most of the day, and then the decision was made for me. There was static white light above us to the right. I leant back. 'Nearly at the nice warm van, Mary, not long.'

My tone, I hoped, made it sound like this was a good thing we had going on here. Maybe I was trying to convince myself more than Mary.

Jack was soon directly in my headlight, silhouetted against the side of the van. Its lights were on, and the exhaust coughed out a cloud of vapour. At the top of the hill, the snow was coming down much more heavily.

I stopped about twenty short of the junction and swung the ATV to my right until it straddled the track. Any follow-up would be slowed, but not for long. I threw it into park, killed the engine, grabbed the key, and turned to Mary. 'Let's go. The van is going to be a lot warmer.'

Jack had sort of run downhill to meet us, swaying on his metal leg. I put my arm around Mary and began to coax her towards the van, not dragging her, just letting her know somebody was there to guide her.

Rio got Jack up to speed as he put his feet down onto the track. 'I'm fucked. It's fractured. Get the fuel, I'll make my own way up.'

Mary and I reached the van and I ushered her through the open side door, staying outside to give Rio more room to sort himself out. 'Lie down if you like, get comfortable. There's some snacks and yoghurt for you when you're ready.'

She collapsed on the bed, and the interior lights showed a stare that was more focused, yet still very vulnerable. It wasn't herself she was concerned about. 'Gedi? Kirill?' She went to push herself up from the mattress, and I put a hand on her shoulder. 'Gedi's okay. They're both okay. I'm sorry.'

She looked at me hard. 'I know. We forgive you.'

I almost laughed. 'Really? I don't think so.'

'You're wrong. You will always be forgiven. Remember that.'

Jack ran past me, a jerry-can in each hand. He threw them into the footwell and passenger seat of the cab, and was soon turning back downhill for the other two.

Rio was ready to embark so I moved aside, prepared to give him a push if needed. He stepped up gingerly, nursing his injured arm. He would know as well as I did that unless the ends of the break were realigned soon, he could lose circulation and, in turn, the whole limb.

Rio had broken a bone, but something had been slowly breaking inside my head. I suddenly had a feeling that I was about to fuck everything up for myself and, even worse, the other two. It was a feeling I'd never had before. My body was burning up, and my heart was pounding as if something was fighting from inside me, trying to burst out of my body.

Rio had his back to me as he manoeuvred into the space behind the driver's seat, finally easing himself round and sliding to the floor, his back against the seat for support. He smiled through the pain. 'Easy. Who needs arms, yeah?'

'I'm staying.'

The smile vanished. 'What? What you on about?'

'I'm staying here. I'm going back down.'

Rio got it the second time. 'No, no, no, no. None of that shit, mate. Get in, close the door. Come on, let's go.'

Jack ran past with the last two jerry-cans and took them straight to the front of the van. 'Vehicles – there's vehicles below. They'll be up here soon. Let's go.'

Rio shouted back as the last jerry-can was loaded. 'He wants to stay! He says he's staying!'

'What?' Jack slammed the passenger door shut and came

running round the front of the van, cutting across the headlights. 'What do you mean, staying?'

I wasn't sure if he was talking to me or Rio, but it was my eyes that his were drilling into.

'Mate, this is where I want to be. It's okay. You haven't been down there – you don't know. It's going to be okay.'

Down in the valley, I could just make out the revving of ATVs.

'Listen, Jack, I'll run into them on the track, stall them. Take my cash. I'm through. I'm going.'

Jack took the remaining couple of steps to the sliding door and launched his head towards my face. I jerked back but his forehead connected, and I stumbled forwards onto the snow. The next thing I knew, he was kicking into me.

'Get in the fucking van!'

He might not have had his full complement of legs, but he was a big unit. He hauled me off my hands and knees and pushed me into the van. Immediately, Rio's legs gripped me like a vice. He cried out in pain and Mary screamed to join in the chaos.

I heard the sliding door slam shut and then the van lurched as Jack jumped into the driver's seat, the door closed, and the engine revved up.

Jack yelled out at no one but himself, 'Stay? I'm going to stay? Fuck sake, you dickhead!'

58

Straight away we were moving.

I stopped the struggle. My head was still spinning, and they were right: now wasn't the time to fuck about with the plan. We still had a job to do. Me bailing out would have put their lives at risk, and I was never going to do that. I hadn't been thinking straight. I had to clear my head, set my priorities. I needed to get this job done, and fulfil my responsibilities to the other two, and only then could I think about sorting out my own shit.

My back was against the bed, with Mary above me and Rio over to my left, his back still against the driver's seat. Jack drove slower than we would have liked in the snow. He was the only one with a clear head as he kept rigid focus through the windscreen, past the wipers thrashing backwards and forwards and into the tunnel the headlights carved through the snowfall. I looked up and forward as Jack jerked the wheel left and right to avoid potholes that would be increasingly hard to spot, and wasn't always successful. Each time a wheel lurched into one, the pile of crockery in the sink rattled and clanked and Rio shouted different versions of 'You fucker!'

Jack yelled louder than he needed to at me. 'Listen in, dickhead. Enough of that woo-woo shit. Get it all sorted out after the job. Get on the mobile and call us in. It's going to take longer than thirty in this . . . maybe forty.'

I shouted back. 'On it.' My hand went into my parka and I retrieved the iPhone, warm in the knowledge that in our world a head-butting was a sign of affection.

The Owl answered on the first ring.

'We're on our way. We got Mary, and it's going to take longer, about four-zero.'

The Owl wasn't fussed one way or the other. Thirty or forty minutes, what did he care? 'Mary?'

'She's good.'

He closed down.

I shrugged at Rio. Even with his pain to think about, he was still trying to process what had happened. 'Oi, Your Holiness. What the fuck was that all about?'

I didn't answer immediately.

He took a gasp of breath as we jolted into another pothole.

Mary looked at him, concerned. 'We've got to do something. Is there a first-aid kit in here?' Her feet hit the floor to my right.

'Mary?' I pointed at the rear window, which was covered. 'While you're up, can you open that curtain?'

Rio would be in a good position to have eyes on any white light following us up in the darkness.

Mary moved it aside and was soon throwing open drawers and cupboards.

I got back to Rio and Jack. 'Lads – I'm sorry. I fucked up. It was just something that came over me, a feeling. I don't know what I was thinking. I won't let you down again.'

Jack shouted, 'You said to grip you if you became an

arsehole. You became an arsehole. You got gripped. Let's move on.'

Mary had found a small green plastic first-aid box. She knelt by Rio and opened it. I could see a traditional collection of bandages and general first-aid shit. She seemed to know what she was doing. Positioning a triangular bandage under the arrangement of salad servers and duct tape, she tied the ends carefully around his neck so the broken limb was supported in the sling, then unpacked a couple of crêpe bandages and wrapped them around his upper arm and torso for extra stability. Rio looked like a mummy and could no longer help himself, so she had to put two painkillers in his mouth, then another two because Rio wanted more. She held a bottle of water to his lips while he drank, before attempting to wipe the blood away from his face.

I pushed myself up from the floor and got onto the bed. Mary gave me a pack of gauze to sort out my nose, which felt five times bigger and was leaking. I'd have expected her to be more frightened and confused than she was, certainly after the seizure, but she was composed, not exactly happy, but certainly not scared. Maybe, now rebooted, she realized we didn't present a danger to her.

'What happens to me now, Nick?'

'We're going to hand you over to some people, who are then going to take you to Oslo for your treatment – your deprogramming – then back to LA.' My eyes were on the rear window but all I could see was the gentle glow of the van's lights turning the snow near them red. No white light chasing us – yet.

Hearing about the next stage of her drama didn't freak her out. When I looked back at her, she was smiling.

'Nick, you're right, I will be back. What I have in here' – her still gloved hand went to her heart, just as Cameron's had done – 'can't be deprogrammed. They can't delete it. All they will do is make it stronger.'

I nodded. I believed her. 'Just play the game, nod and agree with anything they say. Once you get back to LA, you're free. Yeah?'

She kept her hand on her heart as she gave a slow nod of understanding. 'You know what, Nick? I think you have it in your heart, too. That's why you wanted to stay. Your head had no part in what happened earlier. It was your heart speaking to you. Money and emotions are confusing you as they fight for control. But that's a good thing.'

I shrugged. She might have a point. 'Maybe.'

Jack cut the silence that followed. 'Two minutes.'

59

I craned my neck to look ahead, and Rio shuffled himself so he could do the same. The headlights swept through the car park, illuminating two identical vehicles and beyond them a boat in the harbour, light seeping through the cabin hatches. The two Shoguns should have been white, but they were covered with grime. The windscreens were just two half-moons. There was movement at the Shoguns as the occupants of one climbed out.

Jack brought the van to a stop and I yanked on the sliding door. I checked the bodies moving towards us, and jumped out. There were four, and as they got closer, I could make out two women, two bouncers.

The guy with a beard had a US accent. 'You being followed?'

'Possibly.'

'Okay. We need to move this on.'

The two men turned back towards the Shoguns but the two women kept walking. 'Mary?' Also American.

I jerked my head at the van.

'Hello, Mary.'

I turned, and she was smiling at them. No hint of fear. She almost seemed to be enjoying herself, knowing all this was a waste of time. She'd be back to marry in the spring.

'Hello.'

One of the Shoguns crunched over the snow and drove out of the car park, back towards the village.

The woman talking to Mary sounded caring but firm. 'Mary, can you tell me your full name?'

She complied.

'Thank you. And your date of birth?'

'April fourth, 1998.'

'Thank you. And your parents' names?'

'Michelle and Tripp Gaskell.'

'Thank you, Mary. Do you have your medications with you?'

She nodded.

'Thank you. Will you please now come with us?'

'Sure.' She slid off the bed and said her goodbyes to the other two, before stopping next to me.

'Don't worry, Nick. It'll be fine. Remember, I forgive you – and they will, too. Who knows? I might even see you in the village and you can tell them yourself.'

She walked unaided with her inquisitor towards the quayside, where the boat's mast lights swayed from side to side. I felt relief that all that mattered now was getting Rio to Tromsø to have that arm sorted. Then that feeling was swamped by an almost overwhelming sense of loss.

The other woman had stayed, and waited until Mary was out of earshot. 'Our boss wants you on the boat with her.' She spoke firmly, and it was clear I was being told, not asked. Jack would have to get Rio to Tromsø on his own.

I tried to look for positives. One was that maybe I'd get to see Mary walk away from Oslo and return down the hill. 'Okay, give me a minute.'

'You have to hurry, Nick. It could be unsafe here. Think of Mary.'

I jumped into the van and grabbed the yoghurt with a couple of protein bars. 'Lads, you heard it. No problem.'

As I spoke, I pulled out my Samsung and gave the cut-throat sign with the other hand.

'You two just get that arm sorted, then back to the plan. I'll see you in the UK.'

They looked at me and nodded.

'And, lads – again, sorry. I fucked up.'

Rio was first on it. 'Yeah, we know. What makes it worse is soppy bollocks here had all the fun, know what I mean?'

I couldn't do anything but agree as I slipped out of the van. 'See you in Tulse Hill.'

I slid the door shut. Jack immediately found first gear and the wheels rolled. Soon their lights had disappeared, heading south, and all that was left was the second Shogun, engine ticking over, no lights. I couldn't see who was inside.

At the edge of the stone quayside I tossed the Samsung into the water. That had been the plan. Once we started moving – what was the point in splitting up if we still had comms?

A body was waiting on the side of the large fishing boat, hand outstretched.

'Hello! Hello! Welcome!'

Grisha gripped my wrist for me to scramble aboard.

'Hello, mate. You get about, don't you?'

The mega-smile got even wider. 'Please, follow me.'

We went forward.

'Where's Mary?'

He looked back without breaking step. 'She's below. She is safe. Come, please – this way.'

Grisha ushered me into the wheelhouse, but stayed on deck, closing the door behind me. I was hit by a wall of heat. US-accented radio traffic hummed low from a wall speaker next to the steel wheel and instrument panel.

'Sit down, Nick.'

I spun round. The Owl was on one of the bulkhead benches that formed the seating for a table in the right-hand corner of the wheelhouse. He was nursing a mug of something in one hand and pushing his hair back with the other. He looked absolutely done in. He'd had just as busy a time of it as us.

That said, he didn't look as fucked as I knew I was about to be – why else would he be there?

60

'Where's Mary? She okay?'

The Owl gave a dismissive wave of his hand, half of it hidden by parka sleeve. His Canada Goose was box-fresh, a couple of sizes too big, and probably on its one and only outing. 'She's been sedated. She needs to rest before it all starts for her tomorrow.' His eyes narrowed. 'But unfortunately, Nick, not with you. That part of your life is over. It's been a success, you've been paid – so now it's done.'

I didn't bite. From the look on his face, the explanation was on its way as to why he wanted me on board.

'It's not going to work, you know, deprogramming. She'll be back.'

Another wave of the hand. 'She'll want to, but that simply isn't going to happen. For her and you, that's all done.' He tapped the tabletop. 'Come, sit.'

I unzipped my parka and joined him, inhaling the coffee vapour coming off his mug.

He pointed at my face, still swelling from the head-butt. 'Another little boating accident?'

I nodded as he gave himself a pat on the back for his funny.

'Mary's safe – so now it's my turn.'

Stupid of me to have thought I couldn't feel any worse than I already did.

'The dial is about to turn up on the Cold War. Things are going to get hotter than we could ever have expected. We have to prepare for it. We have to *pre-empt* it. It looks like the old-guard baby boomers . . .' he pointed over his shoulder in the direction of Russia '. . . well, one of them for sure, they want their last stand-off, and whatever it is, it won't end well. Never does, does it?'

Now wasn't the time to engage. I didn't know what he wanted from me but it felt worse than just going back in to carry out a recce. But did I care? I was finished: no more of this shit for me. I didn't say so. It needed to stay in my head for now. I decided just to listen. It's always a bad move to bare your neck to a wolf.

'Putin and his circle, they have a sense that time is running out for them to fulfil their destiny, to restore the Motherland's greatness. Forgive the history lesson, Nick, but I like to keep reminding myself I'm on the side of right.

'We forget how personally Putin took it when the USSR collapsed, as bad as Hitler did after Germany's defeat in 1918. The Kremlin's still convinced the West wants to keep Russia down and drive them out of power.' A flicker of a smile. 'Mind you, that's kind of true. We have the same generation of post-war babies, white-haired white guys in their matching grey suits trying to do exactly that. Our guys like to claim some kinda moral leadership of the world rather than bringing back the good old days.'

He studied his coffee mug, like looking thoughtful was part of his sales pitch. 'The problem we have, Nick, is we've got two opposing systems, and both of them are dysfunctional organizations. Their decisions are . . . insular. It's not a good mix, Nick – certainly if you want to mow your lawn without manoeuvring round bomb craters.

'But on the good side of crap, Nick, they're all going to die soon. Maybe our right wing takes the Capitol, or some of their guys take the Kremlin, before they pass their sell-by. However it happens, we can only hope the next generation will do a better job. But until then, we have to fight to contain both sides. We must keep the lid on dysfunction.' He jerked his thumb at Russia again. 'Our leadership-analysis team, they know something's going on over there but that's the problem – understanding what they plan to do next. That's not an easy gig. But whatever it is, it won't be good. It never is.'

He sat back and extended his hands to me as if I was part of the conversation, then ploughed on regardless. 'That's the challenge, Nick: understanding what's happening in Russia, understanding what the next move is going to be. Are we looking at a conventional confrontation – is he going to move in to take, say, Estonia or Lithuania, NATO countries, but reasoning that we're not going to back them? Between you and me, Nick, the political climate at home makes me wonder. Small nations, would we start a Third World War just to stop regime change? It wouldn't be the first time we'd stepped back from international agreements. But if we support, we have craters on our lawns. You get what I'm saying?'

I didn't understand why he always ended with a question he didn't want the answer to.

'There's a lot of dark matter out there, Nick. And governments – well, they're just too ridiculous to solve these problems. Hell, they made them. It's up to us to solve them for our own sakes – everyone's sakes, I guess.'

He lifted his mug in both hands as if to take a mouthful, but stalled. Grisha had come back into the wheelhouse and The Owl raised his voice for him to hear. 'This guy here's been working on the operation for a year.'

Grisha grinned as he took the last few steps to the wheel. 'Sixteen months, Sam, sixteen months.' He did some boat stuff with the radar and controls, then peered out at the snowfall. The water was about to get even deeper, I thought, just like the shit I felt myself sinking into.

The Owl lowered his voice and got back into it. 'Say it's not going to be conventional, localized action in Europe. What if he's planning a big cyber-attack? Closing down our critical IT? Maybe cutting the data cables. Can you imagine if the New York and London stock exchanges stopped trading? It could be our cyber Pearl Harbor, Nick.

'Direct conflict with Putin – what do you think? What would China, Iran, North Korea think about that? Maybe a conventional hit like Estonia would be a better option for us all, keep it contained kinda thing.' He let it hang, and then he had another idea. 'Hey, Grisha – you got some coffee for our friend here?'

Grisha was busy scanning the inky blackness outside as the engines throbbed below us. He didn't turn round. 'Coming up. You take sugar, Nick? No milk, sorry.'

'That'd be good.'

The heavy anchor chain rattled as Grisha got on the radio.

An American accent monotoned back. 'Roger D. We need ten minutes' warning.'

Grisha signed off and played about inside a fifty-litre daysack before dragging out the world's biggest Thermos. The traffic was one of the Shoguns, and it sounded like they were standing off the car park, waiting for their ten-minute warning to go back there and clear it in case of a follow-up from the village.

This wasn't good. It meant that the boat was going back.

Grisha filled two plastic mugs and hit all the lights. All that was left was a gentle glow from the orange and red LEDs of the instruments as he passed me one of the mugs with a spoon in it.

It was then, as the boat swayed gently from side to side, that The Owl announced what he had in mind for me.

'What it all boils down to, Nick, is that you have to kill the person at the centre of all this. You have to kill Matvey.'

61

'What the fuck, *Sam*?'

I hit his name hard in some sort of stab at sarcasm, but if he heard it, my protest went straight over The Owl's head. 'Because Grisha and I don't want bomb craters on our lawns – and you shouldn't either, *Nick*.'

He let that rest awhile.

'It's the Zero-Day problem. There's a cyber arms race out there and Russia's getting far too many from Matvey. That bastard is giving Russia God-like access to our critical civil and defence infrastructure. Unacceptable. You know what unacceptable means, Nick, and you know the remedy. Kill him, make it look internal, same as with Isar. I've got to tell you, Nick, I'm not a fan of this guy.'

I knew what I wanted to say, but now wasn't the time to say it. I could think it. I just needed to make sure he couldn't read it.

'So none of this was ever about Mary? You set her up?'

All I got was a slow shake of the head.

'She was happy in the village, and you know it. I know

why she was happy. I know why she left her fucked-up life for all of them down there. They've got their lives squared away. You saying Mary wasn't a set-up?'

The Owl shook his head again but then he smiled into his mug. 'Just you, Nick. Her meeting the Austrian guy was too good an opportunity to pass up. But you know what? I'm a little disappointed in you. I didn't have you down as a happy-clappy kinda guy. I told you it was easy to get dragged in, didn't I?'

Tapping a few keys on his iPhone, he looked up at Grisha and caught his eye. 'I told him it could happen to anyone – the more confident you are that you won't succumb, the easier it is for them to suck you in. It's happened to him before, when he was a teenager, but he likes to ignore that truth.' He looked down. 'Ah – here it is.' He hit the speaker button and up came the rant in the van about me wanting to go back down to the village and Jack head-butting me.

Grisha liked what he heard. He pointed at my nose. 'Quite an evening, then, Nick?'

The Owl was right, of course. I'd been sucked into the military cult at the age of sixteen, and then was too scared to get out. All those persuasive techniques: I'd been gripped. I'd been in the military cult, I'd come out into a private military world cult, and I was even now in a cult working for The Owl. My cult had groomed me well. Now that I'd finally decided to make the leap to freedom, I couldn't.

His eyes reverted to me. 'You've only got yourself to blame, Nick. All I wanted was some pictures of Matvey and a recce of the IT centre to get more information, his contacts, that kinda thing. He would be killed at some stage once we knew more. It's you who pushed events along. We've got our own escalation going on here. You've created this situation yourself by wanting to join them.' He pursed his lips, maybe thinking I'd really believe that. 'But now Grisha gets to go home earlier. So, in the round, it's kinda worked out neat, don't you think?'

He sounded very pleased with himself. A hint of the mattress salesman's smile crossed his face as he took a swig of coffee, but it disappeared just as fast. He lowered his voice. 'So, Nick, kill him. It has to be now, and it has to be you. No one else can get here before the snow. And it goes without saying, it has to be deniable.'

Straight to the money shot. No qualifiers, like 'try to' or 'see if you can'.

'You're getting rid of him because you don't like his asking price for Zero Days? Is that it?'

His face was impassive. 'It's not at all like Isar. Matvey is not a middleman. As for asking prices, the fact is, we'd very much like to buy anything he has, but we can't. He doesn't want to sell it to us. Everything he does is for his own country. He supplies a well-stocked attack platform and it's aimed at us. The Russians buy it, but they don't pay fortunes. Didn't you ask yourself how come the village is straight out of *Homes & Gardens*? The Kremlin let him make as much money as he wants from the West, from hacks, ransomware and such, but it's the Zero Days, Nick, that's the issue, as long as he doesn't play his games in Russia – and his Zero Days stay in-country. Why do you think Matvey's never had a picture taken, never crossed the bridge to Norway? Come on, Nick – you really think it's the Sunday collection plate that's paying for all that down there?'

It was starting to make sense, and I was getting pissed off. 'So God's Word on Earth isn't real? It's actually a front to make money and Matvey's running it?'

'Correct. It's a front, cover, protection, whatever you want to call it. It's fake.'

I didn't believe him. Or, more precisely, I didn't want to believe him. But, then, I wouldn't, would I, if I'd been sucked in by Saynab's sales patter? Maybe I was one of those stupid people who thought they were too smart to be converted. It had happened to me before, so why not now? 'I need more. How do you know all this?'

The Owl lifted his coffee, which must have been cold by now. He took one sip and put it down again. It was Grisha who answered. He leant in closer, like he was sharing a playground secret. 'Because he is Snuggly Bear.'

'The daycare centre?'

Grisha nodded. 'Cosy, Fancy, Sunny, they love those names. He's having fun with it.'

He stared across the table at The Owl as if I wasn't there. 'I still like Shadow Brokers – that's a really cool name, better than all this bear talk. Gives bears a bad name.'

Grisha liked his joke and The Owl smiled patiently, like he'd heard it before. I was starting to experience a feeling I didn't like. It was much too close to the one I'd had at the top of the track. 'Fuck the bears. Who are you two?'

The Owl exchanged a glance with Grisha. This was between those two. 'Nick, a good question, one I ask myself. In this one, think of me as the real world's No News Guy. No news, especially no bad news, is good news. Am I right?'

He wanted a reply from me but all I wanted was for him to get on with it.

'So, Nick, what I have done, with the help of Grisha for the last year, is provide no news.'

Grisha liked that, but for one detail. 'Last sixteen months.'

'Think of me as the bridge between the CIA and the

NSA – and that includes your GCHQ guys. These people don't like *any* news about them. They like no news. So, I get the tasks from them to stop anything that may become news concerning them, and then task guys like you. I tried to have Matvey hit in 'seventeen, in St Petersburg, but got the wrong guy.

'Grisha's here to make sure I get the right target this time, the right Matvey. Now we've pinpointed him, you will do the defence-in-depth work by killing him. So, there's no news about any cyber-weapons race, Zero Days, nothing to worry real people. It's neat, don't you think?'

Even in what little light there was in the wheelhouse he must have seen I didn't think it was neat at all. 'Nick, I get it. You've fallen for the spiel down there. The guy's smart. He knows how to push people's buttons. Grisha has seen his converts come and go, and the fact is, there's no way of knowing how he uses his villagers who go round the planet. Are they going out to work on his attacks in Europe, in the US? Who knows? But we must stop it. We must de-escalate the situation. We must kill Matvey.'

Grisha leant in once more. '"You may not be interested in war, but war is interested in you." You know who said that?'

He didn't wait for me to supply my guess as he got off the bench and headed back to the wheel. 'Leon Trotsky. There's a man who knew the world.'

62

As the anchor clanked its way up from the seabed, The Owl put his hands together, almost in prayer. 'We're bonded, Nick. We're fighting the same bad guys, and today it's Snuggly Bear, selling Zero-Day exploits exclusively to the Russians. You understand that?' He didn't wait to find out. 'That's why the village looks like an upscale ski resort and the nuts-and-bolts side of it is in Russia. This guy's been making a fortune. He's been hacking the Pentagon, NSA and GCHQ since 2016.

'Thanks in large part to his efforts, the Kremlin have played with the US elections, the UK Brexit vote, and have been adding to their cyber-weapons stockpile week by week. Thanks to Matvey, Putin keeps getting all the keys to our kingdom – the codes, the algorithms, you name it – and that has to stop. We're heading into dangerous times, Nick. We need the keys to the kingdom back before whatever they're planning on the other side of this inlet kicks off.'

I felt like I was burning up. My heart pounded as if something was fighting inside me to burst out of my chest. I knew what it was, but the result here wouldn't be a head-butt and a move on. The water I could disappear into was very, very deep.

Even in the gloom, he could spot there was something wrong. 'Nick, are you still with us? You do understand, don't you?'

The throb of the engines wasn't the only noise in my head. Unfortunately, I was still very much with him, but I couldn't stop the war zone in my chest. At the same time, all the electricity in my head was trying to burst out through my skull. Instead, it came out of my mouth.

'I'm not doing it.'

I waited for the explosion, but it didn't come. No shock, no surprise, just a pause as if they were waiting for me to carry on.

'I'm not going to do it. I'm not going to kill Matvey.'

The Owl blanked it. 'What I was thinking was that maybe you would kill him by suicide. Maybe the aggrieved villager – an avenger, even better, since Matvey is a fake prophet – or something to do with Mary. Now you've rescued her, your anger has taken over and you want the cult leader dead to save others, kind of thing. They know nothing about you that's traceable. Would that work for you?'

The boat swayed. We were on the move.

'I said I'm not doing it.'

Still no blowback. I felt a huge release, but there had to be consequences.

He steepled his fingers again. 'Nick, that condition of yours, whatever it is. Our guys reckon it's Parkinson's. Whatever, you don't have that long as a more or less fully functioning operator, do you? I mean, you might have years, let's hope you do, but you're not going to like just waiting to die, are you? There's a market for people like you in our world – you helped create it. People like you who've got no hope, and need to be compensated for being dead. A sort of Dignitas for your kinda guys. You know it works. You proved it in France.'

Of course, he knew I was ill. Why wouldn't he? What the fuck didn't he know?

'So, Nick, I was thinking, why not use your illness for good? Just like Gabriel. Don't waste it – don't waste away your final months. Matvey is your bad guy too. He is helping to disable the West, so don't you want to do your bit to stop that?'

What he didn't know was that I had been shown there was a glimmer of hope for me in the village. And there still was a chance of me experiencing peace. 'I'm not doing it.'

He wouldn't stop. 'Okay, Nick, I understand. I understand why you feel that way. He's got you – he's got your mind. Anything I say will be attacking what he's already planted in your head. I understand that. You need deprogramming, but there's not enough time for that. So, let's make this personal to get that head space of yours back into the real world. Just like Gabe, when you die, no matter how, you're going to leave people behind. There'll only be two of your crew left once you've gone, and you want the best for them, don't you? Like any family. They are your family, am I right?'

I knew what was coming, and I almost couldn't breathe. I didn't want to hear any more.

'Yeah, yeah, I get it. If I don't do the job, you're not going to use them, no more work, no more anything.'

I was totally on the wrong track. The Owl uncoupled his hands and shook a finger. 'No, no, no, Nick. Nothing as petulant as that.' He paused. I waited, and as I did, I knew that what he was about to say would press down hard on my shoulders.

'If you don't do this work for me, Nick, they become loose ends. I can't do anything with them and it'll be your fault.'

And there it was: two death sentences.

The words fired out of my mouth without filters. 'Sam, you're a cunt.'

He sat back and rubbed his face to try to get some human into it. 'Nick, you're not the only one with a personal – let's call it an emotional – connection to this situation. I want you to understand that this is very important to me, and why you will carry out this one last task. You get the Matvey problem, we all do. That wasn't enough for you, so here it is. Matvey's Zero-Day exploits killed my mother.'

The conversation he'd had with Tripp. Covid hit her.

'She was waiting for a ventilator. If the hospitals hadn't been attacked, if they hadn't been using pen and paper to move people and get people in place, she would have been in the system and taken straight to where she needed to be. So, you see, Nick, I want payback. This is my back-atcha moment. I will do anything to achieve it, and as we all know, Nick, shit rolls downhill.'

Grisha reappeared with the daysack in his hands. He placed it on the table with a metallic clunk. 'Better to die on your feet, my friend, than live on your knees.'

The Owl leant in. 'You have the means to kill him – make sure he's dead and make sure it looks good.' He held out his palm. 'Take the bag, Nick. And give me the iPhone. You don't need it any more.'

I had a bigger concern than a phone handover. 'What if I fuck up? What if he lives, and I die? The deal is still the same for the other two?'

'Of course. All I can do is let you loose. I trust you because they are all you have.'

I put the iPhone into his hands as if it was sealing the deal, before pulling the daysack across the table and reaching inside. The moment my hand closed round the first hard object I knew what it was. Out came a Russian-designed RGN hand grenade, and then another. Next out was a Ukrainian-made Fort 14 semi-automatic pistol with three mags and, finally, an Ikea freezer bag of loose rounds. I couldn't help myself: I split the pins holding the grenades' handles in place even further apart than the factory default. Once the pin comes out and the handle is pushed away by a spring, these things would detonate as soon as they made contact with anything solid, including snow and water, or after a delay of four seconds. With a killing area of six metres, that was the last thing I wanted to happen as they bounced around in the daysack.

I then set about loading the twelve-round mags. The Owl pointed at the pistol, which looked much the same as any other 9mm semi-automatic. I had never been a weapons geek. If it went bang when you pulled the trigger and the round went where you wanted it to, that was enough for me. A weapon could be a hundred years old, but if it was capable of those two details it would still kill.

'It's all deniable – the war.'

The well-worn Fort 14 had probably been used to shoot at Russians in the Donbas, but the RGNs could have come from either side. They were manufactured and used by both.

Grisha came over, shoved the Thermos into the daysack and grinned. 'It's going to be a long night for you, my friend.'

PART SIX

63

Day Four: Monday, 11 October 2021

I only stopped running when I reached the junction where the road met the track down to the village. Hiding in the tree-line, bent over, hands on my thighs, I gulped in air, trying to slow my heart rate. Snow gathered on the daysack at my feet. My parka was secured inside it, along with the RGNs, and the Fort was in my waistband, spare mags in my front pockets. I wasn't expecting to have to use it at this stage but what a dick I would have been if I'd needed it and the thing was stowed in my parka.

As predicted, the Shogun had driven back to secure the harbour area for the boat to come in and throw me ashore. Even before I'd got from the quayside to the road, the lights of the boat had swung round as it pushed out of the harbour, soon extinguishing altogether as they reached the open sea, destination Vardø. From there it would be a flight to Oslo for Mary. It was done.

I'd followed the tyre tracks all the way down to the

junction. With no wind, the snowfall was settling in them fast. That was a good thing, but at the same time some wind would have helped to keep the noise down as my feet crunched in the snow and I breathed like a warthog.

I had passed the Shogun's handiwork on the road to stop any ATV follow-up. The snow had been churned up in a frenzy and the reason why made me move into the treeline to get past. Handfuls of tyre spikes had been scattered like confetti from the Shogun to deter followers. I picked one up. These three-centimetre triangular stars were designed to take out tyres, like a police Stinger system. Landowners used them to deter poachers, and they'd certainly done the job here. The whole area had been rotovated as the Phantoms' tyres had burst or deflated, and wheels had spun uncontrollably as the drivers fought to turn the vehicles round and nurse them back towards the hill.

With my breath near normal and the sweat on my back starting to chill, I lifted the daysack's top flap and retrieved my parka. A quick shake to get some air into the flattened goose down and it was back on, preventing what was left of my body heat from escaping.

I was back in work mode, my boots crunching methodically and mechanically into the snow as I followed the contours of the hill downwards. I had to be over the bridge and hidden in the Russia treeline before first light. Using the bridge wouldn't be secure, but what were my options?

The snow was dumping more heavily, finally penetrating the tree cover, and darkness engulfed me. It wasn't just the sense of fuck-it to everything that had taken hold. What I truly understood now was what Gabe must also have felt: the feeling of wanting to get it over with, while at least leaving some benefit in my wake. I didn't care about The Owl keeping a lid on the world order or stopping any escalation with the old grey guys on the other side of the inlet so they wouldn't fuck up his lawn. Quite frankly, he was lucky to have a lawn. I didn't care if he was lying about Matvey or not. I didn't even care if the entire village was a lie. Fake or not, it had shown me there was another way, that no matter how fucked up my past was, I was nearly there, nearly able to take the last step and embrace it. It didn't make me angry to know that a better life than the one I'd had up until now was out there for me yet I would never be able to grab it. The feeling was more of relief: that I was getting all this Elvis bollocks over and done with. I didn't need to sign up for training at the Paradise Facility: all I had to do was give Matvey a big hug with a RGN in each hand and go out with a bang – literally.

The only reason I was totally focused on the job and switched off to everything else was because I wanted the only two people remaining in my life to be left alone, and to be left with some control of when they got dead, not have it decided by somebody like The Owl. Back in Tulse Hill, I had promised them I'd never do anything to put them in danger. I'd already failed in that promise once by not wanting to get into the van, but not this time.

Twenty minutes of downhill got me just short of the entrance to the village, and I moved into the treeline, roughly in the area where Rio had waited for me. The village was awake. Lights were on in the buildings, and bodies moved from building to building, most of the foot traffic being in and out of the dining hall. It didn't take long for a wheelchair to emerge from its doors, helped along by Elaine. Cameron was right: I was dim, not that smart at all really, or I wouldn't be tucked up under this tree in the dark watching him like a stalker.

Inside there would be hot drinks and food laid out and lots of group hugs happening for sure, as they tried to make sense of the night's events. Mary was gone, abducted by Nick – with violence. They would be asking themselves why, and they weren't the only ones.

And then, to make the situation worse, Saynab and Poppy materialized from the gloom. They stopped and hugged and talked with Elaine and Cameron. Snow gathered on their beanies and shoulders as Poppy hugged into her mother's stomach and Saynab, in turn, comforted the child.

I wanted to start moving to avoid seeing this, get on with what I was there for, but I couldn't. Were they talking about being betrayed by me? Did they feel like I expected Kirill did right now, wanting to get his massive tattooed hands around my neck?

I couldn't pull myself away from under the tree as the four of them talked and more snow drove down. What if they weren't wanting to wring my neck? What if they really cared about me as well as Mary, Gedi and Kirill? What if they really did forgive?

Fuck – this has to stop. You have to cut away.

I looped the village, trying to circumnavigate my way to the bridge. I had a job to do. That should have been the only thing that was in my head. But it wasn't, and now I had guilt fighting for dominance over the feeling of relief that it would soon be over. I didn't care which won the fight because they both served the same purpose.

64

The snow was nearly knee deep, even in the treeline where I kept to minimize sign.

My thoughts turned to Saynab and Poppy, Elaine and Cameron. What was going to happen to them, post-Matvey, if the community didn't survive? If they had to accept the whole thing had been a charade, how did they get on with their lives? Would they need deprogramming too? Or did they fade away, disillusioned, with nowhere to go, no dream left? Without the support of the others, did Elaine and Cameron go back to Scotland and he die slowly and painfully, throwing away two grand a week for the privilege of watching the traffic drive past his nursing home?

Guilt was winning out, and I decided I liked relief better.

If the people in the village truly believed, they would start afresh, set up somewhere else, find a way to carry on. Maybe another benefactor would come to the rescue, only this time someone who wasn't working out how to close down the West's IT systems. Or, the most unfeasible thought of all, life just went on in the village. That made the guilt pull back a little.

And then something else took over, and I found myself looking forward to the relief that it was all about to end.

Fuck it, everything was far too confusing. I'd just concentrate on putting one foot in front of the other.

Dead ahead, the rush of the Jakobselv was almost deafening. Twenty or so more strides and it was clear why. The river was working overtime, taking the snow downstream towards the bridge, the current crashing over rocks scattered the whole twenty metres to the other side. I swung left to follow the flow down towards the village, looking at the whitecaps where rocks tried their hardest to keep their peaks above the water surging towards the sea.

The closer I got to the village, the more sign I was crunching into the snow. On the plus side, I could soon see the lights of the bridge illuminating the route across the water into Russia.

I'd been hoping to find the village in lockdown after Mary's abduction, no one about, but that wasn't the case. Every few seconds, two or three bodies crossed the low half-lights of the bridge, going into Russia or coming back into Norway. Maybe Matvey had organized patrols. Beyond the bridge, the lights were on in the two-storey church. Maybe the villagers had been summoned for an emergency meeting, or to huddle together while they waited the day or two it would take for outside help to arrive. Whatever, a decision had been made for me. I couldn't use the bridge. It simply wasn't worth the risk of compromise. I turned back.

I scanned the darkness, tried to find a safe place to cross. Wherever I chose, it was going to be a major drama. If I'd doubted the strength of the current I had only to look at the size of the whitecaps where water sluiced over the top of the rocks . . . and there was no way of telling how deep it was.

The quickest and safest crossing point into Russia was going to have to be where the whitecaps were closest together and stretched the full twenty metres. Finally, I checked along the opposite bank, following the current to my left, trying to work out where I might end up. It was futile. The current would be in charge, not me.

My eye traced a route, and from that moment there was no time to lose. Tearing off my parka, I spread it out on the snow. The inside pocket was stuffed with blister packs of Rasagiline. I grabbed handfuls and threw them into the river, because I wanted it registered in my head that crossing this thing was the start line, the start of the job with no return. I almost laughed when I realized there were going to be some fish with very steady fins swimming about very soon.

As soon as my fleece was off, the cold bit into me. But once committed, I had no choice. The weight of trapped water in clothing can slow you down, then drown you even before they become saturated and therefore useless once on the other side. As if to underline the point, just feet away the water crashed angrily against the rocks.

I ripped off the rest of my clothes and dumped them on the parka. The Fort and mags went into its pockets before I wrapped it up into a bundle and crammed it into the daysack. My boots followed, and I secured the top flap. The quicker I could complete the job cold, the quicker I could start to get my body heat back. It was all about keeping those clothes dry, ready for the job the other side. All I could do was take the pain, then get to the other bank, get that dry kit back on as soon as I could, and Grisha's coffee in me before I went down with Russian hypothermia.

I took my first steps into the water.

65

It was even colder than I'd been expecting, but I told my brain the cold was just signals telling my body to feel the numbness in my feet. The freezing sensation climbed up my body as I took another step into the torrent, the daysack up in the air. Soon I was shin deep, and the weight of water was already almost too strong to resist.

The first big rock that I might be able to use as a support was a metre ahead. I lifted the daysack onto my shoulder and steadied it with my neoprene hand. My good one was needed to counterbalance and steady myself, while I did my best to lean into the current and keep stable. I braced myself for the next bound.

The sanctuary of the next rock was another metre or so ahead, but the water was deeper, the weight of the current stronger. My toes tried to grip into the riverbed but I had lost all sensation in them. This was no longer about avoiding compromise: it was about avoiding hypothermia. I had to speed up.

My lead foot hit a submerged rock that I tried to use as a hold, something stable to push down on, but then it happened. A combination of bad footing and the current, and I was over.

Reflexively, my hands stretched out, but the water caught the daysack. My neoprene hand couldn't grip it sufficiently, and my left flailed to make better contact, but the bag was lost in a second, shooting downstream. I pushed my head up and over the current, scanning the darkness, hoping to see its shape snagged on one of the rocks. But the sheer weight of water had won. It was bouncing its way towards the sea.

No time to think about that. It was done.

Not a single therm of body heat could be wasted now. I had to get out of the water before it killed me. I had to get body warmth back.

I kicked and thrashed to keep afloat and make some progress towards the opposite bank, but the surge was dragging me under. I kicked back up to the surface, forcing myself to breathe in through my nose, only to choke as I took down yet more icy water, but only for a moment. Then the water dragged me under again. As I came up, fighting for air, I looked, but saw nothing in the torrent.

I was in fast-flowing water, tons of it, tearing at my legs, threatening to throw me off balance again.

I was dragged back down and inhaled more river, but this time, as I scrabbled my way to the surface, the current had carried me almost to the far bank. It wasn't weakening, though. The river curved there, and I was on the outside of the bend, where the force of the water was at its fiercest. An eddy caught me and threw me against the bank. I flung out my hands, trying to grasp at anything I could.

I forced my eyes open again but they stung too much. Thrashing around blindly, my left hand connected with something solid. I made a grab, but whatever it was gave way. The next thing I knew, my right arm had hooked into a root. The current swung me round, pressed me against the bank, and my feet touched the riverbed. I clung to the root and took a series of deep breaths.

I struggled against the weight of water until I could reach out with my free hand and grab another root higher up the bank. I hauled myself up until only my legs were left in the water.

Suddenly I was lying on the bank, chest heaving. As soon as some strength returned to my limbs, I rolled onto all fours, then staggered to my feet.

I had hit the bank maybe fifteen short of the bridge. I could do nothing but run towards it for cover, my legs trying to recover from the numbness, my head shaking uncontrollably. I took in deep breaths, trying to calm down, trying to get oxygen into my body, telling myself the cold wasn't real, but my body was telling me otherwise.

I fell onto my knees just below the bridge, as a couple of concerned male voices drifted over towards Russia. I took really deep breaths trying not to cough, trying not to wheeze, trying not to make any noise breathing, trying to control it, and trying to keep quiet. I wanted these people to get out of the way. But it wasn't enough creating body heat by moving: I had no clothing so I had no way of holding it. I needed shelter, and I needed heat.

The body has a thermostat, located in a small piece of nerve tissue at the base of the brain, which controls the production or dissipation of heat and monitors all parts of the body in order to maintain a constant temperature.

When the body starts to go into hypothermia, its thermostat responds by ordering heat to be drawn from the extremities into the core. Your hands and feet will start to stiffen. As the core temperature drops, the body also draws heat from the head. When this happens, circulation slows and you don't get the oxygen or sugar the brain needs: the sugar the brain ordinarily feeds on is being burnt to produce heat.

As the brain begins to slow down, the body stops shivering and irrational behaviour begins. This is a sure danger sign, but it's hard to recognize it in yourself because one of the first things hypothermia does is take away your will to help yourself. You stop shivering and you stop worrying. You're dying, in fact, and you couldn't care less. At this point, your body loses its ability to reheat itself. Even if you have a sleeping bag to crawl into, you will continue to cool off. Your pulse will get irregular, drowsiness will become semi-consciousness, which will become unconsciousness. Your only hope is to add heat from an external source – a fire, hot drinks, another body.

It was then that I realized I was feeling light-headed. I was suffering from the first stages of hypothermia.

The voices faded, and as I staggered up onto the bank I saw the bodies go left on the pathway towards the church. There would be coats hanging, but that wasn't enough. I couldn't stay in the heat of the church, and I needed more clothing if I was going to be outside.

One rapid scan of the bridge looking back towards Norway, and I was up and stumbling, using the pathway for speed, taking a chance of compromise. If I didn't recover soon, compromise wouldn't matter. I would be dead.

I stumbled on, my legs slowly gaining some form of co-ordination. I needed shelter and warmth, and to use that as a launch pad to find Matvey.

The building that the happy French voices had come out of: that was where I needed to go.

66

The wind whipped the snow against my body. Freezing flakes blasted their way into every exposed pore. My body was pleading to be allowed to lie down and sleep, but I knew that if I did that there would be no waking up. Shivering in almost uncontrollable bursts, I forced myself on, slipping and sliding along the pathway, falling, my knees banging through the snow onto the concrete. I couldn't feel the pain. I was losing my core heat and was starting to spiral down through the spectrum of hypothermia.

I staggered past the Spiritual Centre on my left, heading blindly for the log cabins that I hoped were accommodation: that meant hot water. A huge part of me just wanted to run into the church and give up, grab a hot drink from someone's hand, pull the coat off their back, anything to get life restored to my freezing hands and feet. I was almost past caring, and it wasn't a good sign. I had to force myself to remember what was happening and what the remedy was.

I kept staggering. I tried hard to take in oxygen, but I

couldn't. It was like my lungs were frozen and I couldn't actually force more air in. But I was still shivering, and that was the only sign I hadn't gone down completely yet, that all this drunken movement to get to a source of heat wasn't a waste of time. Shivering meant my body-heat regulation system was still active and fighting the downward spiral. Shivering generates heat, but it won't go on for ever.

The lights were on in the two-storey house on my right as I lurched past. Then, through blurred vision, I saw a kaleidoscope of lights and windows ahead. And the one thing I was so desperate to see: a door.

I didn't care about the lights being on. If somebody was inside, maybe they would get me warm before the drama started when they recognized who I was.

My hands were so cold, it took for ever to stop them shaking enough to guide them onto the handle and push it down, but eventually, somehow, it happened, and I fell headlong over the threshold and crashed onto the floor.

The warmth was instant and intense, and I felt it first in my nostrils and throat as I fought for oxygen. All the room lights were on, but no one was there to confront me. I slithered further inside, using my feet to close the door. I tried to push myself upright, my hands fumbling like a frightened child's, unable to coordinate my digits with my brain, as I struggled to grasp the key hanging on the frame. After several futile attempts, I had to give up. My fingers just weren't capable. Fuck it – I couldn't waste any more time trying to secure the door. I could be dead soon if I didn't move on.

I hauled myself up the wall and swayed and staggered into the kitchen. The set-up was the same as mine. I knew where to look. Grabbing a bread knife between my frozen fists I stumbled into the bedroom and on into the bathroom, dropping the blade into the shower tray. My next battle was with the shower controls, but I eventually managed to force the dial to the max before collapsing onto the tray below it.

Hot water felt like molten lava as it hit my body and I curled up into a ball.

I got my mouth down to the drain and slurped from the pool of hot fluid. After what felt like many minutes my left hand had thawed enough for me to use it as a scoop, and I gulped hot water until I could take no more. I was way past caring if anyone came into the cabin and found me. There was nothing I could do anyway until I'd recovered enough to be able to use the knife to defend myself.

Maybe fifteen minutes later, I began to feel pins and needles attacking my hands. It was a good sign, along with my lobster red skin. My core heat was restored; my thermostat was releasing blood again to the extremities and capillaries. I sat up and enjoyed the water cascading off the top of my head. I was out of the danger zone, but I had to get moving. I could recover fully while getting stuff done.

Pulling myself to my feet, I gave myself another minute of heat, my face pointed at the shower rose, drinking in yet more hot water. I turned the shower off and removed the neoprene sheath from my hand, so wet it would do more harm than good until it was dry. I grabbed a big towel and wrapped it around myself as I headed back into the bedroom. With luck, I would find clothes that might fit. It didn't matter to me what sex they belonged to, as long as they retained the heat I'd now generated.

The wardrobe told me a couple was living there. Whoever it was, their jeans were too small for me. The thermals were okay though, as were the tracksuit bottoms, two fleeces, and thick woollen socks.

I moved to the kitchen to get the kettle on, then rifled through the cupboards. I got a handful of chocolate biscuits down my neck, hoping to generate yet more heat from calories. Like Grisha said, it was going to be a long night.

The kettle clicked off and I mixed up some chocolate powder, thick enough for the spoon to stand up in. Mug in hand, I went and squatted down to check the boots by the front door, and felt the sting of scraped skin on my knees being stretched. At least I had feeling back. A beanie hanging on a hook was soon covering my wet hair, and a nylon windproof went on over the fleeces. I could just about squeeze into the larger pair of black wellingtons. I scalded my lips on a gulp of hot chocolate and headed back to the kitchen and the biscuits, put the kettle on again and looked around for a Thermos.

It was a very strange feeling, funny even, realizing I was saving my life so I could kill myself later. The attempt on Matvey was going to be a whole lot harder now that the pistol and the RGNs had gone. The bread knife went inside the elastic waistband of my thermal leggings, with the tracksuit bottoms cord tied as tightly as possible to keep it in place down the left side of my arse. If this thing had to be pulled before I planned, I wasn't going to risk my right hand doing the job.

Zipping up the windproof, gloves on, pulling down on the beanie, a Thermos under my arm, I headed for the door to find my target. I'd investigate the house next door first, followed by the IT room. I would need to be fast, before the happy couple realized some of their kit had been taken by someone needing a shower, and asked themselves why.

I eased the door open and quickly checked outside before stepping over the threshold. I only had time to register that the hands that grabbed me were tattooed, and then that one was squeezing hard into my windpipe and the other was gripping my face while pushing me back into the room.

67

It didn't matter if I could see him or not, I knew who he was, and the very raspy 'In! In! In! In!' confirmed it as the Thermos dropped away onto the floor. He was calm but firm with his command. Not that I had much choice but to comply, with one of his hands around my throat and the other pressed into my face, thrusting me back over the threshold. Behind him, in the blur, I saw more heads.

As Kirill forced me down onto the floor I curled up, eyes closed, head tucked in, waiting for the pain as they went for payback. But none came. All I heard was the shuffle of boots around the room, and then the door being closed.

'It is Nick. It is the same guy.' A French accent I recognized. 'They are my clothes.'

Still I hadn't been searched, but maybe the accent answered the question. Why would I be searched if Mathulla had seen me running around naked trying to get into a building, or had come in and seen me in the shower, or even afterwards, while I was in the kitchen? He'd assume I was harmless and unarmed. But I wasn't. I was still breathing, and I had a weapon. It wasn't going to do me any good right now, but it made me feel a lot better about the situation – whatever that situation was about to be.

Kirill was on his knees, his mouth up close and personal with my ear. He had to work hard to get the words out after the remote had been shoved down his throat. 'Open your eyes, Nick.' His whisper was sandpapery. 'Nothing's going to happen to you. Open your eyes.'

I did what he asked, lying in a foetal position, my head resting on the tiles. Close to my face were pairs of boots, the snow left on them melting to join what had already been deposited on the floor. There were four pairs in all, and as I craned my neck I could see one of them belonged to Gedi. He had a couple of bruises about to develop on his face, but on top of that he looked totally shattered, his features red and blotched. It didn't look like cold damage, more like the aftermath of pain and tears and being physically and emotionally shaken by events. Then there was Kirill, still very close, still on his knees, staring into me. His face, too, was the worse for wear. 'Where's Mary?' Again, the sandpaper. 'What have you done with her?'

I couldn't tell if he was angry or not. There was a glazed look in his eyes, as if he was drunk, but he was close enough for me not to smell alcohol. But why would there be? There was no alcohol down here. It could have been drugs, but I very much doubted it. Behind him, Mathulla had the trendy Bang & Olufsen phone to his ear, and he was telling whoever it was at the other end that they'd found me. To his left, Gedi was inconsolable. 'Where is she? Nick – her medication, she needs her medication.'

I slowly nodded at Kirill. Gedi was past understanding much of what was happening. He should be under medication himself.

'She's got it.'

Kirill turned to him, still on his knees, and held up a comforting hand, before turning back to me with his faraway, unblinking eyes. 'I'm treating this as a test of my faith, Nick. I'm trying to be a better man.' He held up both of his fists and straightened his fingers so the backs of his hands could remind me of what he once was. 'Is she safe?'

He studied me, waiting for an answer, as Mathulla finished the call and looked over. 'They're coming.'

Kirill's eyes screamed of the internal fight going on between what he would like to do to me, and what he knew was the bigger picture: finding it in himself to forgive.

I was calmer than I should have been, and I was conscious of that. Maybe it was because these were my last hours, and the fuck-it factor was going off in my brain, like a Coke bottle full of Mentos. But Kirill wasn't the only one with an internal fight, though in many ways mine was easier than his. For me, the bigger picture was simply making sure Matvey got dead so Jack and Rio didn't.

I held his blank gaze. 'She's okay. She's on her way to Oslo to be deprogrammed. She's not hurt, and she knows what's happening to her.'

Gedi's hands shot to his face, as he towered above us. He buckled, either from the news of the deprogramming or from relief she was safe. Kirill ignored him. He focused on me with greater concerns. 'The Black guy. Where is he? There any more with you?'

I shook my head as best I could with my skull on the tiles. 'He's gone. The deprogrammers have got Mary. They've all gone south. She really is safe – but she'll be back. They won't take any of this place,' I nodded upwards to Gedi, 'or him out of her heart. She told me.'

A couple of bodies moved to the kitchen and I heard them making brews. Another couple helped Gedi onto a stool at the breakfast bar, and attempted to comfort him as they explained she'd be back with him soon. Gedi was a big lad but his head wasn't made for this.

Kirill's head, on the other hand, was, and I was glad he was taking ever deeper breaths as his internal battle raged. 'Nick – why? Why did you do this?'

Whether he intended it or not, it came out sounding more like concern for my emotional wellbeing than hard-nosed interrogation. If he was genuinely worried for me, despite the natural inclination to kick the shit out of me, then maybe he was a much better person than most I'd ever met.

'Just money, mate. That's all it was. Her family wanted her back and were willing to pay for it.'

The door opened and a gust of cold air blew over me until it closed again. Boots began to move out of the way. Kirill stood up, but gestured for me to stay where I was as he made room for the voice I knew so well.

'Nick, are you okay? You could have died crossing the river.'

I twisted my head and my body to see her in a jacket covered with snow, as she pulled down the neck of her jumper so I could see her smile. 'Thank God you didn't. He wants you alive, here, in Heaven.'

68

'Matvey – I want to talk to Matvey.'

'That's okay, Nick. That will not be a problem. Please, sit.' Saynab indicated the *über*-smart sofa that looked brand new. 'Be comfortable. Rest, you have been through so much today.' She turned to the group and said everything was okay, they could go back to their families.

I pushed myself up onto my knees, very conscious about not exposing the knife, and went and sat down.

Saynab was having a final hug with Gedi, who then left, supported by Mathulla. Kirill stayed behind. It flashed across my mind she was clearing the decks so there were no witnesses to me getting filled in. But surely Saynab wasn't the vengeful type. She came and sat next to me and it was clear that she wasn't. Kirill stayed by the sink, probably in case it was me who wanted the violence.

Saynab rested a hand on my shoulder. 'You don't need to explain anything, Nick, but, please, is Mary really okay? Is she really going to Oslo? We all love and care for her so much, as I'm sure you do.'

I nodded, but felt a big pang of guilt. 'Yep. The deprogramming won't work, though, will it? She'll come back for Gedi. They love each other, right?' I wanted to keep to truths, to keep my mind off the future of the village once Matvey had gone.

Saynab agreed. 'Yes, they do. Very much.'

Guilt had got me now. It had won the fight because I was desperate to know if she really did believe what she had so passionately told me in the Spiritual Centre. Would she find it in herself to forgive me?

'Nick, you had your reasons.'

Kirill had the raspy answer. 'Money. Her parents.'

Saynab gave a knowing nod. She'd seen this before.

'Is that why you came back to speak with Matvey? To explain?'

I nodded and shrugged at the same time, trying hard to avoid an answer.

'Matvey will forgive you, Nick. Because what are we, if we can't forgive?' Even now she was concerned for me. 'Your drugs?'

'Gone.'

I got a pat on my thigh and a genuine look of concern.

'I'll get you some. You must stay well.'

She stood up slowly with her hand out, and Kirill took a pace closer, just in case. 'Come, first let's give Madeleine and Mathulla's home back to them. I'll take you to Matvey and you can speak with him for as long as you want.'

I stood and nodded, my hand still in hers. 'Thank you.' I felt like shit, but what else could I do?

We all zipped up and headed out of the cabin and along the path, with Kirill never more than a step behind. I didn't mind that: I liked the idea of more than one person knowing my cover story, just enough for what happened next to make sense. Saynab's hood was up and pulled down over her forehead, and the polo-neck covered so much of the bottom of her face I could only make out her eyes in the light coming from the two-storey house.

'Matvey – he's a fake. You know that, don't you?' I wasn't sure if she'd heard me, so I turned back to make sure Kirill had. 'Matvey is a false prophet. I will tell him to his face. He's got you all brainwashed. Don't you see that, Kirill?'

I wasn't really bothered how he answered. If they were all brainwashed, they wouldn't see it anyway.

The Russian gave me a slow shake of the head as we passed the house, but Saynab put it into words. 'It's okay, Nick. Wait till you talk with Matvey. You'll feel his love. You'll know he is real.' The voice faded inside the hood and we hit the main path and took the right towards the warehouse. She stopped suddenly and turned back to Kirill.

'Please, everything's fine here and Esther has Poppy. Please go home to your family and kiss Poppy for me. Tell her I'll pick her up soon.'

Kirill wasn't having any of it. 'No, I should stay.'

She rested a hand on his upper arm. 'It's okay. It's normal that people doubt us. Didn't you in the beginning? But look how strongly your faith guided you this evening. You should feel so proud of yourself. I know Esther does. Nick just needs time. Matvey will guide him.'

He wasn't convinced, but she was. The hood rustled as she turned and looked up at me. 'It's going to be fine, isn't it, Nick?'

'Yep, it's all good, Saynab.'

Kirill still wasn't happy with the situation. 'You call if you need anything. I'll wait up and be ready. Anything, just call.'

She accepted the offer and waved goodbye to a still not convinced Kirill, and he turned back to Norway as we headed deeper into Russia.

69

We went in via the door next to the shutters. I wasn't expecting a warehouse to be heated, but it was just as warm inside as in the cabin. The advantage of Russia having all that surplus gas, I supposed. The strip lighting was almost blindingly bright, and the vast space looked like a Costco superstore, with aisles of palleted goods from foodstuffs to toilet rolls, even a section with building materials, and some plant machinery with spare tyres. What interested me most were the two Phantoms to the right of the door. These hadn't been involved in the chase as the tyres were inflated and ready to roll. Parked alongside them was a pair of electric forklifts, which had leads in and were charging up, and a couple of steel snow shovels. They'd be ready to clear the hard standing outside for the forklifts to do their unloading thing when trucks arrived with resupply. Ahead of us were two blue and windowed Portakabins, stacked one on top of the other, with a steel staircase leading to the upper one. She pointed, 'Nick, please,' and she followed me up the stairs.

The administration office we walked into was Scandi-chic-furnished and sparse, with a light wooden desk supporting three Mac monitors and a keyboard, reminding me of a City boy's trading desk. Three high-end leather recliners were round it, one for the screen, two on the other side, and against the wall there was an equally trendy wooden cabinet on which stood a Nespresso machine, bottles of water, and all the makings in a very smart Nespresso-designed tray. I got working on it as Saynab made herself comfortable in one of the recliners on the visitors' side of the desk. I turned back from the coffee-making, and offered her one. She declined.

The coffee oozed out and I opened four sachets of sugar and emptied them into a stackable mug. My body was still craving it after my exertions in the river.

Was this Matvey's office? Was he about to appear? I was going to have to use my left hand. There couldn't be any room for a fuck-up when the time came. The bread knife wasn't the most efficient tool for what needed to happen. It was designed for cutting, not digging into.

'Where's Matvey? Is he coming here?' I went and sat opposite her in the other visitor's chair and we swivelled round to face each other. I had a flashback to our meet-and-greet session at the Spiritual Centre, but it was me now asking the questions. It was good there'd be a witness who was aware of the cover story, but I was sorry it had to be her. I would try to make the kill as quick, and so less traumatic, as possible for her. If there was such a thing as a less traumatic killing.

Saynab perched forward to make the recliner tilt so she could rest her feet on the floor. She looked at me, elbows on her thighs. 'He will soon. He's checking on Mary. We have friends in Oslo, people who know the clinic where she'll be taken. He wants to make sure she is okay. Check on the whole situation, that sort of thing.'

'These friends, are they going to bust her out or something?'

Saynab sat up a bit, and unzipped her jacket. She pulled down once more on the polo-neck and the smile was so not pirate it almost had me wanting to confess. 'No, no, no, of course not. Mary's her own person, just like you, just like all of us. She knows that Gedi, and all of us, we are all here for her.'

I took a gulp of the very sweet black coffee. 'Does the same go for me? I created all this emotion, drama and pain for money. It must be hard not to hate me.'

She smiled. 'Of course I don't, Nick. Whatever you think or feel, you must say it to Matvey. He will show you there is nothing fake here, nothing but love, so you can be at peace and, in turn, you can live a life. Just as God wants you to.'

'What about you? Do you forgive me?'

She shifted her weight and the recliner tipped back till her toes only just touched the tiles. 'Yes, I do. This is a bad moment in your life. But we have all had them. Remember what we spoke about on Saturday? All that matters is today. You came back, wanting to confront Matvey, discover the truth, because you want to believe, you want to have a life. That is coming from a good person, Nick.'

She stood up and I did the same. She threw her arms around me, and I kept my distance a bit like an awkward family embrace. I didn't want her discovering the knife. We parted, but she held my hands. 'Nick, you're free to leave whenever you want. But please stay. Wait here for Matvey. I don't know how long he will be, but Matvey will come. I will bring you more drugs.'

'Thank you.'

'I'll go and kiss my child, collect your drugs, and I'll be back. Maybe Matvey will be here before me, but I'll be back. I promise.'

She left, and my eyes followed her across the Costco floor.

Until this moment I hadn't concerned myself with what happened to me after Matvey was dead, because I would be, too. That had changed: I would probably still be alive after Matvey was down, now that there were no RGNs. But what did I do after that?

As Saynab disappeared through the door into the snow, I suddenly understood what I was going to do afterwards – and, more importantly, why.

I was now here just to destroy Matvey. I would keep going. You can't die until you've done what God put you here to do and that is to live. When you die, you need to know in your heart that you have lived rather than simply won or lost at life.

I still didn't go for the God bit, but Matvey dying meant others would live, including me. I wanted to make sure I didn't fuck this life business up. I wanted to live a real life for however long I had left, and that meant doing right by Jack and Rio, and then doing right by me.

Yet for all that rationale I was still fighting back the guilt, but fuck it: I had to distance myself from that and get on with what I was there for.

70

I double-checked, and there was no CCTV, either outside or inside the office, no surveillance covering the warehouse at all. But, then, why would there be here in the middle of nowhere? To deter who?

Back in the office, I rifled the desk drawers in the slim hope of finding something that fired rounds. But they were empty, apart from three pairs of identical glasses, Matvey's, in identical black cases. The drawers were just like the desktop, sparse, functional, not even a pen or a Post-it. No problem. I had two weapons already: I had the knife, and I had my hands – well, one hand.

I had to get on. I headed down the staircase two steps at a time, landing as gently as I could on the steel to stop my wellies echoing round the vast space. I had no idea when Matvey was going to turn up, but Saynab was right. Of course I would wait. I checked out the lower Portakabin – nothing but notice boards with papers clinging to them, a desk full of running-the-shop shit. This was the admin office, not upstairs.

Flicking on the ignition of each Phantom, I checked their fuel status. The best one was just over half full. I had no idea how far that would get me in this weather, but it really didn't matter as long as it got me out of the immediate area fast. I'd have to stay in Russia: I couldn't take the chance of crossing the bridge into Norway, and then the heavier snowfall making it impossible to get up the hill. But that didn't matter either. The Russian coast wasn't that far, and there was a decent road heading that way. I'd worry about escaping the country when I got to that part of the plan, which was pretty sketchy so far. The inescapable fact was that Matvey still had to die, and that was all that mattered at the moment. If I died attacking him, that was still okay because I'd never know if I was dead and the other two would still be safe. But if not, what? It was simple: get out of the danger zone, make distance, and work out what to do next to get me back to Tulse Hill and start living.

I took the Phantom's keys and now controlled that vehicle's destiny. I checked out the shutter mechanism, and found the control panel was to the left of it on the small piece of wall between the door frame and the shutter. One push on the red button and the motors started to lift the shutter. I let it go a few more centimetres, pressed the black Stop, then the green to let it drop back down. Good: I could get out.

The warehouse manager must have been very proud of the signage and directions for all of the different areas, and I was glad the official language in the village was English. In the clothing section I dug in the boxes and crates for a decent set of bottoms, boots, and another thick Canada Goose.

Matvey could appear at any minute, and I was starting to get a bit of a sweat up as I threw a set of ski salopettes over the tracksuit bottoms, then dug about in the boxes of boots for more Sorels my size, while adjusting the braces on the salopettes bib. I put the boots on but wouldn't lace them up yet. I needed more kit. I found the parkas and was soon wearing a black one just like The Owl's. Gloves and a thicker beanie followed. I had no idea how long I might be exposed out there trying to cross the border, so the more kit and layers the better. The bread knife fitted in the big chest pocket of the salopettes and was covered by the parka.

I tipped the contents out of one of the packing boxes and took it with me as I headed for the foodstuffs. It wouldn't matter what I threw in as long as it was made of calories that could be burnt. I stuffed the box with Alenka and protein bars, and my pockets with biscuits and cranberry-juice boxes.

I ran to the Phantom and shoved the box into the footwell, then realised the front seat could be raised for helmets or whatever to be stowed, so I threw all the bars into the space and put the seat back down.

I was nearly ready for the target.

71

I'd always managed to dehumanize the people I was up against. To me they were targets, the same as boats, houses or warehouses. In the final stages of a job I wouldn't refer to them, or even think of them, as people. I couldn't, or I wouldn't be able to do the job. Why not? I'd never liked to analyse myself too much on that one because I wasn't sure I'd like what I found. I knew I'd done some really terrible things. I had killed, but I didn't feel like a killer, and I didn't think I was too bad a person. Saynab seemed to agree.

The question that always bugged me more was, why was I doing this shit in the first place? My whole life had been spent sitting in shit-holes. Even when I was in the army I'd ask myself the same thing: why? I couldn't answer fully then, but I could now. Even as a kid I was just odd socks and scabs. My mother, well, everyone, was always telling me I'd never amount to anything. Maybe they were right, but that was then, and this was now. Today I was saving lives that mattered to me by taking a life that didn't, and that started to feel good because it was no longer Matvey but a target. At least there were no Pearly Gates with St Peter standing beside them with a reckoning book. Like Saynab said, this, here and now, was Heaven, and I wanted a piece of it.

Matvey was a High Value Target, a danger to the state.

I had a weapon, and I had the means of escape.

Except I wasn't entirely happy about the bread knife. Until the shutters rattled up or the door opened, I had time to look for an upgrade. I needed something small enough to be hidden but that could kill him instantly. That would be good for both of us. I ran to the hardware area.

Shovels and axes were no good to me: with what I had in mind for the attack, those types of weapons were too cumbersome. I rummaged in a box until I discovered it contained vegetable and flower seeds, then looked around for the next container. Sitting on a shelf at eye level, among rolls of brown parcel tape and balls of string, was exactly what I needed. The yellow DeWalt folding lock-back retractable utility knife – in my language, a box-cutter – would be perfect.

Wrestling it out of its blister packing, I unfolded it and checked that the razor-sharp blade was in place and secure. This would be far more efficient than the bread knife, but that would stay with me as well. There'd be a long journey ahead once this was done and it might be needed.

The box-cutter wouldn't kill the target immediately, but as long as I got it where it needed to be there was no way even the best trauma consultant could keep him alive.

I needed to flesh out the plan. My line of work had never been a science. People might have an image, picked up from spy movies, of precision and perfection, and assume it all runs like clockwork. In reality it doesn't, for the simple reason that we're all human beings, and human beings are liable to fuck up – I knew I did about 40 per cent of the time. Add to that the fact that the people we're working against are also fallible, and it isn't a formula for guaranteed success. The only true measure of human intelligence is the speed and versatility with which people can adapt to new situations. Certainly, once you're on the ground, you have to be as flexible as a rubber band, and what helps you there are planning and preparation. With luck, when the inevitable fuck-up did occur, I wouldn't be a rabbit frozen in the headlights. As Von Clausewitz, or some other general, said, 'If your opponent has only two possible options, you can be sure that he will take the third.'

The only entrances to the warehouse were the shutter and the door to the side of it. I therefore needed to be concealed as the target entered the warehouse by either means, then passed me, enabling me to attack from behind. I couldn't afford another fuck-up. I had one chance at this. If I fucked up, that was all three of us down.

I knew the perfect spot, behind the forklifts. With my back against the side panel of the furthest truck from the door, and with my arse liking the parka's padding as I sat on the concrete, I tightened my laces and pulled out some Alenka and cranberry juice. It was anyone's guess how long I'd be there, so I'd make the best use of it and take on some calories, while at the same time closing my eyes and visualizing the attack. Athletes, actors, doctors, they all did this, they all visualized, and so did special forces. If it worked for me then, it would just as well work for me now. If you visualize situations, you can usually work out in advance how to deal with them. The more you visualize, the better you'll deal with them. It might sound like something from a tree-huggers' workshop, but it gets the job done.

My aim was to visualize every step of the way, trying to

create a film in my head of what I wanted to happen, starting with the target's entry, as if my eyes were the camera lens and my ears the recording kit.

The pictures in my head were all in slow motion so I wouldn't miss a thing. The door or the shutters would open, the target would walk or drive in, but no matter how he arrived, he would have to be on foot at the point where he passed the forklifts and ATVs to get up the stairs to the office. My killing ground was those three or four metres just before the stairs. In my slow-motion movie I saw the target with four others around him, to make it as problematic as possible. In my mind's eye I gripped the DeWalt tight in my left hand, taking deep breaths to prepare for the body burst as the group passed me. One last check to make sure the blade was facing me, then I focused on the back of the target's head.

Taking one more deep breath and launching myself towards the head, ignoring the others, ignoring their shouts, I had to get to the target before he could turn, my right hand reaching round to his face and grabbing it, my fingers getting involved in his glasses as they came off the bridge of his nose, and all the time I was pulling the back of his head onto my chest, and pulling it up to present his neck. I visualized my left arm bent, making it easier to get to the right of the target's neck, digging the blade in deep before pulling back, using all my strength to keep the pressure on, to keep that blade dug into the target's neck as I gouged it round to the left, cutting through first one carotid artery, then his windpipe, and then the final carotid. I then visualized letting the target drop to the ground. No matter what movements or noises he made, no matter what help the others tried to give, he would bleed and oxygen out.

I kept planning the kill over and over again, like a sprinter visualizing bursting out of the blocks. The first few strides are under your control. It's the longer part, the race that develops, that's the bit that can't be completely planned for.

I next considered different escape routes. I visualized running through the door if driving the ATV through the open shutters wasn't an option, if there were bodies trying to stop me. It would be out into the darkness and turn left, and run, run, run – staying on the concrete as much as I could and keeping moving. Whatever happened after that, it happened: I had no control of that. All I had control of was getting my feet moving and keeping them moving.

The last permutation I visualized was having Saynab alongside the target. The kill would be the same, nothing could alter that, but in my slow-motion film as I went through the scenarios before opening the shutter, I said sorry to Saynab and asked to be forgiven.

I tried to hear her telling me I was, but it didn't happen. I decided I would just apologize, explain why, and hope to be forgiven, then get the shutters up and go. But that didn't work, either.

I bit into the Alenka and tried to imagine a version in which I explained why, then apologized without waiting for her reply. That felt much better: I could always try to bluff myself that she had forgiven me. It felt strange. I was spending more time visualizing the situation with Saynab than I was thinking about the target.

It made me feel better to stick with the final cut, and I played it out in my head many more times as I continued to top myself up with calories.

It must have been two hours, maybe more, before I heard engine noises behind the shuttering. I moved off my arse and onto my knees, pressed myself hard against the forklift.

Crouched, I took deep breaths to oxygenate myself, and checked yet again that the box-cutter was in my left hand, the blade facing towards me.

Any second, the shutters would rattle their way up.

But no rattle came. It was the door that opened, and headlights poured through, illuminating the snow that fell between the ATV and the building.

The light show was blocked as the target came through the doorway.

And at the target's side was Poppy.

72

Fuck, fuck – I hadn't visualized this and it wasn't the place for a child. Events like this can even fuck up adults for ever.

There was no going back. It had to be on. As soon as the target was down, I'd grab Poppy and place her in the admin office to get her away from the scene. I would be fast on the kill, fast to get her away. It takes a while for an action to sink in if it's totally unexpected and unrecognizable; maybe the confusion of what was about to happen would remain just that for Poppy. Maybe.

She was covered with snow and brushing herself down. The target was clean of it, just some gathered on his beanie and shoulders. They weren't talking animatedly, weren't taking urgent strides towards the stairs. It was leisurely, when I wanted it to be fast. Let's get them past me so I can do what I have to do, and get away.

They came level with the forklifts and I took a final deep breath, ready for the burst. My body was rigid. I couldn't risk the parka rustling. My eyes flicked down for a final check on the box-cutter, left hand clamped around it as tight as it could.

Eyes now on the target's head.

Poppy was to his left. My whole focus shifted to his blue beanie. Just like in my visualization, and feeling like it was in slow motion, I moved up from behind the forklift, right arm out, hand open in readiness to grab his face and pull back to present his neck, left arm hooked, the blade primed to sweep across his throat, dig in, and pull back violently.

No reaction from either of them. They couldn't hear me. Maybe the engine noise, I didn't know.

I had maybe five steps left.

Then, from behind me, a loud shout.

Startled, the target began to spin round. The back of the beanie was replaced by the side of his face, and then his glasses were reflecting the warehouse's lights. He faced me square on and his eyes were as wide as saucers when he saw what was coming for him.

He yelled, pushing Poppy away from danger.

I had got to within two bounds of him. The kill would take longer now it was a neck not a throat. I focused on the left side to take out a carotid.

And then something hit the back of my head so hard it felt like I'd walked into the path of a speeding car. Stars exploded behind my eyes. My legs buckled. The box-cutter fell from my hand and I followed it to the floor as another blow crashed down on my back forcing the side of my head to slam against the concrete.

Hollering and screaming came from everywhere: from me, from them as my head kept spinning. It felt like it was swelling to bursting point. I was going to black out.

I forced my eyes open, trying so hard to recover, to gulp in oxygen, and Saynab was a blur as she threw the steel snow shovel she'd been wielding onto the floor and gathered a hysterical Poppy into her arms.

The target moved in on me as I went in and out of blackness.

Game over.

73

My left cheek was on cold concrete; everything else was a blur. I heard the long protesting rasp of tape as it was torn from a roll and the next thing I knew, my wrists were grabbed and being bound together. I caught sight of brown parcel tape, and the hands wrapping it around me. No tattoos. This was happening, but there wasn't a lot I could do about it. Blood thumped in my head and the occasional red or white star still burst. My only coherent thought was that at least my wrists were being taped in front of me rather than Gedi and Kirill style. It gave me a chance. More and more tape came, and I was powerless to do anything but let the target get on with it.

He crouched over me as he worked. 'I'm sorry, Nick. I know you understand.'

He finished doing a not very good job of it, and stepped out of my line of sight.

I glanced round for Poppy and Saynab but saw no one. That was a good thing. I flexed my feet and tried to shift myself, the parka scraping against concrete as I struggled and failed to make the metre or so back to the forklifts. I wanted to sit up and support my back. I needed to recover quickly, while there were just the two of us.

Hands came through my armpits from behind. 'Let me help you.' He pulled me up, then left me to make the final adjustments. I was where I'd wanted to be, with my legs straight out, hands on my lap.

He crouched down again. 'Nick, I'm sorry, but . . .'

I was already shaking my head, even though it hurt my brain. He didn't need to say anything. 'Poppy – she okay?'

He gave a cursory nod. 'Saynab's taken her next door. She'll be fine. Unfortunately, she's seen worse. The war.'

The news didn't make me feel any better.

The target studied my face. 'So, who sent you? Americans? The UK?'

I tried to look confused, but he was several moves ahead of me. Of course – why wouldn't he know he was a target?

'I don't buy it. You were sent to rescue Mary, then come back and kill me because I'm a fake. Her family responsible for part two? No, of course they aren't. Besides, there has been too much commitment. Why nearly die for money? There's more to you, Nick. Much more.'

I played dumb, easing my hands to the bib to feel for the bread knife, but I knew it wasn't there. The parka had been unzipped. I worked my hands up to my head, trying to rub out the pain. What now? I still had a job to do. With what? The box-cutter wasn't anywhere to be seen on the floor, just the bars that had been left in my parka, now scattered about after the search, along with the ATV key. If the target's drills securing me were anything to go by, he was just as switched on and the weapon was well gone. But why wouldn't he be, if he was an HVT?

The target carried on: 'Nick, you're not the first to have tried.'

I was still trying. 'Mate, I've got to stand. Can you help me? My legs are numb.' I moved them out straight and arched them again. 'I can't feel them.'

I rolled over onto my knees, and the target let me get on with it. I made it onto all fours, part bluffing, part genuinely in a shit state. 'I need to stand. I need to walk. My legs, mate.'

He came in behind to assist me, his hands once again through my armpits to get me upright. I needed to be firmly on my feet and behind him. I visualized getting my taped wrists over his head and against his throat, then pulling as hard as I could towards me before dropping back to my knees, all the time leaning forward so his head bent down, crushing his windpipe as the tape acted as a garotte.

Finally, I was on my feet. 'Thanks. I just need to move around a bit.'

The target let go and I staggered a little, still half bluff, half for real. I turned to face him, vision still blurry. The next stage was going to be a gang-fuck unless he turned round, but most of the night had been, so why change now?

I tottered about, testing my legs, giving time for the target to turn. But he didn't. His face was etched with concern. 'How is it, Nick? You feeling better?'

I nodded and hobbled about, edging closer.

He was still facing me.

Fuck it. Now or never.

Thrusting my taped hands out dead ahead, I raised them above my head and threw myself into the target. For a split second his expression said he couldn't work out if I'd lost my balance or was attacking, but as soon as he realized what was what, there was yelling.

He tried to push me away, but by now my hands were over his head and against his neck. I jerked back hard and as I pulled so I got his face into me, his glasses fell between us. I felt his cheek against mine and then I let myself drop like liquid. My knees hit the concrete hard. Pain would come, but not yet.

Hands and tape against the back of his neck, still pulling him into me, I fell onto my back so he was half on top of me, his face aimed at the concrete. He kicked out, bucked, his hands trying to push himself away as I now swung a leg round to get over the back of him.

The target wasn't giving up. Both of us flailed and writhed, and I did my best to keep his face as tight into mine as I could so he couldn't butt me.

The door must have opened.

Shouts were closing in on me, and a boot flew into my ribs at the same time as a fist came down on the side of my head. I saw another round of starbursts before hands were wrenching me away from the target. A frenzy of kicks rained in and I curled into a ball, my head tucked in as far as it would go. There was nothing I could do but take the pain.

'Stop! Stop!' It was the target shouting. 'Stop!'

There was no way the heavy breathing above me came from Saynab, but I wasn't about to expose my head to see who it was. It would be small consolation knowing my attacker's identity, now that I'd fucked up even more and was back at the start line.

Whoever it was, their boots retreated and the rustle of nylon jacket faded in the direction of the shout.

'I'm fine.' The target again. 'It's all okay, Kirill. Thank you.'

'Go upstairs. I'll take care of him.'

The target was full of concern. 'No, please.'

'Not like that. I'm just going to make sure we're all safe from him.'

The target wasn't interested. It was a soft, gentle voice as he fought to get his breath. 'We've got to understand him, Kirill. Know why this has happened. We have to help him.'

The target's voice came closer. My head was still tucked in, eyes closed.

'Nick? No one's going to harm you. Please, can you look up? Just look up, Nick.'

He was right next to me now, his voice nearly in my ear.

'Nick, look. I want to help you.'

I moved my head just enough to get my eyes on the target, now just inches away. Above and slightly behind, Kirill was standing by, no doubt to launch himself on me as soon as he could.

Deprived of glasses, the target's eyes narrowed to focus. 'I want to help you, Nick. I want to understand you. Come, let's get you up.'

Kirill stood ready and eager, as I pushed myself onto my knees and the target helped me finally to reach my feet. 'Come. Please.'

He supported me on my left as we walked towards the staircase. Kirill picked up the target's glasses and inspected a smashed lens before handing them over. The target looked down at them and gave a little laugh. About what, I hadn't a clue. I certainly wasn't laughing. The only upside as far as I could see was that at least we were going where there was some coffee.

74

The chair was the one I'd sat in before with Saynab, but this time the company was different. Kirill was behind me making coffee. The target had been on the other side of the desk, retrieving a pair of his spare glasses.

'I'm always sitting on them or losing them, but this is a first.'

Now he had come round from the desk and sat facing me, therapy style. The Nespresso machine gurgled away, filling another cup, on top of the four sugars I'd asked for, as the target finished polishing his new eyewear.

'Nick, I think it must have been the Americans who sent you.' The target leant forward and rested his forearms on his thighs. 'But why Mary as a cover just to get to me? I can't work it out – it's all so intricate when it needn't be. Why make it so?' He rubbed the back of his neck, either to relieve any pain still lingering from the garotte, or because he was literally scratching his head about what was going on.

'I mean, Nick, really? The parents? Twice you attack – I really don't think it's the parents, do you?' The question was clearly rhetorical, because he hardly drew breath. 'But that's okay, Nick. You have your reasons, I understand that.'

I nodded. I was trying to do some working out of my own, wondering what lay in store. The coffees arrived and were placed on the desk between us, before Kirill grabbed the spare chair the other side of the desk and wheeled it over to the door.

'But you know what, Nick?' The rhetorical questions weren't finished. He pointed at the back of the sleek steel monitors. 'I would really like you to understand that the work I do with these things is totally in sync with the ethos of the village. It's all about doing our best to make sure we all live in peace.'

I picked up the hot brew and chanced a sip. My jaw felt like it needed oiling at the joints, like it was going to let out a loud creak after the battering. What *was* next for me? As far as I was concerned, I still had a job to do. Returning to Tulse Hill was back on the cards, but it could only happen after I knew, a hundred per cent, that the target was dead. And at that, I surely had just one more chance.

It was time for me to start talking, to mark time a bit while I looked for an opportunity to attack. Hopefully, third time lucky, though Kirill had taken up station by the door, facing us. He wasn't making it easy for me.

'You're right. It's the Americans.' I took another sip of very sweet coffee. If I was going to see this through, I needed those calories. 'They're the ones who want you dead. But that said, the Mary thing, that's real. Her parents do want her back, but the operation was used to get me here to you. You're right. Complicated.'

I jerked my head at the monitors. 'You play about with these things too well. That's why you like being called Snuggly Bear, isn't it?'

I smiled at him. What else was I supposed to do? Be angry? Go off on one? Give him a bollocking for being a naughty bear? Fuck it, why not keep smiling, try to get some dialogue going, try to keep in the game, try to keep alive?

He smiled back, before looking across at Kirill, and soon all three of us were smiling. Was I completely sure this wasn't a cult?

The springs tilted the target's chair as he sat back. 'One thing about the Americans, they are persistent, aren't they?'

I shrugged, pretending not to know what he was on about. 'Who knows? But they're worried about you. I suppose you're just too good at what you do. All those Zero Days have got them worried.'

The target swivelled on his chair to reach across the desk for his own brew. He rested the mug on his thigh, thinking of an answer. 'Nick, by doing what I'm doing, I'm keeping the peace. I'm not making the potential for war, but doing everything in my power to stop it. As for what we have here, do you really think all this is fake? That I'm not true? What I believe isn't true? What we all believe isn't true?'

I really did want to know if it was or not, and I really did want to believe, but above all else I wanted time and opportunity to kill him.

I shrugged again. 'I really don't know. I find it hard to reconcile the two things.'

'Nick, I'm going to explain why I work so hard creating these cyber-weapons. I want you to believe this place isn't fake. This place is true, and I want you to believe.'

75

'Why bother?' I asked. 'I'm working for the Americans. Why don't you just kill me and get this over and done with?'

His eyes brimmed with concern as he leant forward and stared directly into mine. It looked real, but what was real, these days?

'No, Nick, never, never. I understand that you will not stop, and that's why Kirill there has to stay with us. But I want you to know one thing: that I forgive you, because you don't know the truth.' He pointed at the monitors again. 'You don't know the real story about these things, and you don't know the truth about us.' He glanced at Kirill. 'So, it's okay. You're not going to die by my hand. That's God's job. He'll decide when you die. My job is to let you live to your full potential – because this is Heaven, Nick, where we are right here and now. What I'm trying to do is stop it being destroyed piece by piece.'

It all sounded good, but love, peace and goodwill to all men weren't the vibes I was getting from Kirill.

'Nick, did you realize the Cold War never ended? In fact, it's about to get worse.'

'You mean the Baltic states probably being invaded by your country?'

The target didn't miss a beat. 'Ah, so that's why you're so keen to get me out of the picture. No, it's nothing as dangerous as that. Not NATO. It's Ukraine.'

'Ukraine? Why? The Russians took Crimea years ago. We just let it happen.'

He put his hands up. 'Exactly. 2014. I don't know why they might invade again, and I don't know what they intend doing once they get there. I just know that both sides are deluding themselves, thinking that we're on the brink of something, when the fact is it's been a reality for such a long time.

'So far it's been contained. It hasn't been allowed to escalate, and I've helped that happen. My Zero Days give both East and West a mutual deterrent, by levelling up Russia's cyber-weapons capability. If one side is more powerful than the other, especially in terms of cyber or nuclear arms, then the whole architecture of security as we know it collapses. So what we do here, Nick, is help enforce that neutrality, keep that mutual cyber deterrence alive and kicking.'

He put his mug back on the desk without touching a drop. He was in full flow now. 'Obama did everything he could to prevent a war over Ukraine in 2014. But one of his own generals was plotting in private to overrule him and escalate tensions – can you imagine that, Nick, acting against a direct order from his own commander-in-chief?'

I knew who he was talking about, and it wasn't just any top-echelon officer. General Philip Breedlove was the Supreme Commander of NATO forces in Europe, and he had a grievance. Breedlove considered Obama's order to his NATO generals 'not to start a war' with Russia over the 2014 war in Ukraine a very bad idea. Breedlove didn't want to breed any love in Europe. Unfortunately for him, the Russians intercepted his emails plotting with senior US politicians and policymakers to bypass the commander-in-chief and get the ball rolling, and leaked them. Obama might not want war, was the gist, but it was about time we had one.

It had sometimes been an advantage having Gabe, the Royal Signals geek, about the place. He loved reading about this shit, and now I wished I'd listened more when he ranted from his sofa about whatever he was reading on his laptop.

The target pushed on: 'So, one of the first decisions Trump made when he came in was to take huge swathes of the Republican Party along with him on the notion that Ukraine belongs to Putin.'

The target paused. He'd had a thought. 'Have you ever seen *Dr Strangelove*, Nick?'

I tried to remember the title, but going to the pictures had been right up there with music as a non-event in my life.

'You need to see it. You need to see those good old boys. They don't care if they go to war – it's all about beating the other guy. These people have the same mentality as a child in the playground, no idea how to control the escalation of an argument. To the hawks, it's all about not backing down, not losing face.

'And these hawks, Nick, they're on both sides. We have to keep doing our best to stop them escalating tensions, and mutually assured destruction at the cyber level really puts the brakes on.'

The target's face was almost radiant with conviction. There wasn't a shadow of doubt in his mind. He believed this as firmly as he believed in his God and his village. 'If Russia does go into Ukraine, with even bigger territorial aspirations than it has already, the conflict needs to stay conventional – just armour and aircraft. It also needs to stay contained. And it will in the beginning, because both sides will use the war as a weapons-testing playground. The West will send different weapon systems, as they'll want to see how they perform against Eastern tech under real conditions, as will Russia. But we don't want it spilling into NATO. We don't want escalation. We don't want the generals, the old men, to think it's their time.

'That's why Obama in 'fourteen and Trump in 'seventeen let Putin get on with it. The Dr Strangeloves on both sides want the ultimate showdown. They want to see who's the last man standing before they all die. That's where my Zero Days come in, and why they are so important. Cyber mutually assured destruction, the status quo, is the only barrier that keeps both sides from walking straight to their nuclear options.

'I'm very proud that I've been able to make that happen. I'm very proud it was me who let the world know about Breedlove. I'm so proud that I leaked those emails so all the Dr Strangeloves were exposed for what they were, drum-bangers for war.

'That's why we need to be where we are now: both sides staring mutually assured destruction in the face if it happens again, if Putin is crazy enough to go into Ukraine. Hospitals, banks, police computers, military equipment, power stations, airports, the list goes on and on – anything with software or hardware involved. All in meltdown. If he does invade and it escalates, Nick, it's not just Europe we have to worry about. China and Iran would get involved, as well as any other player joining in to carve up their own piece of the pie.

'The next world war could start because of a country no one has cared about since the fall of the Soviets. But I, the village . . .' he leant over to his screens and tapped the one nearest to him '. . . we care.'

The target finally picked up his mug and took a mouthful of coffee that must have been cold by now.

'Here's a thought, Nick. "You may not be interested in war, but war is interested in you." You know who said that?'

'Trotsky. He knew the world, right?'

If I closed my eyes and had an accent filter, I could have been back on the boat with The Owl and Grisha.

76

'You and I both, Nick, we're trying to stop war. We're trying to have peace. We're both the same, except that your way brings escalation. But only because you don't know the whole story – and I want you to know the truth. What's happening here isn't fake. It's really about living a life here on earth – in Heaven. That's what it's all about. Peace.'

'So, tell me, then.' I wanted him to tell me more, because it meant more time with him, more time to work out what to do with him. And yet, at the same time, deep down, I really did want to know. Above all, I wanted the village to be real.

But before that happened, the door opened and Saynab appeared. My instant reaction was to be pleased to see her, but then it hit me that she was one more body to stop me doing my job and, even worse, it had to be Saynab witnessing it.

Her eyes were still the only thing showing above her polo-neck. The corners were creased, giving away a smile.

I began to get to my feet as if to greet her but Kirill jumped from his seat to make sure I didn't. I sat down again. 'How's

Poppy? I'm sorry, I wasn't expecting anything like that to happen. I don't know what else to say, except sorry.'

Kirill offered her his chair and she nodded in thanks as he pushed it towards us, the wheels clattering on the wooden floor.

'She's sleeping at Esther's. She'll be fine.'

She looked me straight in the eye and it felt like she was more concerned about me than her daughter. 'Nick, I'm the one who's sorry. I had to do something. Here.' She handed me a green plastic first-aid box.

Kirill positioned the chair between me and the target, and as she sat down, she pulled a carton of Rasagiline blister packs from her coat pocket. 'Please forgive, Nick.'

I felt even more of a shit now that she should be asking for forgiveness on top of providing me with this box that would help me kill the target. I smiled. 'Yes, of course. But I'm the one who needs to say sorry. I've come into your lives and created all this drama, something you didn't need. I'm sorry. I'm sorry for everything.'

The moment I lifted the lid, Kirill was all over me. He grabbed it out of my hands and confiscated the only decent thing that could have been a weapon, a pair of angled scissors. He gave it back and I ripped open some antiseptic wipes to clean my face, a natural thing to work on first, considering it probably looked like bubble-wrap.

The target brought an end to the apology fest. 'Nick's here because of the Zero Days. The Americans have sent him to kill me.'

Kirill jumped in. 'He's tried twice.'

Saynab's eyes again conveyed more concern than anger or disappointment. 'But Mary?'

I shrugged. 'This came later.'

She held out a hand and touched my arm. Did she get that I was coerced into this shit? I hoped so. Maybe she would just leave, and I could get on with it. I had finished cleaning up my face and the cuts still stung. It felt good, like the antiseptic was scrubbing away the guilt.

I took the wrapping off a bandage and set about binding it around my fucked hand. It seemed the natural thing to do to support it, especially as I needed it to be as strong as it could be to do whatever I had to do to kill the target and get the fuck out of there.

Saynab wasn't going anywhere. 'But why, Nick? Didn't you feel that we were true, that Matvey, the village are authentic? Can't you feel it? What went wrong, Nick? I thought you wanted to be here with us. I thought you felt the same as me, that it would be good for you and the village to be here . . . living your life. Was that all a lie? Please don't tell me it was.' She started to well up.

'I wanted to believe, I still want to believe, but my life just can't work out that way. I want it to, but it can't. You and the village have shown me that there is another way, but I can't go there.'

The target knew the score. 'Nick, I understand you have no choice. But what I don't understand is why. It's not about money or ideologies, is it? Maybe if all you have is a hammer, everything else looks like a nail. But you must believe us. We can help you think differently about life. This is the real deal. Snuggly Bear is here to make God's word function on earth. We are trying to keep God's Heaven from destroying itself.

'We know we're just a drop in the ocean. We know we might fail. But God made this world for us to live in, not to kill each other. So, we're just trying to spread the word of God on earth – and that word is peace. You know it, you've heard this. If we can spread the word, get others to believe, and they in turn spread the word, then maybe, just maybe, we'll have a little more peace than we've got now.'

Which sort of made sense. I certainly wanted it to, because I wanted it to be the real deal. 'So Snuggly Bear, the village, it's all about the Zero Days?'

I finished binding my hand. It felt good, tight, ready to fight.

Saynab looked shocked. 'No, Nick. Of course not.' She pointed at the screens. 'Matvey *is* Snuggly Bear. This room – the three of us, and now you – we're the only ones who know. The village is out there doing great work, spreading peace. They are real. Just like us and, deep down, I think, like you.'

77

She had a point, but there was a problem. She was talking just about me, and that wasn't good enough. I had Jack and Rio to think about.

How was I going to drop the target with Kirill watching me like an eagle, and Saynab on hand to help Kirill haul me off him?

The only immediate method I could think of was to grip his throat with my bare hands and keep squeezing the life out of him even as the other two tried to drag me off, but it wasn't likely to succeed. My hand would be better now it was bandaged, but still not as good as it once was. What was more, it would take time to make sure he was dead, and that meant more time for Kirill and Saynab to make sure he wasn't. Worse, I would be left alive, since the target and Saynab wouldn't let Kirill kill me. I would have failed.

The only other option was to wait and see what was in store for me, what opportunities there might be once we were outside the office – but that also presented problems. I had no control of what happened next. Would the target even be there?

Then another option hit me, and it made all kinds of sense: to just go for it, with such violence that Kirill would have no option but to respond to what I was doing, and kill me before I killed first.

Death by villager.

The target's eyes burnt into me. Clearly I was sitting too quietly. He knew what was going on in my head. 'Nick, you don't have to keep on like a machine trying to kill me. I'm not afraid of that, but I am afraid that my work and the village's work will be for nothing. There must be a solution to this . . .'

He was right, and it was a quick one. Everything became very clear in my head. 'I get it. I believe you.' Even half hidden under her polo-neck, Saynab couldn't contain her happiness. 'I believe all of you, but you need to know you're wrong about me. I might want peace, but I've got a gun to my head.' I nodded at the target. 'I've got to keep going at you, like a hammer, because if I don't, two people who mean a lot to me will be killed.'

Saynab gasped, and her eyes narrowed. I understood what she wanted to know.

'I'm sorry. I had to keep them from you. One of them is the Black guy, and the other was waiting for us at the top of the track. They really are the only two people in my life. They are all I have so you have to understand my situation. So, yes, there is a solution.' I looked at all three of them in turn. 'You must kill me.'

Saynab and the target looked like they were the ones who'd been slammed with a snow shovel. Kirill was intrigued, and I focused on him. 'I'm sure you'd do it. Or I'll go back into the snow and let the weather get me.'

The target took a breath and I turned back to him, trying to appeal to his pragmatism. 'It's very simple. If I get killed trying to kill you, then my boss will know I died trying, and my two friends are safe.'

There was silence from all three, but Kirill was the important one now. My eyes went back to him.

Still no one spoke. If there was no answer soon, I was going to launch myself anyway, literally go for the jugular. Kirill would know what to do, and I'd like it. In fact, I'd help him get it over and done with as fast as possible.

Saynab was the first to fuck up the scheme. 'No, Nick, no. Why would you think that? No, we can't do that.' The smile had evaporated, and her eyes were almost closed as she fought back the tears. She turned to the target, who agreed.

And then it hit me. There was a way of squaring the circle, of Matvey and me both staying alive, him so he could continue his work. Me, so I could continue to . . . Well, I'd work that out.

I outlined my plan, and they listened intently. Not everyone liked what they heard.

Kirill took strides towards us. 'No, this is wrong.' He pointed a finger angrily at me. 'He must die.'

Matvey raised a hand. 'Please, please. No one's going to die. I'll do what Nick suggests. It might be the only way out – unless anyone can think of something better?'

There was silence.

Saynab had started getting out of her chair and collapsed on her knees beside him. Her hands clasped his, as he gently soothed her. 'It's okay, Saynab. We always knew something like this might happen. It's time for you to take over. This is the succession we've worked towards, so let's get on with it. We have more important work, Saynab. Peace.'

Tears streamed down her face and her head fell onto their hands, still clasped together.

Matvey fixed his gaze on Kirill. 'You must stay here – you have your family to think of.'

Kirill nodded slowly, but clearly didn't like what he was hearing. He glowered at me, the cause of his world imploding.

I just wanted to get out. 'So, Matvey, what happens now?'

His voice became a monotone. 'We have money. I'll make more. The banks hardly see their losses. Four million here, seven million there.' He gave a fleeting smile. 'Even when they do, not a word of it ever escapes the boardroom. Who would trust a bank that lets money disappear?'

I had to agree, and joined in with a smile of my own that was very far from a pirate's. I liked him. 'No one.'

'Correct, Nick. No one.'

His smile broadened and I joined in once more. 'Are we good?'

Saynab had regained some of her composure. 'You know, Nick, honouring your friends like that is being the best person you can be. I knew I was right about you. You have started to live a life in Heaven.'

Her eyes creased up once more, but this time not from tears but from pure happiness as she put both of her hands to her heart. 'Enjoy.'

78

Kirill was waiting for me astride an ATV as I came out onto the snow. His face was hidden behind a ski mask and goggles, but from the way his chest was thrust out and his chin jutted high, I knew he was seething. Matvey and Saynab might have bought into my idea, but he hadn't. I finished stuffing my parka pockets with chocolate and protein bars from the ATV inside the warehouse, and Saynab and Matvey were behind me, coming to say their final goodbyes.

Shivering in just her polo-neck, Saynab gave me a hug, and this time I could return it. There were tears in her eyes, but I doubted they were caused by me leaving. She'd been promoted up the God's Word on Earth ladder, but not in the happy circumstances she would have wanted.

We took a step back from each other, but once again she kept my hands in hers. 'Nick, please enjoy your life. Please do not forget about us.'

I tried to smile. 'Saynab, that will never be a problem, because it simply won't happen. You and the village are in my head.'

Matvey came in for a hug so strong it hurt my back, still sore from Saynab snow-shovelling it. 'Peace, Nick.'

Kirill's chin went higher, and his arms tensed on the handlebars. He'd had enough. He jerked his head and I jumped on behind him, having to grip the seat as he immediately swung the Phantom round and twisted the throttle wide open.

As we sped along the snow-covered pathways, I squeezed the wiring in my hood to minimize wind-chill. I would have put my gloved hands in my pockets, but the parka bulged with more than chocolate. I'd been provided with a fistful of krones and euros, spare hat, gloves and a mobile, closed down to preserve the battery. I was going to exfil via Norway, and it could be a long journey.

Matvey had offered to get me out far more easily via Russia, but that would have raised questions from The Owl. Instead, Kirill was going to take me to the bottom of the hill, and from there I would push on up to the road on foot. I needed to show The Owl I'd made a hard exit from the village and needed help to get out of the country.

We shot past the Spiritual Centre and the church before hitting the bridge, and I allowed myself a brief smile. Crossing the river was a lot drier and warmer this time than last. Moments later, we were bouncing off the bridge and into Norway.

The plan was simple. I'd contact The Owl, telling him the job was done and I needed a way out to get back to Tulse Hill. Maybe I'd wait in the chapel, out of the cold, for Grisha in his boat or a vehicle coming from the road, though that seemed unlikely in the snow conditions. Or maybe The Owl would just fuck me off and tell me to sort myself out. In which case, I wouldn't risk stealing a boat or a vehicle. I'd have to wait until the other two returned to the UK, then get hold of them to come back with my real docs and we'd work out what to do from there. Who knew? Who cared? But it wasn't a problem, because I had no choice – and, most importantly, if this plan worked, I was free and the other two were alive.

Kirill contoured his way to the bottom of the hill and stopped the ATV, but kept the engine running. I started to dismount. I knew I wouldn't be getting a hug from him, but he rammed out his arm for me to stay put, then swivelled round to make sure I heard him from under his ski mask.

'It's not too deep here yet. I'm going to try to get you up as far as I can.'

I liked the idea. Better to make distance with wheels than feet. I nodded and muttered, 'Thanks.' At the same time, I wanted to be away from him as fast as I could. Kirill wasn't stupid. He would have worked out that once we started going up the hill we were alone, and it would be easier for him to leave me out here dead. He'd just have to say I'd attacked him, it was self-defence – death by villager – to ensure his friends would be safe. The icing on the cake for Kirill would be that it kept Matvey online at the village. I was sure Kirill could live with one or two lies under his belt.

We got to the first incline and the ATV slowed, inching forward with Kirill upright in the footwell, his arms rigid on the controls. He braked to a halt and turned back to me. 'I might be able to get you up a lot higher. I want you out of here quickly. I want you out of our lives.' It wasn't exactly a fond farewell, but what was I expecting?

He didn't give me time to answer before giving another angry twist of the throttle, and soon we were taking the steeper gradients of the hill. I was pushed back on my seat as the ATV ascended slowly but steeply, and we bounced along for maybe another five minutes before he stopped the ATV again, and stood up, arms still straight, hands still on the handlebars, inspecting the snow in front of us. He pulled off his goggles and jumped into the snow to have a closer look. We were losing time. I wanted to get moving, so I lifted my leg to get off. He swung round to me, grabbed the rim of my hood with both hands, and yanked me off the Phantom. My knees collapsed into the deep snow.

I put my hands up, trying to grab his wrists and dislodge them from my hood, but with no luck. This was a big man with intention. He yelled and pulled his body weight backwards, yanking my parka hard into my armpits. Within seconds I was face down in the snow.

He let go, because he was going to do something else. Whatever it was, I wanted to see it, and I wanted to get out of its way. I needed to get up, and then, somehow, I needed to start running.

I made an attempt to twist my torso and rise, but Kirill was having none of it. He hurled himself astride my chest, crushing the air from my lungs, keeping my arms pinioned with his legs. I arched my back, kicking, bucking, struggling to get my hands up. He dropped his hooded head to butt me, and I jerked my head away just in time. The side of his head crashed hard against my chin. My teeth weren't clenched, and I bit my tongue. Blood flooded into my mouth with that horrible taste of iron. He kept his head down. He wasn't going to try it again. He was angry that he'd missed. He hissed out his words. 'You're a bad person. I have no problem hurting a bad person.'

It would have been pointless trying to reason, beg or even insult him, not that I could have spoken. My swollen tongue felt three times its normal size. What was most important was breaking free.

I could see his mind whirring. As he lay with his face to one side of mine, his body weight pressing down, controlling me as I tried to buck around, I could see him working out what to do.

Hurt me, without a doubt. Kill me, maybe.

He made his decision.

79

Releasing my arms, Kirill jumped so that his knees came down onto my shoulders, his hands up to his mouth as he bit to pull away his gloves. His massive tattooed fingers thrust their way past my parka and my clothing, working to close around my throat. He pushed his chin down, his face flushed with the effort of tightening the compression. Fuck, he was big. He adjusted his thumbs under my Adam's apple and flecks of his saliva sprayed into my face as he strained to push it out through the back of my neck. My face swelled to bursting point. My head felt like it was going to explode. There was nothing I could do but kick, buck and writhe like a madman. I threw my hands skywards to force them around his throat, but his muscles tensed like steel hawsers under my weakened fingers. I shifted them down to grip the lapels of his jacket, using the jacket as leverage to try to dig my thumbs into the soft, fleshy area between the collarbones, at the base of his throat, but there was just too much material.

My strength was ebbing. As a last resort, I propelled my hands upwards again, this time around the back of his neck, and then jerked him down towards me. He pulled back but I tightened my grip. I redoubled my effort, trying to pull myself up to achieve that extra couple of centimetres, until finally I could feel the material of his ski mask against my cheek.

He froze. He realized what was happening. He knew I was going to try to finish this with my teeth.

With my final ounces of strength, I pulled again, and when his nose was only millimetres from mine, I got my chance. I lunged, and my teeth caught him just on the bridge. I bit down on the hard bone and kept going. He flung his head from side to side in an attempt to shake me off, but I was like a terrier hanging on to a stick. If this didn't work, then I got dead. But then he just took the pain, breathing like a warthog through gritted teeth, his face static, knowing not to pull away. He changed tactic, pushing down, trying to force his head into my face to prise my teeth away from him.

I responded by biting as hard as I could, working my head from side to side as I did so.

My jaws closed and the bone crunched under the hood like a fortune cookie. His sinuses exploded. As he let out a scream of rage and pain, blood and snot oozed through the hood and into my mouth.

I jerked away from him, unlocked my teeth, kicked, punched, whatever it took to get him off me. But he still hung on, trying to hold me, to control me.

It was stalemate, and we both knew it. Both of us lay in the snow, fucked. I wanted oxygen, to just lie there and breathe, but I couldn't do it. I had to be up first and I had to start making distance.

Kirill also knew he had to be the first up. We both rolled onto our knees, and all I could do was throw myself against him, make sure I was on top when both of us went back down into the snow.

My tongue had swollen to the roof of my mouth. My Adam's apple felt like it had been kicked right against the back of my throat. I gobbed out our blood.

But I had to make myself as clear as I could.

'We are better than this.'

I got nothing back. I bear-hugged him to get my mouth right against his ear as I spat out each word.

'We - are - better - than - this!'

I collapsed on top of him. There was no movement beneath me, just laboured breathing, his chest rising and falling as he took the pain. I took a chance, pushed myself off him, and rolled away slowly. I wanted it to be quicker, but I was fucked.

I staggered to my feet and started walking up the hill, looking back only once. Kirill lay in the snow, still taking the pain, still taking in oxygen. I continued ploughing through the knee-deep snow, trying to swallow, trying to re-engage my Adam's apple. It was agony, but physical injuries heal. All it takes is time.

And then in the distance, maybe half a kilometre below me, I heard the rev of an ATV engine . . . but it got quieter, not louder.

Kirill really was a much better person than most I'd ever met.

PART SEVEN

80

Westfield Shopping Centre, Shepherd's Bush, London
Tuesday, 14 December 2021

Jack was waiting outside Pret for me and Rio. It was a mixture of masks on, masks off in the mall, and Jack and I had both gone for faces covered. It hid us a bit from the CCTV and, as far as I was concerned, that was another little win.

I'd had to buy something and get it Christmas-wrapped. Rio had gone to pick up his Model 3 from the Tesla showroom, minus a mask – not that covering up would have made much difference for the CCTV, with his dreadlocks and missing arm.

It was originally meant to be Jack getting the car, but after Rio went with Jack on the test drive, his mind was made up. For reasons we couldn't fathom, he wanted one so much he wasn't prepared to put himself on the waiting list for a new one, and went for a nearly-new 2020 model.

Jack was checking his mobile and saw me coming. 'He's still upstairs. I'll get him a tuna.'

We went into a packed store and picked up baguettes, crisps, and cans of drink.

Jack checked back at his phone. 'That writer's done a great job on me.'

He shoved his screen to my face for me to see his new dating profile. The head shot, which he'd paid to have professionally taken, made him so much younger and better-looking he could have been charged with fraud. Below were a couple of paragraphs the writer had concocted, basically telling prospective girlfriends that he was very kind, considerate and, of course, liked long country walks with his faithful Labrador. Jack didn't have a Labrador, but he'd registered on a dog-walking site. If he got any dates he'd just borrow one for the day.

'Good luck, mate.'

He was feeling up for it, on more than one level. 'You think he'll take us two on?'

Hands full of lunch, we took a bench and started to unwrap. Things always taste better when they aren't paid for. I couldn't remember when we'd started this, but if the line was too long, we just peeled off and sat down. Old habits die hard.

'It's why we're meeting. It makes sense. There's going to be plenty of work if this Russia thing really happens.'

I couldn't be arsed waiting. I bit into my tuna and cucumber and took stock. It had taken a little while for me to get back to Tulse Hill. The exfil had had to be via the second option, because The Owl wanted nothing to do with me until I was safely back in the UK. I contacted the other two, then took a two-day walk to Varangerbotn, about halfway to Vardø, then three coaches and a ferry for another two-day, four-hundred-kilometre journey to Tromsø. Jack and Rio were waiting for me. Once they'd made it back to London, they'd retrieved my real docs from the flat and come all the way back out again. We then flew to Brussels, had a celebration mussels-and-chips before Eurostarring it to St Pancras, and finally got an Uber to Tulse Hill. When I met up with The Owl a couple of days later I'd tried to reclaim all the fares on expenses just to see the look on his face.

The debrief hadn't taken as long as I'd expected. I sat in the passenger seat of a Ford Eco Sport as The Owl drove, badly, around north London. Matvey, I'd explained, had been double-tapped with the Fort 14 in the IT room. I'd checked he was dead, and run. The Owl confirmed there had been an announcement online of his death, a tragic heart attack from a condition he'd had since childhood. He had been buried in the place he loved, in a new plot near the Spiritual Centre created just for him. Matvey would have liked that, I said. And so did I, because I was now out of this shit. I'd told The Owl so enough times, and he had finally accepted it.

Jack took a swig of green smoothie. 'This is going to be a really big deal for me and Rio. Maybe do a couple years, get involved in the Russian thing if it's going to happen, and then, like you, we're history. I'm going to get out there and enjoy myself.' He held up his phone full of romantic possibilities. 'Maybe settle down – wife, kids, a better Tesla than Rio's, who knows?'

I nodded him a very-pleased-for-you smile, and as I opened my packet of ready-salted my phone beeped. It was twelve o'clock: Rasagiline time. I pushed a capsule from the blister pack with my neoprene hand and washed it down with a swig of Coke. I liked using my fucked hand: it made me feel that everything was going to be okay.

Rio finally strode through the door. 'Let's go, for fuck's

sake!' He made it sound as if we'd been delaying him. 'I've only got an hour's free parking.' He picked up his tuna baguette and left the drink and the crisps for us to carry for him as he turned on his heel. 'Come on!'

Jack muttered, 'The fucker's been an eco-warrior for ten minutes and he thinks he's our leader.'

We took the lift down to the underground car park, where Rio displayed his sleek grey Tesla with a proud wave of the arm. 'Dog's bollocks or what?'

I wasn't going to say so, but it did look good. The Tesla lads had even managed to fit a black steel suicide spinner on the wheel to match the black pretend-leather interior. The spinner was needed because Rio was a one-handed wonder, but he also still had a Velcro cast on his broken forearm. There was no way legally he should have been driving.

Jack made straight for the front seat as it was always better for his leg. I liked it in the back anyway: more room to spread out. Rio stayed on the concrete, holding his door while he waited for us to climb in. As soon as we sat down, farting noises came out of the speakers. Rio was like a child on Christmas morning. 'Now you see why I wanted one? My girls are going to love it.'

Jack looked at me. 'Because it reminds them of their father?'

The noises continued as he settled into the driver's seat, and it was very clear the girls weren't the only ones who were going to enjoy having a fart car. Plus – it now had a name.

Rio made a show of inhaling deeply. 'Come on, breathe, breathe in.'

We did what he wanted, just to shut him up. That didn't work.

'It's not that new car smell, but what is it? What's the smell?'

Neither of us answered because we knew it was leading to a bad joke.

'Elon Musk! Get it? He owns—'

'Shut the fuck up and drive, knob.' Jack had had enough.

We glided away silently with Jack being the perfect front-seat driver. 'You sure you know what to do with this, shit-for-brains? It's not a car, it's a computer – not really your thing.'

We approached the barrier, and as Rio worked the suicide spinner to get close enough to reach the ticket machine, he scraped a front alloy on the kerb. Jack and I doubled up, but before we could jump in with a piss-take Rio was there: 'It'll add character. Shut the fuck up or you can go full eco and walk.'

81

We exited the car park into a grey but dry day, and headed towards Notting Hill Gate. There was a car park just past the café and the Russian embassy.

The two of them had had the full brief from me on what happened after Mary got dropped off, and the only thing they latched onto, even above me volunteering to die for them, was letting Kirill go. Jack said I was becoming far too woo-woo. Then the jokes started about crystals hanging from the ceiling in Tulse Hill and candles burning twenty-four/seven. Yep, it was good to be back. Even with me leaving the SNS, I was still going to live with them until I sorted myself out . . . one day.

They were right about one thing: my views had changed since leaving the village, whatever that meant, and I felt really good about it.

'Lads, one more thing before the meet.'

Rio hit the stalk to indicate left and the car gave us a series of farts. He checked in his rear-view. 'What are you on about in the cheap seats there?'

'How's Gillian? Did you get to see her? He's going to ask.'

'No, mate. I'm waiting till after all this. She's all right.'

'Give her a call now. See how she's doing. I'm telling you, he'll be checking on her, and he'll be checking on us. Well – me.'

The showroom guy had already linked Rio's phone to the Bluetooth. He shouted: 'Hey, Siri. Call Gillian the Jock.'

I laughed. It wasn't so much about the Jock thing, as Rio thinking he needed to add that keyword into his Contacts so he knew which Gillian he was calling.

The phone rang a bit too long before the answer machine came on with the BT generic message.

Rio kicked in. ''Allo, mate, it's Rio. How are you and the kids? Listen, I'll call—'

She picked up. 'Good timing! Nearly missed you. I just got in and was bringing out the shopping . . .'

I didn't believe a word. She was already over-explaining. But so what? We all do it.

Rio kept chatting away as if she was his oldest mate. 'How are you doing, Jocky McJockface?'

She didn't sound as casual in her reply, and nowhere near as happy. 'I'm good. The boys are good. Have you heard anything?'

'About what?'

'I don't know. It's just been so quiet here with you not calling, is all.'

'No drama this end. I'll come up and see you soon, yeah? Make sure everything's okay.'

She gave a very bland reply. 'That'd be nice. I have to go now – the boys will be back soon.'

'Yeah, yeah, see you.'

He closed down. 'See? She's soundo.'

As Rio hit the indicators for more farts and laughs, I leant forward to get my head between the front seats. 'What do you think about that call? Didn't she sound strange – wanting to get away? The boys coming home? What time does school stop?'

Rio waved it away. 'Listen, mate, she's sound, no problem. I'll see her soon. I'll keep it all sweet.'

We passed Notting Hill Gate tube and I pointed out the café on the left, then the tall brick walls of the Russian embassy on the right of Kensington Palace Gardens. I wondered if the Russian taxpayer knew the average house price there was around the thirty-five-million mark.

Maybe two hundred metres further on was the car park for Kensington Gardens and the Diana Memorial Park. Sam and Tom heaven.

Rio abandoned the Tesla rather than parked it, and we headed to the main, passing the Russian embassy, then crossed the road. We were finally approaching the café.

I had just one more thing for them. 'Lads, remember – he and Tom are obsessed with this Diana stuff, so no piss-taking, no matter what. And don't call him The Owl. Let me do the talking and see where it takes us, yeah?'

They nodded and waved their hands. 'Yeah, yeah, yeah.'

Rio was curious about my plastic carrier bag. 'Present for Teacher?'

'Something like that. Just remember: ears open, mouth shut.'

82

For once, The Owl was there first. And, going by the empty teacup and half-eaten sandwich on the table in front of him, he'd been there a while. His head jerked up the moment the door opened, and his face creased into its default service-with-a-smile mode. Even his mattress salesman's uniform was back: navy blazer, buttoned-up polo shirt straining at the neck and waist, jeans and loafers.

He stood up ceremoniously and held out his hand for the other two, who had to drag themselves away from the wonders on the wall. Those pictures were always overwhelming for a newbie. I could tell Rio already had Diana piss-takes bubbling up in his head. I needed to get this meeting over with quickly.

He shook hands with both of them. 'Well, now, how do you do?'

Thankfully they responded with nice-to-meet sounds. As I sat down next to him on the four-chair table, and the other two sat opposite, they were still checking out the pictures, which worried me. I placed the bag under my seat. The Owl approved of their Diana appreciation. 'I know, amazing, right?'

They nodded respectfully, but Rio couldn't help himself. 'She was the queen of my heart as well.'

I didn't want to lock eyes with him because he would probably have started laughing. But The Owl liked that, a kindred spirit instead of a sarcastic twat. He kept his smile on full-beam as he leant across the table and spoke in an almost conspiratorial murmur. 'I just want to say thank you to you guys for your service. You wear your sacrifices with dignity. You should be proud, as I am. I haven't had to defend freedom in such an awesome way.'

He sat back, smile unabated, tone slightly louder. 'So, thank you, both.'

Rio was the first. 'No problem, no problem.'

Jack came in a very close second. 'Thank you.' They both looked a bit taken aback. It was probably the first time anybody had ever said well done for having lumps blown off them and thrown about the desert.

A server came over. It was a different woman every time we were here, and this one was older than the last few and a Brit. 'What can I get you gents for drinks – and do you want a menu?'

I ordered a cappuccino and left it at that, and the other two followed suit. We'd deliberately had something to eat at Pret because I didn't want any of us hungry and tempted to stay long. The sooner this was done, the better.

The server went back to the bar with the orders, only for The Owl to beam with good news. 'So, Mary – she's back in the village.' He checked out all three of us for the surprised look that never came. It didn't matter to him. He just pushed on. 'I know, right? Amazing – she got back home, got everyone thinking all was good. But within a week she flew to Murmansk. The village picked her up, and now she's back with that Austrian guy. True love, eh?'

That sounded good to me. In fact, it made me just a little jealous. Maybe come the spring the village would pick me up too and take me back down the hill.

Jack agreed. 'Yep, that's good news.'

The Owl was still all smiles and happiness as the coffees arrived, and we said our thanks, waiting for her to leave.

Then he did it: 'Anyhoo . . .'

Anyone who'd had any connection with any American, anytime, anywhere, knew that when you heard that, they were getting to the point.

He put his hands together and rubbed them as if he was conjuring up whatever was about to be said next. 'Our boat friend has confirmed that they did indeed bury our bear friend in a new burial plot, well, a shrine to him really. Like we already knew, an unexpected death due to a heart condition.' He raised his teacup and proposed a toast. 'To our bear friend.'

We sort of joined in, and I was very relieved. My plan had worked.

His teacup went onto the saucer with exaggerated precision. The prelims for why we were really there were over.

'So, Jack, Rio. It's good to meet you after all of— What is it, six years?'

They knew better than to answer. They let him move on.

'It's so unfortunate that our friend here is leaving us, but our arrangement can continue. I think it's a good idea. What say you?'

He smiled at them both and waited for what he wanted. Both of them agreed. 'Yep, good idea.'

The Owl liked what he heard, as if a different answer had ever been on the cards. 'That is so cool. Thank you. Do you know what? I like the SNS. I like all three-letter organizations. You guys are the ideal cover. Your conditions and your black-and-white thing are good for me. It's such a shame that Nick is going to leave us, but like the end of all eras, a new age will dawn. The king is dead, long live the kings. What do you think?'

They nodded.

'That's so cool. Maybe at a later date you'll bring other people in, and maybe I might introduce others into the group. And that'll all be cool. But whatever happens, I just want to deal with you two. Same as I used to with our friend.'

It was as if I was no longer at the table.

His smile widened to display gleaming teeth as he raised his teacup once more. 'To the new era.'

The other two raised their mugs and I didn't need to join in. The deal was done. Good: a quick sip of cappuccino and let's get out. I started to get off my chair, but it wasn't to be.

The Owl lifted a hand at me. 'We've got just one last piece of old business to deal with.'

I sat down. I knew it wasn't going to be good. It never was.

83

The Owl adjusted himself on his chair so he faced me side-on, now ignoring the other two. 'So – the Scottish thing. How is it?'

'It's all good. We spoke to her just now on the way here.'

He looked at me, like a disappointed schoolteacher. 'But it's not good, is it, Nick?' He paused and waited for me, not interested in the other two. They were now on the team. Me, I was history – and I didn't feel good about what was coming.

'Nick, she's been asking questions at the bank. Where's the money coming from? That kind of thing. Can she follow the trail? I assume you've done your job and she can't. The next thing, she'll be spending taxpayers' cash, which we gave her, to get an investigator to ask the questions now that she's hit a wall. Hasn't she told you this? Hasn't she told you about her concerns?'

I didn't acknowledge.

'Nick, you should have known. You're my go-to guy on

this.' His face was still the concerned schoolteacher, disappointed in his failed pupil. 'You should have made sure that her only concerns were her family.'

'I'll go and see her, find out what's happening and make it okay.'

A couple were taking their time heading for the door as they checked out the walls one more time, and we waited for them to pass. I tried to make sure he kept his focus on me. I didn't want the other two to fuck up by weighing in to help solve the problem. This one wasn't going to be solved in any other way than what I knew he was about to say.

He gave a big smile, because that had been the answer he wanted. 'Thanks, Nick. After all, it was you who said she wouldn't be a problem. But now she is, and so could those boys be.' His hand went across the table to the other two. 'I'm sorry to have you here for this, but I need to make sure Nick sorts out this final loose end of the Isar job, closes it off for good. Then you guys can continue with no baggage pulling you down.'

He turned back to me. 'Think of it as a parting gift to the new team. You'll go today?'

My thoughts were instantly back with Saynab, Matvey, even Kirill . . . and I was determined to live my life until the end, without all of this shit. I didn't have a war zone in my chest this time. There was no electricity buzzing around my head trying to burst its way out through my skull. In fact, I felt remarkably clear-headed and calm. The village had made me better than this.

I stood, picked up the bag from under the seat, as The Owl waited for the reply he was expecting: 'I'm on it.'

But instead, he got a simple: 'No.'

I headed for the door, making sure I was distancing myself

from the other two. They might have to take on the job, but that was their choice. I had no problems with that. This was just about me, and wanting to live a life for however long it might last. I had a feeling I wouldn't be needing too many more blister packs of Rasagiline now The Owl had another loose end to deal with. In fact, I might as well cancel the prescription right now.

84

It was cold outside, and coming up to last light. Christmas lights shone out from the shops and lampposts, and from somewhere came the strains of 'Silent Night'. As I turned right, heading for the tube station, my head was still as clear and calm as it had been a moment ago. I felt a bit of what Saynab had called a lifting into the light, and it was good. I even had the fantasy flash again of being a teacher somewhere in the world, doing my bad Elvis impersonation as I popped handfuls of pills in front of my class.

And then, from behind, over the sound of the carol and my giggling class, I heard: 'Oi, dickhead!'

I spun round. The other two were hurrying towards me. Rio was running, Jack was a bit behind, working his leg to get some speed.

Rio came up level, his breath hanging in a cloud.

I shook my head. 'What are you doing, mate? This isn't about you two.'

Rio had other ideas. 'The fuck it isn't. We're all we've got, right?' He wasn't even looking at me – he was looking behind him, waiting for Jack to catch up.

When he did, his face was far more serious than Rio's. 'Listen, we've got to get a grip of Gillian, and we stay together. Fuck The Owl, fuck what happens next. We can't control that. All we can do is back each other up and go head on with whatever comes our way, right?'

I thought of Cameron and his wheelchair philosophy after our mindfulness session. We might not express it the way that Cameron did, but I was getting love from these two fuckers and I was giving it back. My life was full. And so were theirs.

Of course I wasn't going to say anything about that to these two dickheads. You only tell the truth to those who don't matter. Instead, I agreed with Jack, and I was relieved that they not only had my back but also were genuinely concerned. They were right: fuck it. I nodded, and we turned round and started off in the direction of the fart car, crossing the road to avoid the café.

It wasn't long before Rio started playing about, trying to check out the bag. 'What have you got in there?'

We were outside the Russian embassy's tall wall. I looked up at the flag of the Russian Federation, then back down at the bag.

I opened it to reveal a large tub shape covered with Christmas wrapping. 'Strawberry, her favourite. I'm going to courier it to the village via Russia. Can't get it there in time for Christmas any other way because of the snow.'

They didn't get it, and as we carried on, Jack slapped my back with all the force of a snow shovel. 'Tell you what, dickhead, you'd better be quick sending that before Putin kicks off with shit, know what I mean?'

THE END

From the day he was found in a carrier bag on the steps of Guy's Hospital in London, **Andy McNab** has led an extraordinary life.

As a teenage delinquent, Andy McNab kicked against society. As a young soldier, he waged war against the IRA in the streets and fields of South Armagh. As a member of 22 SAS, he was at the centre of covert operations for nine years, on five continents. During the Gulf War he commanded Bravo Two Zero, a patrol that, in the words of his commanding officer, 'will remain in regimental history for ever'. Awarded both the Distinguished Conduct Medal (DCM) and Military Medal (MM) during his military career, McNab was the British Army's most highly decorated serving soldier when he finally left the SAS.

Since then Andy McNab has become one of the world's best-selling writers, drawing on his insider knowledge and experience. As well as several non-fiction best-sellers – including *Bravo Two Zero*, the biggest selling British work of military history – he is the author of the best-selling Nick Stone and Tom Buckingham thrillers. He has also written a number of books for children.

Besides his writing work, he lectures to security and intelligence agencies in both the USA and UK, and works in the film industry advising Hollywood on everything from covert procedure to training civilian actors to act like soldiers. He continues to be a spokesperson and fundraiser for both military and literacy charities.